AF215983

What readers love about Jo Thomas:

'Each of her books transports you to different places where you **find yourself immersed** in the book page after page'

'When you're having a bad day, read one of Jo's books and it will give you a lift, and you can **forget all your troubles** for a while'

'I was **completely transported** . . . Jo has the most wonderful way with words and I find it so easy to relate to all of the characters'

'Always a **cosy, comfortable read** – just right for the season!'

'Her books are always like a **huge warm hug**'

'I love how Thomas takes **very likeable characters** and throws them in the deep end of a life-changing problem'

'When I think of Jo Thomas, I think of **amazing books, delicious food and exotic locations**'

'I don't need to know what a Jo Thomas book is about; **I just know I will want to read it.** She's taken me around the world to beautiful destinations and treated me to descriptions of mouth-watering foods'

Dear Reader,

Hello and welcome to my world. If you've read my books before, you know what to do: pull up a chair and get ready for some armchair travel. If you're new to my stories, come on in and let me tell you what to expect.

My name is Jo Thomas, and I write feel-good, foodie fiction in places I hope you will want to call home.

As a young adult, I spent time working in a small restaurant in the South of France, and I think this is where my love of food and France comes from. I adored it. The buzz of service and the community of workers when work was done. I fell in love with simple but delicious food: seafood and steaks; barbequed lunches with our toes in the sand by the sea; and one of my favourite meals for a group of friends – mussels in white wine sauce – put on the table for everyone to share with fresh French bread and bottles of white wine. My love affair with food and Europe continued on into Italy when my brother moved there and owned a small olive grove. But at this time, I still hadn't worked out that I wanted to write. That came later, after training and working as a radio producer at BBC Radio 5, Radio Wales and Radio 2. I left to start a family and decided it was time to begin my writing journey. It took me a long time to work out what to write about, what stories I wanted to tell. Then, one evening, I was with my husband in Galway, and we went to a fish restaurant. It had rained and rained. But as we entered the restaurant, the fire was roaring, the candles were lit, and as we sat by a window looking out over Galway Bay, it finally stopped raining. The moon shone and threw a silver shadow over the water. I ordered a platter of oysters, and, oh boy, they were delicious. Fresh, zingy and a blast of the ocean right there. I thought: this . . . this is what I want to write about. These oysters were about to take me by the hand and introduced me to Galway, to the people, the history and the community. I didn't know much about oysters, but I wanted to find out more! And I did. I discovered oyster-shucking contests, visited an oyster farm and travelled on the back of a tractor in the sea with my good friend Katie Fforde. What a wet day!!! And that, I realised, was when I knew the stories I wanted to tell. When you discover the food of a place and it takes you by the hand, catapulting you into a whole new world with the kitchen table at the heart of it, wherever it may be. I wanted to write about food and love. This was my love language.

Since then, I have written about olive oil in Southern Italy, honey in Crete, wine in France, chocolate in Switzerland and maple syrup in Canada, as well as pasta, Iberico ham and lavender fields. Each one has been a journey of discovery for me, and I have wanted to move to each and every place I've written about.

So, for my twenty-first book, I am taking you to Brittany in France, to a quiet little village, beside a large natural lake and a deserted watermill. It's a place holding forgotten secrets within its walls, where the *boulangerie* has been long since closed up. It is a *boulangerie* waiting for new life to be breathed into it, despite the many locals who believe the past should be left where it is: in the past. But, there is pride, passion and plenty of prejudice at play, with love and honour at stake.

Come on! Pull up a chair – let's get ourselves to France. Grab a coffee and a croissant, and let's see who will triumph in the battle of the baguettes. Who will find love and a new beginning, or will the past stay there forever?

Gros bisous,

With love,

Summer at the French Bakery

Jo Thomas is the author of bestselling romantic fiction novels including *The Oyster Catcher* – which won both the RNA Joan Hessayon Award and the Festival of Romance Best Ebook Award – and *Escape to the French Farmhouse*, which was a no.1 Kindle bestseller.

Jo worked for many years as a BBC radio reporter and producer before turning her hand to writing novels. Her kitchen in Pembrokeshire is her happy place, and she can often be found at the kitchen table enjoying meals she has cooked for family and friends, or writing about food, love, laughter and community in places you'll want to call home.

Also by Jo Thomas

Ebook short stories:

Jo Thomas
Summer at the French Bakery

PAN BOOKS

First published 2026 by Pan Books
an imprint of Pan Macmillan
The Smithson, 6 Briset Street, London EC1M 5NR
EU representative: Macmillan Publishers Ireland Limited, 1st Floor,
The Liffey Trust Centre, 117-126 Sheriff Street Upper,
Dublin 1 D01 YC43
Associated companies throughout the world

ISBN 978-1-0350-7750-2

Copyright © Jo Thomas 2026

The right of Jo Thomas to be identified as the author of this work has been
asserted in accordance with the Copyright, Designs and Patents Act 1988.

All rights reserved. No part of this publication may be reproduced,
stored in a retrieval system, or transmitted, in any form, or by any means
(including, without limitation, electronic, mechanical, photocopying, recording
or otherwise) without the prior written permission of the publisher.

Pan Macmillan does not have any control over, or any responsibility for,
any author or third-party websites (including, without limitation, URLs,
emails and QR codes) referred to in or on this book.

1 3 5 7 9 8 6 4 2

A CIP catalogue record for this book is available from the British Library.

Typeset in Apollo MT Std by Six Red Marbles UK, Thetford, Norfolk

Printed and bound in the UK using 100% Renewable Electricity by CPI Group (UK) Ltd

This book is sold subject to the condition that it shall not, by way of trade or otherwise,
be lent, hired out, or otherwise circulated without the publisher's prior consent in any form
of binding or cover other than that in which it is published and without a similar condition
including this condition being imposed on the subsequent purchaser. The publisher does
not authorize the use or reproduction of any part of this book in any manner for the
purpose of training artificial intelligence technologies or systems. The publisher expressly
reserves this book from the Text and Data Mining exception in accordance with
Article 4(3) of the European Union Digital Single Market Directive 2019/790.

Visit **www.panmacmillan.com** to read more
about all our books and to buy them.

Once you learn to live without fear,
life gets sweeter – Joanna Lumley

Is there anything more comforting and enticing than the promise the smell of a freshly baked baguette makes to you? The crack of the crisp golden crust. The scent of the warm fluffy inside, as white and soft and light as a cloud. The crumbs that fall as you crunch. It's all part of the journey you take together, and the joy.

Prologue

'It's a ridiculous idea,' I say, with a high-pitched laugh I don't recognise: part hysteria, part wistful. It would be like agreeing to take on a marathon as the unfit, recovering forty-eight-year-old that I am. I know it would be impossible.

Pete nods, firmly and decisively, beside me. 'Of course it's a ridiculous idea,' he agrees.

We stand side by side and stare at the old stone building as the March rain pitter-patters around us. It is beautiful, despite being neglected. Full of character and charm, but also eerily empty and alone. A building that would have been full of life I imagine, now stagnating and still. The old '*À vendre*' sign is tied to the gates, both of which are listing and peeling with age and abandonment.

'It would take so much work,' I say, my eyes drinking in the building and all its possibilities, filling me with something that feels like a purpose, which I haven't felt in a long time. 'Imagine it as a beautiful bed-and-breakfast beside that lake. With tea rooms. A *salon de thé*. Cakes on pretty stands, bunting, and visitors coming to sit and enjoy the view. I've seen something like it on Instagram. I could spend my days baking cakes for people rather than cleaning at the care home.' I smile. Much as I loved the care home and the residents I worked with – and I hated stopping work when I became ill – this would be my dream. Somewhere people would come to enjoy the cakes I love to bake. 'It would take effort, but could be amazing.'

'Effort . . . and money,' says Pete, and I feel the tiny taste of purpose seep away, like scented bathwater down the plug hole, leaving a grubby residue. 'Money that we don't have to waste,' he says flatly.

I think about the savings account that I've added to every month for every year I've worked and took advice on how to invest it wisely, that has slowly grown and swollen over the years. Just sat there. I could do something purposeful with it.

We fall silent again, lost in our thoughts and different worlds.

In my mind's eye, I can see exactly what this old watermill would be like once it's been renovated. I sigh. Someone will have the same vision and the motivation to take it on. 'Be amazing when it's done up, though,' I say.

'Gorgeous,' he agrees.

'Make a fabulous place for walkers,' I add. 'People exploring the area like us.'

'Or the sort of place that would be good for people on golfing holidays. An afternoon away from the course. Providing they have a course in the area,' he adds. Pete's thoughts are never far from golf these days.

The anorak he is wearing rustles as he walks beside

me: a known brand, bought for this trip. He leans on his new walking poles: top of the range, built to last. Much like his golfing gear, which has expanded over the years and now takes up an entire bedroom, replacing the guest-room touches I'd put in – the comfy chair in the window is now a resting place for a golf bag full of clubs, the dressing-table littered with golf balls and tees. That room was supposed to be for family to visit once the children had left home. I did everything I could to make their stay comfortable, but they rarely came. And now, even if they wanted to, they couldn't, because the room is full of golf accoutrements. Furry puppet heads over drivers and put-ters, a variety of bags, hand towels, ball bags and his fiftieth-birthday present to himself: the electric golf cart, with remote control.

We stand and listen to the peace around us. There's hardly a sound, just the patter of raindrops in the trees, with the smell of the damp spring ground, waking from its winter slumber.

'Yes. Those pig sheds could be self-catering *gîtes*.' I point to the single-storey stone building to the right of the driveway – if you can call it a driveway. It's really a grassy strip, worn down. 'You could do events, wed-dings . . .' Purpose is gathering in my voice again.

'Or retreats for writers and painters, like they do on that TV programme with the châteaux,' he joins in, smil-ing. I can see exactly what he means and I'm grateful he's joining me on my imaginary journey.

'Yes!'

We fall into silence again, and it's as if I'm watching the place come to life before me. A place where people come in the summer sunshine, then head to the lake beyond the building. There'd be bunting hanging from the trees and bushes, leading the way, and fairy lights at night. I sigh again.

Pete's the first to speak. 'We could never do it, though,' he says quietly. I leave just a beat or two to savour the ideas and images in my head before they dissolve into dust, like similar discarded dreams.

'I agree.' I shake my head.

Just then I see a flash of blue, followed by another. I walk a little further up the drive, placing my hand on the cold stone of the old building, and look out over the long grass of the lawn. Then I see them: two beautiful king-fishers darting over the lake in front of the old mill, a flash of colour as they dip across the water from the banks of the lake on one side and back to the other. I take another step or two forwards, then a few more, up the slippery bank, touching the cold wall of the forgotten building as I stare at the two birds. Occasionally they plunge through lily pads into the water, surfacing with small fish in their beaks.

Pete joins me, laying a hand on my shoulder, saying nothing.

'No, we could never do it,' I repeat quietly.

'Come on, or we'll miss lunch at the *brasserie*. I want the lamb again.'

I turn to him. 'You had the lamb yesterday. Don't you want to try something different?'

'No. I liked it. Why mess with a winning formula? You know I'm a creature of habit.'

We couldn't do it. The words circle in my mind as we

turn back and continue our walk, following the map that had led us here, and is now helping us navigate back into the tiny French town to our little holiday rental. It's a peaceful walk, only interrupted by a small turquoise car, moving fast, almost brushing against us – we had to jump into the hedgerow. I recognised him as Monsieur Martin, the owner of the small hotel where we're staying. He's gone as soon as he appeared.

Overhead I see the cranes flying, heralding summer, like a sign of good things to come, better days. A holiday here was as brave as it gets for Pete. In the past, we've gone camping locally with the kids in the summer and, since they left home, spent long weekends at Warners or taken the occasional trip to the West Wales coast, staying in a B&B and going to our usual restaurants and bars. But this year I wanted to do something different. I'd always wanted to visit rural France, to see what it would be like to live here and learn the language. Pete agreed to a week. An early anniversary present and to celebrate finally ringing the hospital bell. I've loved it, ringing that bell and being here.

We could never do it. The words keep repeating in my head. I wish I wasn't walking away from the mill. I could have stayed and watched those kingfishers all day long. But what if I decided to make my idea a reality? What if I took this second shot at life and became the sort of person who followed their dreams? *We* could never do it, but could I?

Chapter 1

'Another one?' Pete's aunt mouths loudly, after three glasses of cava. I don't want to discuss my daughter's partners – not at a family gathering or, actually, at any time. It's no one's business. I make an excuse that I'm hot and start to move towards the glass door of the entrance to the golf-club bar.

'Speech!' someone shouts, and people clap. I glance around at my smartly dressed friends and family. Our children are here, with their partners. Although this one isn't the same woman our daughter Maddie brought with her at our last family meet-up just after New Year. There have been so many over the past couple of years and, while I make a real effort to remember their names, I can't recall this one. I usually try to picture something to remind me of the name – for Belle I saw a little silver bell. Daisy was self-explanatory. But I'm just distracted this evening, and forgot to make a mental image to help me after our introduction. They haven't been together that long, and Maddie's relationships never seem to last. I'd love her to find The One and settle down. But from the way they're holding hands and talking, turned in to each other, forehead to forehead, they seem happy enough right now. That's a good sign. Who knows? This may be it. I just want Maddie to find lasting happiness.

Our son Jake is across the room with his partner, Becky, tanned from their recent holiday. They're looking into business opportunities in Spain and hoping to relocate there. Having spent years at university studying biochemistry, Jake dropped out in his final year and now wants to be a DJ on the European rave circuit, which came as a bit of a shock, and Becky dreams of opening an estate agency on the Costa del Sol. They've been together for years. Becky is very business-minded: she works in mortgages and insurance, setting up her own business during Covid and going from strength to strength, if the holidays are anything to go by. Jake's only recently focused on becoming a DJ. He's moved on from trying to be an online gamer, which didn't work out for him. I have to keep reminding myself that, much as I would love them to be near, they have to live their own lives. That's how we grow as adults, isn't it, deciding which risks to take? I feel helpless, like a mother watching her chick fly the nest, wishing she could turn back the clock, hoping and praying he'll be safe and come home again soon. I can only help and support from the sidelines now.

Saying yes to marriage. That's a risk you take too, I think, contemplating the other people in the room. Most are Pete's golfing friends, some of whom I've met for the first time this evening. *Only you can decide if it's what you want, and if it's still what you want*, a voice in my head says.

'We've been through a rough year!' Pete interrupts my thoughts. His voice is cracking. Someone hands him a glass of fizz and he takes a sip. Everyone seems to have a drink, as instructed when I organised the party with the staff. Everyone, I realise, but me. I wonder if it's strange that Pete didn't wait for me to be by his side to give his speech.

He's unfolding the piece of paper that he's written his speech on, fumbling, trying to juggle paper, microphone and glass. One of his golfing buddies steps forward, takes the glass, and he shakes out the paper, then pulls out his specs from the same top pocket where I suggested he keep them and puts them on.

He clears his throat. 'When Jules first told me she was ill, I thought it was an April Fool!' he says, looking around for a reaction to his badly judged attempt at humour. I wince as it falls on stony ground. He clears his throat and reads on, nervously. 'But it was no joke. Far from it.' The room is silent, listening to him. 'It's been a hell of a year. I've had to stand by, helpless, as Jules has battled this bloody cancer.' The word catches in his throat. 'She's an amazing woman. She's been so strong, supported me and the children when it should be us supporting her. But I hope we have all been there for each other. It's been a scary time.' He gives a hiccup, making tears spring to my eyes. 'You've been amazing, Jules. Like always. You're as determined as the woman I met so many years ago, and we all love you very much.' A tear rolls down my cheek. 'No one could have gone through what you have this last year with such good humour, always putting your family first. But now it's time for us to take care of you. Back in March you rang the bell at the hospital, signalling the end of your treatment. And let's pray that is the end of it.'

A little cheer goes up in the gathered group and I blush, brushing away the tears at the heartfelt words I hadn't expected to hear from Pete. But I also wish there was more to us right now – more than the cancer and the treatment.

'But now,' Pete says, gathering confidence with the words he's rehearsed, 'it's time to look to the future.' I feel a little lift. I don't want to be Jules and the cancer any more: I want to be just Jules . . .

He looks around for me as I stand in the shadows by the door, enjoying the cloak of invisibility it brings me, hiding my blushes and tears. He smiles when he sees me. 'Let's hope everything can go back to how it was. I'm proud of everything we've built together. The life we've created. It's time for us to step back and let the young people have the adventures. With the mortgage paid off,' he raises a glass and his friends give a little cheer and there's a clap. I know how much it meant to him, owning the house outright. 'It's time for us to take things a little easier; put our feet up and look back on everything we've done.'

Something inside me twists – hard. In my heart, my throat and my stomach. Images, as if on a Facebook slideshow, play out in my head. Our wedding day, picking up the keys to the house, having Maddie, then Jake. Watching them grow up. And now, cancer-free, I'm ready for the next stage in my life. His words play in my head: *Time for us to put our feet up*. I'm suddenly frozen with fear. I'm not ready to put my feet up. I'm not ready for matching armchairs and trips to the garden centre on a Sunday. *I want more*, says the voice in my head. I'm ready for adventure. I want to celebrate being alive, not wait for the end. I've fought that one off for the time being! I want to sing from rooftops and dance in the rain! I want to look forwards, not back! As much as I love Pete for being there for me, at every step of my life, as much as I love our kids for the joy they've brought us and who they've become, right now, I want us all to look forward. For the children and Pete to live their own lives without worrying about me. I want us all to move out of the shadow that's hung over us.

'To my best friend . . .' I hear Pete saying, but my head is whirling and wrestling with my heart. My head is saying I should be quiet and grateful, do as Pete suggests and put my feet up, but my heart is telling me I need a new start in life and to live for the moment. '. . . my wife of twenty-five years. Here's to the next twenty-five!' Pete raises a glass. His golfing friends, their wives, our children, his mother and brother are all raising their glasses and cheering. I step back, enough to push the door behind me ajar, enjoying the breeze from the night air through the golf-club reception area. Pete raises his glass a little higher towards me and part of me wants to hug him. Another part wants to head outside to escape the claustrophobia I'm feeling: I'm suffocated by everything the last year has been – exhausting, terrifying and bleak. I want to breathe fresh air.

Pete sips his drink and is distracted by his mate, Fridge – once a rugby friend in their younger days and now a dedicated golfing buddy at weekends. I slide out of the door, making my way across Reception and outside into the early spring evening.

I take a couple of deep breaths, looking out over the car park at the golf buggies and the neatly kept course beyond. I wonder what it's like in France this evening by that lake, still and silent. Then I turn back to the golf club, a stark brightness from overhead lighting in the function room where Pete is chatting with the friends he grew up with, went to school with, plays golf with. Loud laughter fills the air. Pete, my other half for twenty-five years. The constant in my life and the father of my children. I love him, and them.

But as I watch the room, I feel as if I'm watching a film of my life, being played out after I'm gone. I feel so proud of all three of them. It's been horrid for them, not knowing what the future would look like. No one does once the doctor says the words you never want to hear. But with the cancer in my breast removed and the rounds of chemo finished, it's time everyone got back to normal. I've had the all-clear and I'm not ready to go anywhere yet. Every now and again the monkey taps me on the shoulder, reminding me that it could come back at any time, but now I feel more alive than I have done in years, like a bottle of prosecco ready to pop. Twenty-five years. And what was it Pete said? Here's to another twenty-five?

Another twenty-five years of how it's always been? *I can't do it*, I think, watching the party through the big wide window. Another twenty-five years of playing it safe, paying off the mortgage, just to sit back and put our feet up?

No one has noticed I'm not in there, and I realise I'm no longer needed here. I've played my role, organised the party, made sure the invitations went out, the menu was agreed, the drinks bought and flowers arranged. But I've become invisible. Just like in Pete's speech, I'm Jules the wife, the mum and, now, the cancer survivor. I've lost everything else I once felt about life. What am I supposed to do for the next twenty-five years?

The gift of being in remission, of having a second chance, is a constant reminder of how lucky I am to be alive. I want to take risks. I want to be known for being more than the wife, the mum, the cancer survivor. I want to be known for being me.

My phone pings.

It's Annie, a young woman I met at the hospital. We've become close friends. I'd hoped she'd be here tonight, but she's not well enough. *Have a lovely evening. You deserve to celebrate after what you've gone through. Keep going. Seize the day! x* she messages.

I glance through the window again. This isn't really my evening, I think. I may have played a role in Pete's twenty-five-year journey to be here, but we're not celebrating 'us'. We're celebrating getting this far. This is about another trophy to put on the shelf, next to the golfing ones and the Player of the Year cup from the rugby club when we were first going out.

He said I was his lucky mascot and he'd have to marry me. We got engaged first, then married and bought the house. Made all the right moves. We kept fit and active, prepared for retirement with pension plans. But no one prepares you for the rug being pulled out from under your feet, threatening to whip everything away from you, including life. And, actually, it makes me feel angry.

Wish you were here, I type back to Annie.

Me too, she replies. *Enjoy every moment!*

I'm enraged on Annie's behalf, a woman with everything to live for. A husband and young family. Tears gather along the rims of my eyes.

Suddenly there's giggling and laughter as Maddie and her girlfriend come stumbling out in each other's arms, pulling out their vapes and sucking at them, disappearing into clouds of smoke, then falling into a deep kiss.

A little embarrassed by their enthusiastic display of affection, I clear my throat.

'Mum?' Maddie says, and frowns. 'What are you doing out here? I thought you were inside with Dad, celebrating.'

I shake my head. 'No, love. I've been out here, watching.'

There's a pause, and I know Maddie's not sure what to say. I'm not either. I just know I'm feeling something and it's not celebrating the prospect of another twenty-five years of marriage to Pete. We're at a crossroads and seem to be heading in different directions. I'm grateful for everything we've had, but I'm sad too, because I know we're at the end of our road. The one thing holding us together over the last year, the cancer, has gone.

'Are you all right? Do you want me to get Dad?'

I smile. 'I'm fine. Really. Never better.' In fact, I feel drunk, although I haven't had a drink all night. I'm high on life . . . a cliché, I know, but I'm so grateful still to be here with the possibilities I want for myself in front of me. I think about Annie, wishing with all my heart she was standing in my shoes.

'Wait here,' I hear Maddie say to her girlfriend. 'I'm getting Dad.'

'No! I'm fine, really,' I say, and wish she'd listen, but she's gone already and I can see her pushing her way through the throng at the bar, reaching him and pulling him away from telling a story that involves swinging an imaginary golf club.

Pete reluctantly leaves his friends and follows her outside. 'Jules, you okay? Maddie said you weren't feeling well.'

'I'm fine,' I say, trying to calm the fuss that's bubbling around me.

'Shall I get you some water?' Maddie asks.

I know she wants to help and is worried. 'Actually,' I say quickly, 'some water would be great. Take, erm, your friend with you, get a jug.'

'It's Heidi,' Heidi says.

'Heidi, of course. Sorry, I couldn't remember. Warm evening.' I say, knowing that it really isn't. We're barely into spring. 'I've had a lot on my mind.'

But Heidi doesn't seem happy. 'Your *friend*? Do you have lots of friends?' she asks, as the two of them go inside.

As I watch them, I'm hoping I haven't dropped Maddie in it.

Once they're through the doors, Pete turns to me. 'How long have you been out here?' he asks.

I feel a glow of affection, warmth, security, but not the love we once had, giddy with excitement to be with each other. That's gone.

'Long enough,' I say, without needing to add, *long enough to work out what I need to do and say to you.*

'I didn't realise—'

'Pete,' I cut him off. I need to get to the point. No use in prolonging this and making it tricky for either of us. 'I . . . I need some time away.'

'Another holiday? We could go to the coast for a couple of days.'

'It's not you. It's me.' I cringe at how corny that sounds. But I can't stop now. 'I don't think . . .' I look at him. He's clearly confused and hurt, and I hate myself for doing this, but I'm doing it for us both.

'I don't think I can do this for another twenty-five years.'

'Do what?'

'You know, the routine. Coffee at seven thirty, morning news, Sunday lunch at the garden centre . . .'

'I thought you liked the garden centre. We could always go to Deri's café instead, but I didn't think you liked their bacon baps as much.'

'It's not about the garden centre or Deri's baps.'

'You're leaving me, aren't you?' he says, sounding resigned.

'I . . . I just need something more right now. I need to remember I'm alive! I love you, and the life we've had and our kids, but we want different things. You like your Friday nights at the pub, and quiz night. I hate quiz night.'

He laughs. 'I like black-out blinds and you like the curtains open,' he joins in.

'Pete, we haven't shared a bedroom in well over a year.'

'That was the treatment. I wanted you to rest.'

'And I wanted you to get a good night's sleep.'

He sighs. 'To be honest, I saw this coming. That's why I wanted us to have the party – thought it might set us back on track. But it looks like we're heading in different directions,' he says sadly. 'We have been for a while, haven't we?'

I nod. 'We'll always be best friends. Parents to our children. We'll always be family. But, yes, there are different roads for us to explore now. I just need some time away, to feel as though I'm making the most of my life after everything that's happened. I want to embrace adventure and get away from everything that reminds me of Jules with the cancer.'

'How long will you be gone?'

'I'm not sure. But I think it would be good for both of us.' I look at the golf-club doors.

'Someone's bringing the water,' I say.

'That's Mandy. She's the bar manager. Hang on.' He hurries over to her, takes the jug and a glass and reassures her that, yes, everything is fine. 'Mandy thought you might be having a turn. She's been very supportive about the treatment.'

'I don't know her.'

'Oh, she's very nice, you'd like her. On her own since her daughter moved out and her husband left. But she runs a great bar. Always has a good selection of crisps.'

He's waffling now. He stops talking. Then he says slowly, 'This is for real, isn't it?'

I take a deep breath. 'I want us both to be happy. Let's pursue that happiness in our different ways. Do our own thing.' I take hold of his hands and give them a gentle squeeze. 'I need to find out who I am without the treatment going on. What the new Jules looks like.'

He gazes at me. 'But what will I do without you?'

'You'll play golf.' I chuckle. 'And more golf.'

He joins in. 'I do like golf.'

'I know. And you still have work – you love your job at the warehouse. And you enjoy a Sunday drink here.'

He smiles. I put one hand on his forearm.

He pats it. 'Thank you. For everything. I mean it. I want you to be happy,' he says quietly.

'And I want you to be happy. We want the best for each other, so let's just give this a go.'

He slips into practical Pete mode. 'Will you take your car?'

'If that's okay.' Suddenly it feels bizarrely like we're arranging a weekend away with friends, instead of ending our married life.

'It's just been serviced and there's a full tank in it.'

Suddenly the tears threaten to reappear as I realise this is it: I'm walking away, to a new adventure.

'Where will you go?'

'Back to France,' I say. 'See if there's anything there for me.'

He frowns. 'What about the cat?' He seems more worried about that than anything else. 'She likes her routine.'

'A bit like you . . .' I say fondly.

'Yes,' he agrees.

'Let her stay with you,' I say gently.

'And what about the cake?' He points back towards the party.

'You eat it. It's your favourite. Chocolate.'

'I'm a bit more of a lemon-drizzle man, these days,' he says.

'There's a lot we don't know about each other any more, Pete.'

He smiles. 'I know you like yellow roses. They're your favourite.'

'No, Pete, they're yours. You felt red roses were too expensive and could get yellow ones for half the price and have bought them ever since. I like sunflowers and poppies.'

He falls silent. Then: 'When shall we tell the children?'

'Let's tell them in the morning, shall we?' I say.

'What about other people?'

'I bet no one will even notice I've gone.'

'That's not true!'

'Tell them the truth. I'm having "a life pivot". That's what they call them, these days.'

'Life pivot, right,' he says, and stands very still.

I kiss him on the cheek as a best friend would do.

'Will you come back in with me?' he asks. 'Share our last evening together, so to speak?'

I smile and nod, tears in my eyes.

He takes my hand and leads me back into the golf club where Maddie and Jake beckon us to their table with their partners and Fridge says, over the microphone, 'And now we're going to start the quiz.'

I wish I had quietly slipped away. This party isn't for me. It was about trying to hold on to what we once had. But that's okay, I tell myself. We should celebrate what we had. This is one last night as the old Jules. I'm already feeling lighter, freer. Tomorrow I will no longer be Mrs Juliet Townley. I will be whoever I want to be.

A huge wave of excitement and a happiness I haven't experienced in a long time floods me. I may not look like the younger me any more, but something inside me feels it. And I like it. I regard my family around me, all about to spread their wings, and smile as they battle over quiz questions, cherishing the laughter and knowing that, from tomorrow, everything will change. Tomorrow is the start of a new chapter for us all.

Chapter 2

Everything seems to happen very quickly. We speak to Maddie and Jake over toast and tea in the morning, the eggs and bacon I was going to cook all but forgotten as Pete helps me explain that, as much as we love each other, we want different things in life. He wants to stay put and buy a La-Z-Boy chair, and I want to go and explore opportunities in France. We explain to their shocked faces that no one else is involved.

'Mum and I still care very much about each other, which is why we want each other to be happy,' he says.

'But you're Mum and Dad!' ripostes Maddie.

'Yes, but we're also Jules and Pete,' he says, surprising me by explaining so well. 'And now, more than ever, we have to find out what makes us happy and go for it.'

'And you're going now, are you?' asks Jake.

'I am,' I say. 'No time like the present. I'm going to do it while I'm still feeling brave enough. Otherwise I'll get cold feet.' I smile, nervous as a kitten. 'I've packed. Your dad's loaded the car for me. We booked the Eurotunnel online. And I'll be staying in Kent this evening. I've booked an Airbnb. Really close to the tunnel port. I'll be driving onto the train and driving off in France. And Dad's sorted out my satnav, loaded my journey, so I shouldn't get lost.'

It's all happened in such a rush. But now I've said it out loud, I just want to get going. I don't want to lose my nerve. But I can hardly believe what I'm saying, let alone explain it. It's just something I have an urge to do, to take my chance while I can. But now I'm suddenly gripped by fear. What if this is just a stupid wobble? What if I get there and want to come home? And just as I've thought it, Pete says, 'And if Mum wants to come home at any time, that's what she'll do. This is her home, as well as yours, for as long as you and she need it.'

I couldn't be more grateful for everything Pete has done for me and given me in our twenty-five years together. And right now, whether he really wants it or not, he's giving me the best present of all, understanding why I need to go, and why we're not Jules and Pete any more. I'm just Jules. That feels very scary – and exhilarating.

I hug them one by one as we stand by the car, packed with pillows and a duvet that Pete insists I'll need when I finally move into my own place, even though I'll be staying in B&B for a while, and the French have super-markets where I can buy stuff. I take them anyway because it's thoughtful of him and he insists.

I promise to let them know how I'm getting on during the journey and to message when I arrive. And not to talk to strangers! We manage a teary laugh and then, with a final wave, a slam of the car door and a toot on the horn, I'm off. Just me, just Jules, driving away from everything and everyone I've known and loved, with hugs, love and blessings from them all. Tears fill my eyes, so just down the road I pull into a layby and let them fall to clear my vision. I could just turn back and say it was a mistake and I'm too scared to go. Then a message pings through on my phone. It's Annie: *This is amazing. I'm so proud of you! Live your life! You only have one!*

I sit and look at the message on the screen, and take a deep breath. I send a quick one to the family WhatsApp group to make them smile: *Got to the end of the road! On my way!* And get smiley faces back. Even from Pete, who rarely uses more than one word at a time: *Safe journey. Good luck x.* And now, although it will take time for this new 'normal' to settle in, I know it's the right thing to do. My purpose returns to me. I put the car into gear and set off, back to where I need to be right now. Excitement begins to grow. I have sunglasses on, the window open, Dolly Parton playing, and I'm heading south. It feels strange. Strange, but thrilling. I feel alive.

After an overnight stay in an anonymous hotel somewhere near Folkestone, where only a month ago we'd been to start our holiday, I'm here on my own. It's 1 April, and I'm making the Eurotunnel crossing. This is so surreal it almost feels like a joke. I remind myself it's not. It's very much real. And a very long way from where I was in life this time last year, wondering if I had a future at all.

On the train I check my messages.

A WhatsApp from Maddie says: *Proud of you, Mum. YOLO! Jake's coming round to the idea. It's just going to take a little time for it to sink in. He's worried in case you get ill. But I've told him they have doctors in France too. And, as Dad says, you can always come home. #Cool-Mum! xxx*

I smile and send her a picture from inside the train. *On my way! Xx*

When I arrive in France, I file off the train with the other passengers and I know the first thing I want to do, but I have to focus hard on driving on the other side of the road. I take it slow and steady. I stop in the first small town I come to and, as if Fate had a hand in it, I'm opposite a *boulangerie*. I park in the square and head towards where the scent of baking bread is coming from. Next door is a coffee shop, with seats outside. I look at the rows of baguettes and, under the glass of the counter, curls of croissants, puffed up and glazed.

'*Une baguette, s'il vous plaît,*' I say to the woman behind the counter.

'*Bonjour, Madame,*' she says, and I realise I've made my first faux-pas by not saying 'good morning' first.

'*Pardon. Bonjour, Madame.*' I order the baguette and a croissant, and pay. I step out of the shop and find a table and chairs outside the adjoining café, where I order '*Un café au lait, s'il vous plaît.*'

The smell of the baguette and croissant is too much for me to bear. My stomach rumbles, my mouth waters.

As I wait for the coffee, I hold the warm baguette in

one hand and tear off the end. It cracks and little shards of the hard, glazed exterior drop to the ground. Inside, the bread is white, light and airy, warm and welcoming as its comforting smell rises.

I put the piece of bread into my mouth. At first, again, there's the crack and crunch of the exterior . . . not soft like the 'French' bread you get in British supermarkets. It is completely different inside too: soft, salty and beautifully risen. I chew and let the contrast of the two textures, the crunchy coating and fluffy interior, dance on my tongue before I swallow. This is why I'm back. The simple pleasures. A young woman brings me my coffee and wishes me '*Bon appétit.*' The steam from the coffee rises and blends with the aroma of the freshly baked bread. I tear off another piece of baguette, and bite, then sip the coffee.

A message pings on the family WhatsApp group. It's from Maddie again, hoping I'm okay. I tell her I am and I'm in France, stopping for a break and a baguette before driving on to the south of Brittany, to where Dad and I holidayed. I reassure her again that we both love her and her brother, and will always be there for them, when they want us to be. And then I send her a snap of my baguette and coffee.

Looks great. We're home. Hope you loved my DJing at the party! Jake responds.

I did! Xx. Then I add, *Go for your dreams*, with a smiley face, and he sends me a smiley face with hearts. Everyone should be encouraged to go for their dreams, I tell myself, and hold the phone to my lips, as a wave of homesickness washes over me.

I remember the house Pete and I bought when the children were small, the house we had always planned to extend with my small savings pot. But when Maddie and Jake moved out to lead their own lives, we didn't need a bigger house. It suited us well, and it'll carry on suiting Pete — close to the golf course, not far to town, the doctor and the out-of-town supermarket. And, of course, the garden centre for coffee. He's happy there. It's his world. But I couldn't stay there, like him, just waiting for grandchildren to come along.

You too, says Jake. *It's time you did something for you, rather than spending your time worrying about us!*

I send him a smiley face with hearts this time and, not for the first time over the past few hours, brush away proud, happy but sad tears, registering the passing of time. It goes so quickly. One minute I was making Easter bonnets and driving to after-school clubs, looking after them when they were ill in the night, and the next, life had become very quiet after they'd left home. They were the ones coming in to sit with me when I was ill in the night. And now time has marched on again, and it's up to us to keep up with it.

Just follow your heart, I say.

Maybe I will, he says. *Maybe it's time we made the leap and went for it in Spain!*

I reply: *You won't know unless you give it a try. You can always go home if it doesn't work. But at least you'll have tried.*

He sends me a thumbs-up emoji.

I finish the coffee and take the rest of the baguette

back to the car. I'm fired up to complete my journey to Brittany and the little village I left behind.

'You are back?' says the old man, Monsieur Martin, peering at me through his thick glasses, a cigarette hanging from his lower lip. He is wearing nothing but a vest, with braces holding up his trousers, and is clearly drinking *pastis*, judging from the smell on his breath.

'I am,' I say, to the owner of the only hotel in town.

'But you just left?' he says, frowning. 'You forgot something?'

'Yes, I suppose I did,' I reply, thinking that if I told him I'd forgotten *me*, it might take more explaining than is really needed right now. 'But I would like to rent the room again, please.' The one Pete and I had stayed in to celebrate the end of my treatment – a friend of a friend at the golf club had recommended it, for a peaceful, rural escape, with good walking and cheap wine. It was where I may have left a bit of me . . . And certainly my dreams.

'How long for?' he asks, sucking at his cigarette and apparently wondering if he has space in his reservation diary, which I'm pretty sure he does. This is not the sort of hotel people are flocking to. The town is small, quiet and, right now, exactly where I want to be, next to the village with an abandoned mill that I hope will have my name on it one day . . .

'For as long as it takes,' I say, 'at the same rate we stayed when we were here before.'

'As long as it takes?' He shrugs. 'As long as it takes to do what?'

'To find out who owns the old mill in the Village du Grand Lac.'

'*Le moulin*? The old mill.' He looks confused. 'But why? Everybody can use the lake. Why do you want to know who owns it?'

'Because . . . I want to buy it.'

'The mill? But it's . . . old!'

A smile spreads across my face. I'm saying what I've been thinking since we got home just under a month ago. While I was planning and organising the party that Pete wanted for our anniversary, all I've thought about is standing beside the mill and that I didn't want to leave.

Monsieur Martin turns down the corners of his mouth and I fear for the cigarette. Somehow, against the odds, it hangs on determinedly. And why not?

'So, I'd like to rent the room, if I can, until I'm ready to move.'

He opens the door to the mid-terrace townhouse wider, eyeing me suspiciously. He peers out of the door, left and then right. 'Your 'usband?'

I shake my head. 'It's just me,' I say, and make a decision for the new me, tomorrow's me. I revert back to my full name. Not the one Pete called me by, not Jules. 'I'm Juliet,' I say, and start to give my surname, my married name, but then say, 'Just Juliet.'

He turns to his wife, sitting in the front room at the table there. She nods. 'Okay, Just Juliet,' he says. '*Oui*, the room is available.' He begins to list his rules in fast French, just like he did when Pete and I checked in last month. Before everything changed. Before the anniversary party. Before I felt I needed to find me . . . here in a small town, in France, in a little *chambre d'hôte* in the middle of the French countryside with a cockerel to wake me every morning. It didn't make Pete smile. He wanted to leave . . . or wring its neck.

'And no guests,' he adds, handing me the key.

'I promise, no guests.' I smile. 'It's just me from now on.' I move my belongings in, eager to get back to the old mill, find the for-sale sign and ring the telephone number.

Chapter 3

I open my purse, see a single euro and smile. It catches in the early June sunlight. I've been here for eight weeks now and have adjusted to euros not pounds, but with not much call for cash, these days, I've only got a few coins and notes. But I do have a euro, and that is very good. I smile, because a euro is exactly what I need.

I plan to go over to the old mill and have a picnic on the lawn next to the lake. At *my* old mill, I think, and smile to myself. I contemplate the key in my bag and the handshake I shared with the *notaire* once the final paperwork was signed. My initial reaction was to hug him – I was so overjoyed that the mill was finally mine, signed, sealed and paid for at an incredible price. But the horror on his face as I threw open my arms told me that wasn't the right reaction, so I gripped his hand and shook it. Maybe a little over-enthusiastically.

I'm ready to move out of my little room at the *chambre d'hôte*, where I've been for the last eight weeks under the curious eyes of its owners, Monsieur and Madame Martin, wondering why I would buy a run-down old mill in the very quiet Village du Grand Lac. I've been filling my days exploring other towns and villages nearby, getting to know the lie of the land, market days, visiting *brocantes* and planning how I want the mill to look when I turn it into a *salon de thé*. I've also done lots of online research while drinking coffee in cafés. And, of course, I'm learning French online and eating *plat du jour* lunches in small restaurants on my own. Not that I minded that: I was used to it. I'd known it was the beginning of the end when Pete and I stopped eating together. He preferred ready meals by a big-brand producer from the supermarket, but I liked the veg box we had delivered. I made soups and stews from it, filling the freezer with batch cooking, as you do when you're cooking for one. It was just a habit we slipped into.

But it was our holiday to France that brought things to a close for Pete and me. A crossroads. It was supposed to be a celebration of the end of my treatment, waking up here in Brittany, looking out over the fields feeling more alive than I ever have, but something between Pete and me had died. I wanted to grab life, live it for the now. He wanted to carry on as normal . . . whatever normal was. Go back to how we were before I got the diagnosis. Pretend it never happened and it had just gone away. I wanted to do everything I'd never done.

So, we could never have bought the old mill. But I did!

I texted the family WhatsApp group when I came out of the *notaire's* office and sent a picture of the big metal key.

No going back now then! said Maddie.

When can we visit? said Jake.

Whenever you want and I cannot wait!

Pete sent a thumbs-up, which was good. I know he meant it.

I messaged Annie too: *Well, I've done it. I have the key. I own an old watermill in France. I'm scared and thrilled! I'm going to have lunch beside the lake, on my lawn! I can't believe it!*

Eek! she replied. *Me neither! That is amazing! Send pictures! I want to see what it looks like. I want to imagine myself there!*

I will!

So this is it. I'm here, with the key. I've acquired the mill in good time, I'm told, at a good price, it having been on the market for several years. It had been sold by the *mairie*, the town hall, after years of standing empty. The mayor was insistent the sale be straightforward and quick.

So here I am, eight weeks on from arriving on 1 April, the key in my handbag, in the square at Village de Grand Lac, standing under the shade of the line of plane trees facing each other just beyond the *pétanque* pitch. There is a small *tabac* but not much else, which may be a good thing as my idea for the old mill and the *salon de thé* begins to grow. It's lunchtime and the village is deserted, apart from a white cat with brown and black patches on its back, lying out in the sun in front of the old *boulangerie*. People visiting will need somewhere to eat. Maybe I could get some signs done, pointing out of the village and directing them on the ten-minute walk down the lane to the mill. All I need to do now is take my idea to the mayor, explain my plans for my business and apply for a visa to stay on and work. Looks like they could do with more businesses around here, more places for people to eat. I'm sure my idea will be just right for the mill and the village.

I turn and stare at the vending machine in front of me, opposite the *tabac* by the parking spaces. This is a first for me. In the neighbouring town there is a *boulangerie* where I bought croissants every morning and a baguette for lunch. The bread was good, but the woman behind the counter barely smiled. Here, in this smaller village, the *boulangerie* is shut, the yellowing blinds firmly down with a closed sign on the door. Instead, there is this: a vending machine selling fresh baguettes.

I can read the instructions, written in French, thanks to my online lessons and recent Duolingo streak. I slide my euro into the slot. My stomach rumbles at the smell of the goat's cheese I bought from a farmhouse between here and the town where I've been staying, along with some fresh tomatoes from a stall on the side of the road. Their grassy smell reaches my nostrils and tantalises my tastebuds.

I hear the euro drop onto other coins in the machine and lift the flap waiting for my bread to drop. I watch as the baguette shakes behind the glass. It shakes some more and then, when I frown and wonder if I'm going to get my bread, the whirring noise stops.

'It hasn't dropped!' I say to the machine, and lift the flap. 'You didn't drop my baguette!' I say. I give the machine a little nudge to see if my baguette will fall out. But nothing moves.

I give the glass a gentle knock, but the bread still doesn't move.

'Oh, come on!' I look in my purse, but there are no other euro coins. I stick my fingers into the machine and check the coin-return hole. Nothing. I press eject, several times, to get my coin back, but nothing appears.

'I need my baguette,' I tell the machine, and give the clear glass a firmer bash with the flat of my hand, hoping it will shift the stuck loaf. 'This is my special picnic! And you aren't going to stop me!' I'm sounding slightly unhinged, but cheese and tomatoes with no bread is not lunch.

'I'm out of euros!' I try to reason with the machine. It does nothing.

'Okay, well, if you're going to be like that, there's only one thing for it!'

This time I reach my arms around the machine, ready to wrestle and shake it. I'm tired and hungry and I need to eat. And my baguette is just in front of me. My baguette I've paid for. This is my celebration baguette! Everything I've dreamt of since I first got here: eating it on the lawn by the lake.

I shake the machine but the baguette isn't budging. 'Oh, come on, give me my bread!'

'Madame.'

My head snaps up and I realise how this looks. I stand back from the machine and straighten to see a tall, broad-shouldered, good-looking man, with long dark hair and a beard. A very good-looking man indeed.

He raises an eyebrow. 'Can I help you?' he asks, then adds, 'We have laws against vandalism,' an amused smile pulling at the corners of his mouth. My cheeks flush. 'I saw you from there.' He points at the *tabac*, with tables and chairs outside. 'I can see you have a dispute with our bread machine. We would appreciate it if you didn't break it. It is our only way to buy our daily baguettes around here.'

'*Monsieur, bonjour,*' I say, taking another step away from the vending machine and feeling hot. I lift my shoulders and tilt my head. 'This is not what it looks like,' I say evenly. 'I wasn't trying to vandalise it.'

'I see.' He folds his arms across his chest. 'You had your arms around it. Maybe you were embracing it. Madame, have you been drinking? I haven't seen you in the bar. Maybe the sun has affected you. Do you need help? Can I ring someone for you?'

'No,' I say, horrified, and if it weren't so embarrassing, I'd be laughing. 'I'm not sick. It's just my baguette, it's stuck. I only had one euro. And now I have no bread, and that means I have no lunch.'

He holds my gaze and I wonder if he's trying to decide whether to believe me, or is just teasing me. He steps around the vending machine.

'See, that one,' I point to the listing baguette. 'I've paid. It won't drop it,' I say, pointing to the balanced, angled loaf.

He looks at it, arms folded again, his checked shirt rolled back to his elbows, his small hoop earring catching the light. 'You're right. I can see the problem,' he says, staring at the baguette matter-of-factly. 'We all need to eat.'

'I know!' I put my hands on my hips and let out a sigh.

'It doesn't matter.' I wave a hand, backing away. I look around the village square, at the *tabac*, where he's come from. It seems to sell cigarettes, scratch cards, coffee and pastis. Three old men are stepping out of it, in flat caps and short-sleeved shirts, with braces holding up their trousers, clearly coming to watch my frustration with the bread machine. Oh, God, I have an audience! Let's hope none of them had a phone to film me. I very much doubt it. This is rural Brittany, not some suburban sprawl where everyday life is recorded for others' amusement.

'I'm sure it'll work for someone else,' I say, keen to move away from the curious eyes. As I turn I notice a face in the window above the closed *boulangerie*. The sun makes it impossible to see properly. I shade my eyes and squint, but the face has gone.

'Is there anywhere else I can buy food around here?'

He shakes his head.

'What about the *tabac*?'

He shakes his head again, his long hair rippling. 'Sadly, this is all we have now. *C'est dommage.*'

'Yes. It's a shame. Well, I must be going.' I'm keen to remove myself from the centre of attention. I can see the local gossip now: mad, middle-aged British woman hugs baguette machine in the midday sun. That won't help my business plans. '*Au revoir,*' I say, raising a hand.

'*Attend!* I may be able to help,' the man from the *tabac* says. He takes a euro from his top pocket and holds it up. 'It is always advisable to keep a spare euro for moments like this. Always be prepared.'

Then he puts it slowly and deliberately, with a little pressure, into the coin slot. I wonder if there's a technique I don't know about. Another baguette moves and this time releases, knocking mine out of its stuck position. Both land in the tray at the bottom. He lifts the hatch and coolly takes out two baguettes. He hands one to me.

'*Merci,*' I say, realising he may not be quite as fierce as he first appeared.

'You have to have the skills!' He grins.

'What's the secret?'

'Trained engineer!' He laughs, tears off the top of his baguette and tosses it into his mouth and chews and swallows. 'Now, no more vandalising our bread machine. *Bonnes vacances,*' he says, and tears off another piece.

'*Merci,*' I say again, and smile. '*Bon appétit.*'

'Could be better,' he says, raising the bread in his hand. 'Much better. *Au revoir,*' he says, before I have the chance to explain I'm not on holiday but going to be living and building a business here. A van pulls up and the door opens.

I see my baguette rescuer's smile freeze. Suddenly, his expression is stony.

'*Bonjour, Madame*. Laurent,' says the shorter man getting out of the van. I recognise him from the bakery where I've been buying croissants. He pulls out a big bunch of keys, opens the back of the van and then the vending machine.

Laurent nods at him, still eating the end of the baguette.

'*Bon appétit,*' says the man from the van to Laurent, smiling, but not warmly.

Laurent, from the *tabac*, lifts one side of his mouth.

Suddenly the man I thought was attractive is now dark-faced and edgy. 'Too much salt,' Laurent says, tossing another piece of bread into his mouth. 'And could be fresher. But beggars can't be choosers,' he adds rudely, raising his eyebrows.

'You may be a beggar, but I'm doing quite well for myself,' says the baker, gesturing to his clearly expensive, new-looking van.

Laurent rolls his eyes. 'We are the beggars because we have no alternative to this stupid machine! It is just a money-making exercise.'

'Business is good, yes,' says the baker. 'How's yours? Selling enough coffee and _pastis_ to your three customers?'

I'm frozen to the spot. Clearly there is no love lost between the two men. In fact, from where I'm standing, they obviously don't like each other at all. And one is the tabac owner. The sort of place where you can buy cigarettes and tobacco, stamps and lottery tickets and get a coffee or a drink. Clearly not somewhere I'll be spending much time.

The baker laughs as if this exchange of insults is water off a duck's back. He pulls more baguettes from the back of the van and loads the vending machine. 'You should have waited for the fresh ones,' he says to me, brushing his blond hair off his face with a practised swish.

'If you were a good timekeeper, we would know when they were going to be here,' Laurent says. He pulls another euro from his top pocket and tosses it to me. 'For next time,' he says, 'in case you have to battle with this machine again.' He saunters back towards the bar over the square. 'Always be prepared! *Mise en place*. Everything in its place.'

I catch the euro, surprising myself with my swift reaction. But I can't help feeling uncomfortable about the exchange and wish I hadn't been there to witness it. Clearly, Laurent is not the musketeer and rescuer I mistook him for.

'You are on holiday, Madame?' the baker asks. He has filled the machine and locked it. Now he empties the moneybox.

'Actually,' the smile returns to my face under the warm Brittany sun. 'I live here. I've bought the old mill.'

'*Le moulin*? Wow, that is fantastic! I think you say "congratulations"!' he says, as if considering what I'd just said. 'I didn't see that happening! And when do you move in?'

'Today!' I'm beaming. 'I'm going there now!'

I put my hand on my bag, with my bread, tomatoes and a half-bottle of champagne. And then I can't help myself: I blurt out the plans I've been dreaming and hatching since I first saw the old mill. I'm ready now to put them into action.

'I'm hoping to turn it into a *salon de thé*,' I say, my excitement bubbling up, as if it's going to burst out of me. 'I just need the mayor's approval.'

'A *salon de thé*? In that case, you will need bread. Come and see me,' he says, then reaches into the van, hands me a card, and then, from the back, another baguette. 'A fresher one. For your celebration. Remember, let's talk.'

Suddenly this is all very real. My dream of a tea shop on the mill lawn is within touching distance. It will be fine, I think, as long as I steer clear of Laurent, who evidently has a problem with the baker. And once I've seen the mayor and got the business plan in place, the idea rolling out, it will be very real indeed.

'I will. *Merci*,' I say. I put the card and the fresh baguette into my basket.

'I must visit, see what you're going to do with the place,' he says. 'Let me know when would be good for me to call over.'

'That would be lovely. I could do with making some friends.' I smile, feeling warm from the inside out.

'I am Claude. What is your name?'

'Juliet. Just Juliet,' I reply.

'*Bonne chance*, Just Juliet.' He looks me straight in the eyes. I haven't been looked at like that in a long time. 'I look forward to us becoming friends,' he says, his eyes sparkling.

For the first time in years, I feel seen. I put my basket onto my shoulder and head for the car, smiling all the way on the short drive from the village to the old mill, the sun shining, birds singing, the hedgerow bursting over the banks at either side of the road. I'm desperate to get there: everything is falling into place.

Chapter 4

It's hot. I pull up at the gates to the mill, cut the engine and push open the door of my Fiat Panda. The heat hits me like a wall. It might be Brittany, but even here in the north of France it's a flaming hot June day. My life looks very different since I first saw the mill, standing here with Pete. But from what I can see, very little has changed here at the mill itself, except that there is more greenery on the trees. I stare at the mill and my heart quickens as I see it again with fresh eyes because it's mine.

With all the paperwork in place, this is what my small pension pot has bought me. Far better than an extension to our house, or new conservatory furniture. This is exciting. An opportunity. I clutch my basket to me with my baguette, goat's cheese and tomatoes, then pull out my phone and take photographs to send to the family WhatsApp group and Annie. I snap away, picture after picture.

I've been dreaming of this place since we got home after our holiday. While Pete wanted to plan our party, all I could think of was the mill. I've always wanted to have a go at running a business, but Pete thought it was too risky. But once I started baking in lockdown and went on through my treatment, this dream has been percolating, like coffee heating in the pot, aromatic and ready to drink, reviving. And when I saw this place, that day, on our walk, it was like a whole new world opening up to me. A new beginning. And now I'm here, looking at my dream business, I feel as if I've got a second chance. But I've taken on a huge challenge. I mean, it's just me, not like on *Château DIY*, where there's usually two of them, encouraging each other. Am I really going to be able to make it the business I have in my mind's eye?

I send the pictures I've taken to the group, remembering it's Jake's partner Becky's birthday today. *Happy birthday, Becky!* I type. *I'm here!* and attach some pictures of the mill.

We're off to Spain! says Jake. *Time to follow your advice and our hearts!*

Good for you! I reply. *Enjoy it! Maddie? How's things?*

So-so. Off for a weekend with a friend, she replies, and I wonder if this is still Heidi or maybe someone new.

Pete replies with another happy face, which makes me smile. He's a good man . . . just not my man any more. But he'll always be a big part of my life. We've grown apart between shift work, me at the care home, him at the warehouse, having a family and then the illness. He loves his golf and I felt I had sort of disappeared. When the kids left home, I didn't know who I was and then I became Jules with the illness. But that's in the past, I tell myself firmly.

I send the same pictures to Annie, who immediately sends back a picture of herself, giving me the thumbs-up. Despite her thin face and hair to match, she's beaming.

Yay! You did it!!! she types. *This has brightened my day right up! I love the stone work. And the single-storey building on the other side of the drive. It's a lot of brambles to clear but, like you say, it could make a lovely* gîte *some day. Send more pictures!*

I smile, my nose tingling. I rub it. *I can't wait for you and the family to come and see it!*

It's a promise! she replies.

I'm going to hold you to that!

And we both know it's a big promise to make.

By Christmas! she replies.

I'd best get started on making rooms for guests!

Oh, yes! I want to see everything about this place that has stolen your heart and enjoy the journey with you!

You will, I say, and send a kiss. 'You will,' I say aloud.

The *à vendre* sign is still listing on the gate. I step forward, untwist the wire holding it there and pull it off with a flourish. Despite its neglected state, I can picture exactly what the mill will look like once it's had the TLC it deserves. This is what I imagine in the dark of night, when the dread creeps up on me. I force myself to imagine this place when it's finished, with the family here. It's kept me going over the last couple of months.

I leave the car at the gates and walk slowly down the overgrown grassy drive. I breathe in the smell of warm soil and make a mental note to get the drive weeded and raked. I'm listening to the birds and want to remember every bit of this moment. To my right is the one-storey building that may have housed livestock, a piggery perhaps. As I suggested to Pete, one day it will be a self-contained cottage for guests. Maybe Pete will come. It feels strange being here without him to talk to and tell him what I'm thinking. Although we've grown apart, we've still gone through all of life's major milestones together. But this is just me. It's scary but good at the same time. I take a picture of the piggery and send it to Annie, telling her my plans, and that I hope she'll come as soon as I'm ready for guests and she's fit enough. She messages straight back, saying she hopes that too.

Then I look up at the mill. It's built from big stones, with huge corner ones, covered with moss and lichen. I plan to hire a jet wash from a builders' merchant I've found on one of my recces – they need cleaning. I've also found paint suppliers, cheap but cheerful baking equipment in the supermarket, and plenty of crockery and cutlery at the *brocantes* where I've spent hours searching for cups and saucers, napkins and cake forks. They're now boxed up in the boot of my car, ready to move into their new home.

I head for the slope by the side of the building. I'm planning to put steps in to make it easier for people to arrive at the front of the mill, facing the lake. By the time Annie gets here, it'll be straightforward access.

I hold on to the cold stone wall, in the shade on this side of the house, running my hand along the damp mossy stones for stability as I pick my way up the overgrown uneven slope. Thorny brambles run along the edge of the building, catching my bare legs, making me kick at them, and clinging to my dress, snagging it. I take a big leap forward, pulling at my dress and yanking it free, then straighten to gaze at the view in front of me.

It's mesmerising. The green grassy area in front of me needs a good cut, but I can picture it with tables and chairs, large umbrellas and bunting for my *salon de thé*. People sitting and chatting, drinking tea on a Sunday afternoon from the china I've been collecting, eating my homemade cakes and sipping crisp, cold *crémant*. I send the picture to Annie. She says she's put the one of the lake as a screensaver on her iPad so she can dream about getting there. It's helping her through the treatment to have a happy place to focus on, she says. And having Annie pushing me to live my best life is helping me to do it.

A flash of blue catches my eye as it darts across the lake, which is full of reeds and covered with lily pads. It's followed by another flash. The kingfishers are still here! It's like they've stayed to welcome me. I walk up to the water's edge and stare out. An open canoe is tucked into the bank at the corner of the lake, tied up, with two paddles in it. It's not that I'd ever get into it, but it adds to the charm of the place. '*Le moulin*,' I say, as I face it, as if introducing myself to my mill, taking in the stone façade, with shadows from the weeping willows on one side of the water creating dappled patterns and shade.

I make a mental list of things to do: the shutters need repainting; the big green door in the arched stone frame needs washing and its brass handle needs polishing. The door leads into the middle floor of the building. The windows of the room on the third floor, at the top, look out over the lake, and on the other side of the property, where I can hear water trickling, the big wooden wheel on the far wall must once have turned but is silent and still in a dry concrete pit.

This is exactly where I want to be. This place and I will come back to life together. I reach into my bag and pull out the key. I put it into the lock and, with a little effort, push open the door, which squeaks and groans and, as it opens, throws light into the dark, cavernous room.

'I'm home,' I say, taking in the cream stone fireplace, with blackened walls from fires, the metal cogs and stone wheel standing in pride of place. There are piles of junk, wooden boxes and even an old bicycle that all need clearing out, but I can see past all that. Once again, my mind turns to how this will look with the cogs polished as authentic decoration, tables and chairs with white covers and glasses on them. 'I'm home,' I say again.

Chapter 5

It's cool in here, almost chilly, as I climb down the stone steps into dark main room, where I plan to offer my afternoon teas, a set menu and trolley of daily bakes. In the cooler months I'll light the fire and some candles, and in summer, there will be flowers on the tables and more tables outside where visitors can watch the birds.

I walk to the back of the room past the cogs that turned the circular stones that used to grind grain into flour when it was a working mill and that I plan to make a talking point about how this place had a past, but today a whole new lease on life. A bit like me. I put my hand on the cold, worn stones as I pass.

The walls are covered with colourful graffiti – and not the artistic kind. Rough, crude images and words from orange and red spray cans that need to be scrubbed off and painted over. But that shouldn't take me too long. I know where to get the paint and where to hire a ladder.

I walk through the dusty room around the debris on the wooden floorboards that need cleaning and polishing. At the very back, there is an open wooden staircase to the upper floors. Straight ahead I can see a stone step and an archway with a curtain across it, and in front of that, against the whitewashed wall, is a basic kitchen. I pull my new wicker basket off my shoulder and leave it on the wooden work surface, put in for its functionality rather than its appearance I'm guessing. With a bit of paint and maybe some gingham curtains to cover the open shelves, I'm sure I can get it Instagram-ready. I'm excited to make a start and know exactly where I'll find the red and white curtains I want at the Monday market in the next town.

I'll take some pictures now for before-and-after shots. I pull out my phone and photograph the kitchen and the millstone workings in the middle of what will be the dining area. Again, I send them to Annie, and get smiley faces and thumbs-up emojis back. She may be tired now, although still enjoying the pictures. I remember how drained treatment could make me feel.

I venture beyond the kitchen through the archway with the curtain. I pull it back. It's just as I remember it from the viewing I arranged as soon as I arrived here. The estate agent thought I was just a nosy tourist and could barely raise any enthusiasm for the place. He couldn't believe it when I made the offer there and then.

There is a small living area behind the curtain, with a wood-burning stove, and more wooden stairs up to a mezzanine that will be perfect for my living and sleeping area. The small window looks down the drive over fields to the village beyond. I take a few more pictures. This will suit me perfectly. A little studio for one. I have a mattress being delivered later, and the rest of the room will be my living room. I'll put in the television and get a chair, or maybe a sofa. I'll be perfectly cosy here, I think, running my hand over the walls as I head up the stairs to the open-plan first floor, where there is a chute towards the cogs and workings downstairs. I walk over to the windows at the front, overlooking the lake. I take more pictures and put them all in the family WhatsApp group. Later, I'll save them in a folder for my Instagram and Facebook accounts when I open for business.

My phone rings, making me jump. It's Maddie, on video call, and I answer it quickly, hoping nothing's wrong. 'Hello, love. Everything okay?'

'Hi, Mum.' She pauses and I hold my breath. 'Yes, everything's fine. Just . . .' I wait for her to continue. 'It's just weird without you here.'

I give a little laugh of relief. 'Maddie, you don't live at home.'

'I know, but I liked knowing you were there if I needed you.'

I smile affectionately. 'I'm only across the water. You can come any time! Come as soon as you like.'

'I know,' she says quietly. 'But, it's just strange. You and Dad. You were like constant. I don't seem able to stay with the same person for longer than a fortnight before I'm bored. How did you do it, Mum, for all those years?'

'Well, I suppose I married my best friend. We liked being together, doing things together.'

'But not any more.'

'No,' I say, 'not any more. We want different things. But that doesn't mean we don't still care about each other.

We do. We want each other to be happy. We're just not a couple any more. But that's not to say we won't stay friends. Have you spoken to your dad?'

'Yes. He's okay. Keeping to his routines.' We give a gentle laugh. 'He seems happy enough.'

'That's good,' I say, and feel a pang of regret, loss . . . pain for his pain, but also a sort of peace that this is right for us.

'He'll be fine, Mum,' she says. 'Mandy from the golf club is taking him out for coffee this week. They may even make it a regular thing.' I can hear her smile down the phone. 'And he's got a supermarket delivery coming every Wednesday. She showed him how to set up an account.'

I can't help but smile, knowing he's found someone to go for Sunday-morning coffee with. 'And you? You're okay?' I ask. 'And Heidi?'

'We finished.'

'I'm sorry.'

'It's okay. I've met someone else. But it's exhausting going through the whole getting-to-know-you thing again. Sometimes I wish I could be happy on my own.'

'Well, I can recommend it. I'm enjoying just being me.'

'Do you think you'll meet someone else, Mum?'

'Well . . .' I'm suddenly thrown. I hadn't thought about it.

'You're an attractive woman.'

I laugh. 'I wouldn't say that.'

'Don't be hard on yourself. You're not over the hill yet!'

And I laugh again at her direct, slightly tactless style, which is all Maddie.

'Who knows? Maybe I'll meet a charming Frenchman,' I joke back.

'Maybe you will, Mum. Like you said, life is for living.'

I take a moment to let this sink in. It is, and that's what I'm doing. 'I'm here at the mill. I've just sent pictures.'

'I saw them,' she says. 'You sound happy, Mum.' She's much softer than usual Maddie.

'I am.'

'That's good, really good . . . Look, I don't think we realised everything you did when you were here. Always being there when we needed you. I just . . . well, I just wanted to say thank you.'

I feel choked. 'It's fine,' I say, not really knowing what to say. 'I'm still here for you. I'm still Mum. I'm just finding out who Juliet is.'

'I know. Enjoy. And if you're not enjoying, come home,' she says.

Our roles are reversed, it seems, making me laugh. 'I will.'

Our eyes fill with tears and we look at each other through the blurry lens of the phone. Then Maddie sniffs and is back to her to-the-point self. 'Okay, well, stay in touch.'

'Of course!' I say. 'I'm having fun. I'm writing a to-do list!'

'Love you,' she says uncharacteristically.

'And you, lovely. And Dad . . . because we'll always be Mum and Dad even if we're not living together any more. We're just off on different journeys.'

'I know. Bye, Mum.'

'Bye, lovely,' and we hang up.

I head for the stairs, feeling everything has fallen into place now that she understands why I'm here and why I needed to do this. Everything is working out as well as I could have hoped.

My stomach rumbles and I remember my bread and cheese and the glass of champagne, which I'm more than ready for now. I head downstairs to the kitchen area and actually take a little leap down the final step. Just as I do, the wooden trapdoor, leading to the cellar, rattles.

I jump back, a scream catching in my throat. I stare at it. Did I just imagine that? I'm sure that trapdoor just rattled as if something or someone was underneath it. It rattles again.

My heart is racing and I'm terrified. What on earth am I thinking? That this is some romantic story with a happy-ever-after? It's an abandoned watermill, out of the village, with graffitied walls, etched by vandals. Anything could happen to me here. No wonder no one has bought the place. No one said it came with ghosts! Someone should have told me it had history.

I'm frozen to the spot. I can't move. I can't run past it. I can only stare at it. And then the trapdoor starts to lift.

Chapter 6

I do the first thing I can think of and give it a really big kick so that it slams shut.

'Awwwwwh!' I hear a pained cry.

My heart is thundering and my hands are shaking. I'm too terrified to move.

As the trapdoor opens, I see a large hand push it all the way back so it falls flat on the floorboards with a bang. The hand moves around as if checking it's safe for the rest of its body to come out. And it's taking its time.

'What the . . .?' I'm being stupid. Of course it's not a ghost. Ghosts aren't real! But someone is under the floorboards of the mill. My mill.

'Hello? Who's there?' I demand.

A figure starts to climb the steps from the cellar below.

'Who are you? And what are you doing in the cellar?' I say, as a head and shoulders turn to face me. I immediately recognise who they belong to. 'You?'

'You!'

We say it together.

He's still rubbing the back of his head. 'What did you do that for?' He frowns, pushing back his hair with silver-ringed fingers.

'What are you doing down there?' And then, crosser, 'And how did you get in?'

'How did I get in?' asks Laurent, the *tabac* owner from my earlier encounter with the bread-vending machine. 'How did *you* get in? What are you doing here?'

'I came in through the front door! With the key!' I say. 'You?''

'Through the cellar door. It's never locked.'

I make a mental note to remedy that situation. 'Well, if you could shut it on your way out . . .' I say boldly.

He rubs his head again, ruffling his hair, where the trapdoor clearly hit him fair and square. 'How come you have a key?'

'Because I've bought this place.' I walk over to the kitchen counter, put my hand into my bag and pull out the key. 'I own it.'

For a moment he doesn't say anything. He stops rubbing his head and glances around as if the bang has made him see things strangely.

'Look, if you've come for the euro you lent me, for the bread . . .'

He shakes his head. 'No, I am not here for the euro. I'm here to—' He stops mid-sentence, then says, 'You bought the place? You've bought *le moulin*,' he repeats, as if trying to comprehend it.

'Yes. As of today, this place is mine.'

For a moment he says nothing, then, '*Merde.*'

I let my hand, still holding the phone, drop to my side.

'I was telling the baker – Claude, is it? I'm going to make it into a—'

Before I have a chance to tell him about my new business and plans for the place, he reaches for the rope handle on the trapdoor, pulls it towards him, and disappears down the steps. The trapdoor slams, making me jump again, and I listen to the sound of heavy boots on wooden steps and a door banging in the cellar.

'*Au revoir!*' I call crossly after him.

Everything goes silent, apart from the birdsong outside.

I look at the trapdoor to the cellar, then at a dark wooden sideboard in the kitchen area, clearly for crockery. I grab one end and pull. It barely shifts. I pull harder and it moves. I go to the other side and push, so it's right on top of the trapdoor, to make sure there are no more visitors, unless they're invited and come through the front door. I certainly won't be inviting Laurent, that's for sure.

I straighten. I'm going to have to get used to dirty hands, I think, and dust them off. I open the sideboard I've just pulled over the trapdoor and find a small glass inside. In the kitchen, in the sparsely furnished cupboards, I find a wooden board and a sharp knife. It's all I need. My spirits pick up. I grab my basket and go out to the front lawn with my bread, cheese, tomatoes and the bottle of fizz. I'm not going to let Laurent spoil this moment. Turning up here and letting himself in, then taking off like that. Clearly a troublemaker. I'll just have to avoid him.

I head for a fallen tree trunk beside the lake and sit on

it. I hold my face up to the sunshine. But my thoughts return to the *tabac* owner. I must return that euro to him. I don't want to owe him anything. I certainly don't want him turning up unannounced through the mill floor again. But I can't help wondering what he was doing here. He didn't expect me to be at the mill. And why was he so quick to leave when I said I'd bought the place?

Chapter 7

I'm sitting outside the mayor's office the following morning after my first night sleeping in the mill. Although the new mattress was fine and the delivery men did a great job of putting it up on the mezzanine for me, it wasn't the best night's sleep I've had. I kept thinking someone was going to appear from the cellar, even though there was no way the trapdoor could open with the sideboard on top of it. But that didn't stop me worrying as I tried to get to sleep. I must have drifted off eventually, as I woke up to a dawn chorus at full volume and sunshine pouring in through the window where the shutters wouldn't close, reassuring me.

And here I am, dressed to blend in as best I can, with smart trousers, a blue-and-cream-striped top and a scarf I bought at one of the weekly markets, making me feel French already, if a tiny bit self-conscious. I'm ready to introduce myself to the mayor. I know the form. I've read enough online group chats over the past eight weeks to know how this is done. You must tell them who you are and your plans for staying in the town as soon as you arrive, and take a gift. The gift is very important – and is usually whisky.

From inside the office I can hear raised voices and I look to the woman behind the desk, who glances at me while clearly pretending to type: she is also listening intently and, by the look of it, wondering if I am too.

I sit, clutching the bottle of whisky. My *notaire* suggested the brand. In my bag I've made a scrapbook to show the mayor, with my ideas and sketches, exactly how I imagine the old mill will look when I open for business. It's moments like this, though, when I wish I wasn't doing it alone. But this wouldn't have been Pete's idea of fun. He'd've hated it. He liked his routines. His Friday night at the golf club, Sundays at the garden centre, Saturday-night curry. He was happy where things were familiar. He was confident and playful but he didn't find change easy. Adjusting to the babies was difficult for him, but once new routines had been established, he was happy. Washing bottles, making them up so there was enough to go through the night. Laying out school uniforms as the kids got older, always the night before. Bedtime routines and after-school clubs. The thought of something totally different would have had him sweating, I think affectionately. Besides, this is why I'm here: to do things I haven't done before. And I'm not ready to run home yet. If I don't do this, I'll always be wondering, *What if . . .?* So I'm going to present my ideas to the mayor. What's the worst that can happen?

I get a ping on my phone. It's Annie wishing me luck today. *I'm waiting in the mayor's office*, I tell her. *I'm nervous!*

You'll be fine. You've faced worse than this!
You're right!

I remember sitting in that chair in the hospital, the smell of cleaning fluids and the freshly laundered uniforms of the nurses. *How are you feeling today?* I ask, knowing it's a stupid question, but not wanting our text exchanges to be solely about me.

Suddenly the door of the office flies open, banging against the wall. I stuff my phone into my bag and sit up straight, as if I'm preparing for a job interview. I can hear men's voices.

'It was too good to turn down,' I hear, and translate from French to English in my head.

'It was promised! For the commune! You agreed!' It's another voice, deep and full of frustration.

'The commune has bills to pay. It was needed. I couldn't say no!'

'You could! You should have!'

The argument continues and I focus hard to understand the French.

'This village is dying and you're letting that happen. You're letting the people down. Those who worked hard to make it a good place to live. Now we have nothing left and no one here. We even have to rely on a vending machine for bread! It would have my grandfather turning in his grave.'

'You should have returned earlier, then. When you could have helped him.'

There is a silence, and my heart sinks as the tall, broad, now familiar figure of Laurent storms out of the office, slamming the door behind him. He barely stops as he glares at me. I clutch the whisky to my chest, narrowing my eyes and glaring back at him.

The woman on the desk calls after him, half rising from her seat: 'Laurent!'

He doesn't stop. He marches out of the main doors, which clatter on their hinges as he goes. It's like I'm in a Wild West saloon in the aftermath of a shoot-out.

The phone on the receptionist's desk rings. The woman answers. She looks at me, purses her lips, then replaces the receiver. 'I'm sorry,' she says, without a trace of apology, 'the mayor is unavailable today,'

'But I have an appointment,' I say. I know I'm being fobbed off.

'He has had to rearrange. He apologises,' she says, dismissing me with a wave of her hand and her long, painted nails, 'but, *non*, not today.'

I feel my phone vibrate and look down. Annie has sent a smiley face and a thumbs-up. She uses them a lot because she doesn't always have the energy to type more. I touch the screen. I'm doing this because I have been given the chance.

'I don't have time to rearrange. I have plans, and little time to start on them,' I say. I need my project to be approved as quickly as possible so that I can get my visa to stay. Suddenly I feel emboldened, not ready to be told '*non*' before I've even begun. There's a firmness in my voice I haven't heard before. I stand up and lift my head and chin. 'I have only four weeks left of my ninety allowed days here, so it's really important I see the mayor today. As arranged.'

She's surprised, clearly unused to being challenged.

I've been through a lot to get here, Annie has reminded me of that, and I'm not going to let Laurent from the *tabac* or the mayor changing his mind about our meeting stop me. This is my new start. I've earned it and I need it to happen now.

'This way for the mayor?' I ask, and point to his door.

'*Oui, mais . . .*' She puts out her hand to stop me but I carry on anyway. As Annie says, we've faced worse. Suddenly, when reminded that I might not have been here today if the dice hadn't rolled in my favour, I'm feeling much braver than the old me would ever have been.

I march into the mayor's office to find him holding a mobile phone to his ear. He is short and plump, wearing an ill-fitting jacket. He pulls the phone away but still holds it up. 'I'm sorry, I have some business to attend to,' he says, first in French, then repeats in English to be sure I understand, holding up his free hand, a universal gesture of '*non*' I'm coming to realise.

'Yes.' I take a deep breath, trying to channel my inner *Emily in Paris* even though she's half my age. 'You have business with me.' I place the bottle on the desk in front of him. 'A gift,' I say, raising an eyebrow at this ridiculous ritual. It's a tax, that's all. Keeping the mayor sweet and in whisky.

He picks up the bottle and gives the smallest of nods before placing it on his side of the desk and sits, gesturing for me to do the same in the seat opposite.

He nods slowly, then answers in French, and before I have time to translate, repeats it in English.

'So, it is you that has bought *le moulin*. You are here with a family?' It's more of a statement than a question.

I shake my head. 'No, just me.'

He looks at me as if it's British humour, waiting for me to say I'm joking. When I remain silent he finally says, 'An old mill, in the middle of practically nowhere.' He frowns. 'In our quiet village? It's a lonely place for a woman on her own. Why would you do that?' he snorts.

My mouth is dry but I lift my chin again. 'I have plans for the place. I want to turn it into a *salon de thé*, for local people and passing tourists,' I say, pulling out my notebook. 'I have lots of ideas.'

'A *salon de thé*?'

'Yes.' I focus on my notebook. 'I'll be serving afternoon tea, cakes, *patisseries* for local people, walkers or holidaymakers in the area.'

He doesn't look at the notebook but at me. 'So, you are a baker?' he says, tilting his head.

'Yes . . . well, yes,' I say, more firmly the second time. 'I learnt during the Covid lockdowns and then . . .' I stop. He doesn't need to know that baking kept me going through all of my treatment. That it was something else to think about – my safe place when the dread reared its head. It was my sanctuary, considering flavours and designs, learning from mistakes and wanting to get better. And it helped me learn to enjoy eating again. Small bites of sweet comfort. 'Yes, I am a baker,' I say confidently.

He says thoughtfully, 'We need a baker in the village.'

'Well, that's good for both of us, then.' I give a sigh of relief.

'For our *boulangerie*.' He fixes me with a stare.

'Oh, I'm not that type of baker . . . I mean, I bake cakes.'

But he doesn't hear me. 'Our village has no bakery. Just a machine,' he says with disgust. 'What is a town or a village without a bakery?' He throws out an arm, tears in his eyes. 'It is like a village without a soul.' And I wonder if the tears are about to spill.

'Erm, well, you could speak to the baker . . . the one I met from the next village. Claude? Maybe get him to supply to the shop. Then you will have your *boulangerie* back,' I say brightly.

'Oh, no,' says the mayor vehemently, pointing his short, fat finger towards the window and the village square. 'For a *boulangerie*, the bread must be baked on site, in the bakery's kitchen.' He points down and presses his fingertip to the desk. 'It needs to be baked in the village. The bread sold there must be made there. We need someone who will bake in the *boulangerie*.' He eyes me again.

'I'm afraid that's not me,' I say. 'I'm just a home cook who enjoys baking cakes. I'm not a professional bread-maker. As I say, I'm here to set up a tearoom, for local people and anyone who visits the lake at weekends.'

For a moment he says nothing. Then: 'And for that you will need a visa, to stay and work here?' He raises an eyebrow.

'Yes,' I say, slowly and carefully. 'Which is why I am here, visiting you. And praying you approve of my plans so my visa will be granted. As I say, I'll be hoping to open as soon as all my official paperwork is in order.'

'Ah, yes, your paperwork.'

I nod. 'I've done my homework. I know what I need.'
I put my large handbag on the desk and reach into it.

He leans on his elbow. 'You'll need to provide all your
documentation.'

I lift the file from my bag and put it onto the desk. 'I
have it all here.'

He regards the file but doesn't reach for it. 'Visas can
be very hard to get,' he says slowly, holding my gaze.
'You can apply,' he shrugs, 'and hopefully receive a year's
right to stay. To remain here longer, your business needs
to be making a profit.'

I swallow, but hold my nerve. 'Yes, I know. I plan to
work hard to get the *moulin* on the map and known for
its afternoon teas.' If I don't get my visa, I have no idea
what I'll do. I could end up with Pete, sleeping on the
sofa. 'I have all the paperwork right here.' Not to mention
the bottle of expensive whisky I've bought him. 'And I'm
hoping I can bring something to the village. A business
to attract more visitors. I mean isn't that what all villages
need to keep them going? More people coming to visit,
to spend money in the area. And for locals to spend in
their own village rather than going elsewhere.'

'You're right. We do need people with your skills here,'
he agrees. 'Otherwise the village will die. Is dying,' he
says quietly. 'They'll put a road through it and no one
will even notice we were once a community.'

'Surely not . . .'

'It all began with those damn vending machines!' He
bangs his fist on the table.

'Well, I'll admit, I did struggle with it at first, but . . .'

and I remember how kind Claude was, handing me a fresh baguette, welcoming me.

'Vending machines, pah! And why should one bakery serve four villages with bread?' He throws up his hands.

'Well, times change.' I try to calm things a little. 'We all have to move on.'

He gazes at me as if I've said something ridiculous. 'Why?' he says, his hands up again. 'Why do they have to move on? Everyone wants to move on, these days. What is wrong with how things were?'

'I don't know,' I say. 'But I'm not a baker, not like that. *Non, merci.* As I say, I'm not here to open a bakery. I've bought the old mill to make it into a *salon de thé.*'

'But for that you need a visa to stay,' he repeats, and seems to be thinking hard.

'Yes, and, as I said, I have all the paperwork for that.' I gesture at the file.

'It's a very good shop, the *boulangerie*. It served the community well for many years.'

I sigh. He's persistent, I'll give him that. 'And where is the baker now?'

'He left. Very soon after the miller at the old mill died. He just closed up, handed back the keys and left. No reason. There are other mills he could have got flour from, but he just said it was time to go. A few have tried to open it, but they leave as soon as they get here. The shop has been empty for . . .' he thinks '. . . it must be nearly five years now. Once upon a time this village provided everything we needed. A bakery, a shop, a bar and bistro, even a school. Soon there will be nothing left. Why can't we be like other villages with a shop, a pizzeria even? We have nothing!'

'Well,' I give a little cough, 'apart from a *salon de thé*.' I give a light laugh.

'Think about it. The *boulangerie*. It could work for us all if you were to take it over,' he says with a nod, letting me know our meeting is now over.

'It's very kind but, really, it's just me. I definitely can't take that on as well. I'm just here for the old mill and my *salon de thé*.'

And with that I get up to leave, glad that I've stood my ground. Hoping I've done enough to make him see how my plan would work.

Chapter 8

I leave the mayor's office and return to the mill on foot, letting the warm sunshine soothe my soul as I wonder where to start now I'm here, with the keys in my hand and my documentation for my visa on the mayor's desk. Scrubbing away the graffiti and painting the walls is probably as good a place as any. The front door needs washing and painting, as do the shutters. There's plenty of rubbish to get rid of. People seem to have dumped stuff there, like fly-tipping. Or maybe there were squatters. Once the rubbish has been cleared I can clean the floors and start painting the walls. I just hope they won't need plastering.

It's a ten-minute walk from the village to the mill, down the single-track lane. Just enough to stretch my legs, enjoy the sounds and smells around me and let go of the mayor's insistence that I take over the village bakery. That is way out of my league, and not what I came here to do.

I reach the end of the drive and stand by the listing gates to the mill. A car is parked next to the piggery, the boot open, a small figure standing over it. My heart races. I'm not expecting anyone.

I take a few steps down the dusty drive, tentatively approaching the back of the person in green camouflage trousers, sleeveless jacket and khaki bucket hat.

'*Allô, bonjour*?'

The figure turns to me and I'm surprised to see a woman, slight, with a beautiful clear complexion under the bucket hat, folded back at the front to show neatly shaped eyebrows and high cheekbones, dark hair and eyes. She's probably about my age and, if anything, the khaki camouflage outfit adds to her seemingly natural attractiveness.

She smiles, her face even more attractive now under the brim of the hat, which is decorated with brightly coloured feathers and hooks.

'*Bonjour*,' she says, reaching into the boot of her car.

For a moment, I pause. I don't know who she is, or why she's parked on my drive. She pulls out a long bag, which I can only assume contains some sort of weapon.

I summon my courage, which is trying to leave, and wonder what's happening at home, where I know who's going to call and when, and no one parks on my drive without my knowing about it. Where there is always tea in the caddy, a supermarket down the road and a batch of flapjacks in the cake tin on a Friday for the weekend, in case any of the children pop over.

But here it's different. It's new. And that's what I wanted, I remind myself.

'Can I help you?' I ask.

The woman shakes her head. '*Non, merci.*' She smiles

again and unzips the bag. I hold my breath, my mind going into overdrive. What if she's been sent to warn me off, that the mill was 'promised to someone else', like I heard in the mayor's office?

'Look, it might be a surprise that I'm here, and that someone else may have been interested in the old mill, but . . . I didn't know that when I bought it.'

'Ah. So it's you who has bought it. I heard someone had,' she says in English.

She still doesn't clarify why she's parked on the drive or what she intends to do with the weapon bag she's carrying.

'I had no idea. I saw the place was for sale, contacted the agent and bought it. I didn't realise . . .'

'It's good it's going to be restored.' She unzips the bag and slides it off to reveal a fishing rod. I feel a rush of relief. Of course it's a fishing rod! What was I thinking? I must try to calm down. This woman is just fishing!

Despite that, the words of the mayor come back to me: *It's a lonely place for a woman on her own.*

I look back at the old mill. What on earth have I taken on? It's a lot for one person to get this place up and running as I want it to be. Was it all a fantasy, a rush of euphoria after the treatment? Thinking I can shoulder anything? Quite possibly, yes.

I turn my attention back to the woman and the fishing rod. 'So, can I help you?' I say politely.

'No, thank you. I'm just going to fish. In the lake. We always park here.'

'Ah.' Quite a few habits must have been created while the mill was empty.

'The lake is owned by the commune. We come here to fish, talk, clear our minds . . .' She smiles. 'Would you like to join us?'

'No, thank you.' I reply. 'I'm not one for fishing.'

'Well, if you ever change your mind . . .' she says.

'Thank you, but I have work to do.' I point at the mill. 'I have to clean and decorate it, get rid of the graffiti, make it more homely.'

'And you're going to live in it?' she says.

'Yes. And open it as a *salon de thé*,' I say, feeling happier talking about my plans.

'A *salon de thé*? Interesting,' she says.

'For local people, walkers, and people driving out to see the lake,' I say.

'Well, *bonne chance*,' she says, and I have a feeling she thinks I'm going to need it.

I follow her towards the precarious slope at the side of the mill, then to the front door, and am soon snagged in the brambles again.

'Ouch!'

'Oh!' She turns back to me and points. 'No, follow me. Always take the right-hand side up the slope and hold the tree branch here. It's much easier.'

I follow her instructions. It is indeed a much better pathway up the side onto the green at the front of the mill, if not the most direct. '*Merci.*'

'*De rien*,' she says politely, and carries on walking around the side of the lake, picking her way past the shrubs and over the rocks towards a low, flat rock protruding from the bank beyond a clump of yellow gorse.

I look out at the lake again – I could stand and watch it for hours, but I have work to do, so I turn towards the green front door. As I let myself into the cool, dark room, I hear other cars pulling up, and women's voices, greeting each other. The sound of their cheerfulness makes me smile. Here's hoping they may come to the *salon de thé* when it's up and running, rather than just using my drive for parking.

I glance out of the open door, across the lake, hoping to catch sight of the kingfishers, but they're not around. They, too, must be getting on with their jobs in something near paradise.

I grab my cleaning tools, which I bought from Intermarché. They've been sitting in my car for the last few weeks, ready to tackle this job. I make for the big room upstairs, carrying my mop and bucket, broom, dustpan and brush, and throw open the windows. I can see the women at the edge of the lake. Some are being helped by the one I met. Others are sitting side by side on small stools or chairs, their lines in the water, talking intently. Others are laughing, sharing bread and cheese . . . Bottles of water and wine are on a camping table in the shadows of the trees, and I can't help but feel rather envious of the camaraderie they share as I listen to their soft laughter rippling across the water. It's much like the close friendship I share with Annie, both knowing the rollercoaster of emotions we experienced from our diagnosis and needing to be positive even when it didn't feel positive for us and our families.

I send Annie another photograph and tell her she'll soon be sitting at the lakeside too, and how does she fancy trying her hand at fishing? She sends back a laughing face.

I sweep, mop, and scrub at the graffiti on the walls. I think I'm getting somewhere when I hear a small cheer from the ladies at the lakeside and go to the window to see them land a fish in a bucket and congratulate the woman holding it as if she's found the very meaning of life. Maybe she has. She's found a purpose, and that's what it's all about, I think, whether it's landing a fish, reading a book or cleaning an old building to serve tea and cake. Finding a purpose, something that makes you happy, is what's spurred me on recently.

I work away on the walls all afternoon until the sun goes down and I hear the women leave. I'm alone. I head downstairs and sit by the lake in the silence for a little while with a glass of wine. Eventually I go inside, closing the door, and make an omelette for my dinner. Then I head to my living quarters at the back of the building, behind the curtain, for bed.

The following morning, I take my coffee outside and sit on the fallen tree trunk, watching the mist swirl and circle around the lake, where the lily pads float. I breathe in, hoping to glimpse the kingfishers, but I don't spot them. I know they're around, though. They seem to encourage me that I can do this, little by little.

Today, I plan to take on the ground floor, move the rubbish stacked in the middle of the room, then wash the walls with sugar soap, dust away the cobwebs and mop the floor. The women are back by the lakeside for Sunday morning and I can hear the church bells ringing from the village, over the fields.

It's a few hours of hard work, dragging the old blankets, bicycle parts and plastic tubs that were probably fished out of the lake, out of the door, down the slope to outside the cellar door, ready to get to the nearest recycling centre. I stack the rubbish there too, against one wall. Once I've scrubbed the floors and walls, I can start to paint. And it should begin to come to life. Then I can do the fun part and visit the *brocantes* again to furnish the place. I can't wait to start filling it with tables and chairs. I've only made one big purchase so far, and that was my mattress. It's cosy and comfortable and I have plans to paint the room as soon as I can.

But first I want to see what else needs to happen to get the place into shape for my *salon de thé*.

I put my shoulder to the dark wooden sideboard and push until the trapdoor is exposed. I lift it by the rope handle and peer down into the hole. It's dark, dusty and full of cobwebs. I sigh. But the sooner I clean it, the sooner I can have it as I want it. There is a light switch. I flick it and a dull orange glow illuminates the space with a crackle and a fizz. I look at the wooden steps and wonder how to address them. Forwards? Or backwards, like a ladder? Then I remember Laurent's head popping up from the trapdoor and decide to try the latter.

I climb down, seeing more and more of the cellar as I descend.

An axle is propped against the far wall, presumably

from when it was a working mill, harnessing the water and turning the cogs for the stone upstairs. It's a big space, and I could look into taking out the axle, perhaps make it cosier, with sofas and soft lighting. There are small windows level with the lawn, which I push open to let in some air.

The room doesn't look as if it's been used for anything other than storage. There are tools lying here and there, and I start by gathering them all into a toolbag lying open.

As my eyes adjust to the light, I see pencil drawings along the walls of what look like Punch and Judy faces. I pull out my phone and use the torch to get a better look at the words and marks. Next to the doodles are names.

Le mairie . . . and marks in roman numerals.

Le tire bouchon . . . and more marks, counting in bunches of five. It means corkscrew. Maybe the name of a local bar or restaurant.

La boulan . . . I can't read it. But I'm thinking it's the *boulangerie* and a name.

Madame . . . but the rest is rubbed out.

These look like orders for sacks of flour that have been taken for local businesses and families, scrawled quickly onto the wall instead of written down on paper.

In between and over the pencil-written orders, there's more graffiti on the walls too. Someone has had a whale of a time with tins of spray-paint. Clearly a more recent addition. But amongst the spray-paint, high up by the door, leading out of the cellar towards the piggery, I find another pencil drawing: a face with more writing on it.

I wish I knew what it meant. I look around. A coat of whitewash will brighten it all up, I think.

I look at the boxes of parts, small cogs and handles, and wonder where to get rid of it all. Clearly the previous owner isn't coming back for it.

I start to pile the boxes beneath the trapdoor. I'll use the cellar for storage for the time being, and bring in my napkins, cutlery and crockery. Then, when the kitchen is open, I'll use this as my cold store, get some fridges down here. I go to the back door, which is warped, worn and fairly flimsy, and give the handle a twist and a tug, letting in the daylight.

I hear the women approaching, heading for their cars, wishing each other a *bon dimanche* and *bon appétit* – they must be going home for lunch.

I decide to stay in the shadows of the cellar, rather than step out with the boxes. I'll wait for them to pass. I turn away from the open door.

'*Bonjour.*' A voice makes me jump.

'*Madame, bonjour.*' There's another.

Each woman acknowledges me as they pass, fishing gear in hand, with small stools and cool boxes.

'*Bonjour,*' I reply to each one, suddenly realising I've been noticed. And it feels nice.

'*Bon appétit,*' I say, leaning out of the door as they load their equipment into their cars.

'*Merci, à vous,*' they say, and start their engines, moving off the drive and towards the town.

I turn back into the cellar and promptly trip over one of the boxes, sending myself sprawling across the floor. When the noise from the clatter of the box of parts stops,

I lie still, where I am, and listen. I'm all alone. The fisherwomen have gone. All I can hear is the birds outside. I do a quick mental check of myself – nothing broken – and slowly stand, dusting myself down and looking at the debris surrounding me.

I thank my lucky stars I'm not hurt and that nothing is damaged, and begin to pick up the junk and sling it back into the wooden box. I reach out and toss the rusting spanners and old nails back in, wishing I had Sunday lunch almost ready and wondering if the *tabac* in the town serves food. Maybe I should try to make peace there: if I want Laurent to support my business, I should support his. But judging by the look on his face as he left the mayor's office, I don't think it'll be easy. In fact, as nice an idea as it would be, the *tabac* is probably the last place I should go. I pick up a tin, the final bit of junk, and toss it towards the box.

It hits the edge of the box, causing its lid to open and its contents to spill out. I stand and stare. That is not what I was expecting to find in an old coffee tin! Small packets of white powder are scattered about. I'm not daft – I know what it is, packaged up to pass on to customers. I've seen enough episodes of *Crimewatch* to know that it certainly isn't washing powder. Each one is sealed, and now I look into the box of junk, I see scales too.

What on earth?

I think back to Laurent being in the cellar when I moved in. That must have been why he was down here, hiding his stash in the abandoned mill. Well, it's my mill now and I'm not going to have him – or anyone else for that matter – coming here to collect this. All I can think to do is one thing. I go to the kitchen, turn on the taps and, one by one, snip off the tops of the packages and flush away the contents. Then I wash my hands thoroughly – furious that I'm having to be a part of this – when there's a knock at the door.

Chapter 9

'You!' I say, looking up at Laurent. He takes a small step backwards, then dips his head politely.

'*Bonjour, Madame.*'

He waits for me to reply. But I don't. I'm cross that he came here the first time and even crosser that he has the nerve to come again, and now I know what for!

'Look,' he holds out his big hands, with the silver rings, 'we may have got off on the wrong foot. We weren't properly introduced the other day. I apologise.'

For a moment I think of him discovering me wrestling with a bread-vending machine and then appearing through the trapdoor.

'You took me by surprise. I wasn't expecting anyone to be here when I came. No one had told me.'

'And you took me by surprise,' I retort.

He looks up at the mill. 'It's been empty for a long time.'

I nod. 'So I'm told. But it's sold now. And it's not somewhere for people to drop in when they feel like it. Or decorate the walls with their own designs.'

'I understand,' he says. 'Let me introduce myself

properly.' He holds a hand to his broad chest. 'I am Laurent. I rent and run the *tabac* in the town.'

He waits for my response. 'And you are?' he prompts.

None of this is really to make amends, I decide. Most likely he's here to pick up the merchandise I've just flushed down the sink.

I hold him with a steely stare. Maybe I should be scared, but I'm not. I may be here on my own, but this place has a good feeling. Despite the silly graffiti and opportunists using it to hide their stash, I don't feel alone. In fact, I felt more alone during my marriage than I do here right now.

'Juliet,' I say firmly to Laurent. 'I am Juliet,' and leave it at that.

'Well, Juliet,' he smiles, '*enchanté*.' He takes a moment to look past me, clearly noticing the rubbish I've cleared. 'When I appeared the other day, as I said, I didn't realise anyone was here, or that it had been sold. My apologies, but I left some of my belongings here, in my haste.'

'I'll bet,' I say, determined not to be taken for a fool. I won't let the mill be dragged into some grubby drug-dealing scandal before I've even had a go at making it work.

He points to the room behind me. 'If I could just fetch what I need,' he says politely.

'No,' I say firmly. I've come too far to suffer fools gladly.

'Oh.' He raises his eyebrows in surprise and I know I'm being blunt, possibly rude, but I'm not falling for his lies. 'Well, perhaps you could get them for me.'

I narrow my eyes. 'What was it you were looking for?' I raise an eyebrow.

'I left a bag of tools here. In the cellar.' He points in the direction of the trapdoor. 'And a few others about the place.'

'I'll get them.' I wonder if he thinks the coffee tin will be with the tools. 'Wait there.' I hear him sigh. And then I add, 'I'll leave them outside the cellar door for you.' I shut the front door and bolt it. I'm not sure where this new-found bravery has come from, but I quite like it. My heart is pumping a little faster. He could have got nasty, I suppose. I didn't think of that, just acted on impulse. A bit like this whole move. Going with my impulses seems to be the only way I can live my life at the moment. I just wasn't going to let a drug-dealer into my house to discover his drugs are gone.

I climb down the steps into the cellar, gather up the bag of tools and drag it to the back door where Laurent is waiting. I make a mental note to put the sideboard back over the trapdoor before I go to bed tonight.

'Here,' I say, thrusting the bag towards him. 'Anything else that may have been left here has been disposed of,' I say. 'According to the estate agent, everything belongs to me now. So I have cleared the place of any . . . unwanted items.'

'*Merci*,' he says. 'By way of an apology, please come to the *tabac* and I will buy you a coffee or a drink, whatever you would like.'

This takes me by surprise. He's holding the toolbag. He's not asked about the tin and he's inviting me to the *tabac* for a coffee. I'm still not going to let down my guard, or invite him in to search out what he's really come for: the tin is here but the contents aren't.

'Okay. I accept,' I say, and add, 'For my business's sake. This is my new start. I don't want anything ruining it. I want this place to be respectable and popular.'

He nods. 'I understand. Well, *bonne chance*,' he says. He looks up at the building. 'This place holds a lot of secrets,' he says. 'Look after them.'

With that, he drops his head and turns to leave. A lone fisherwoman is returning and they stop to greet each other, clearly exchanging the news about the old mill being sold. Or, probably, about me . . .

I slam the door and head upstairs, drop the trapdoor at the top of the wooden stairs and pull the sideboard over the opening. I then stand with my back to it. I feel slightly unnerved but also a little proud of myself too. Now, hopefully, I can do what I came here to do: open my business.

After an odd start to the day, I decide to cheer myself up with a visit to some of the local *brocantes*, maybe pick up some more crockery. I get into the car and soon I'm boosting my confidence by negotiating a good price for tablecloths and more napkins. I couldn't resist a bargain of tables and chairs from a house clearance that the *brocante* owner will deliver to the mill. So far today I have seen off a drug dealer from my premises and haggled hard for table linen in France. I've spent a big part of what's left of my savings on furniture. I'm committed. All in all, a long way from life back home, and I'm on a journey to create something of my own. It feels really good.

The following day, the sun is shining again and I have my usual morning coffee outside, taking in the mist as it lifts and breathing fresh air. I message the family WhatsApp group and Annie, with a photograph. Maddie replies and so does Jake, saying life in Spain is 'hectic'. I wonder if it's everything he hoped it would be. Pete sends a message to say the window cleaner has been and all is well. Annie takes longer to answer but tells me my new place looks like heaven.

As I stand to go inside, the pretty fisherwoman arrives and heads for her usual spot by the lake. 'Bonjour,' she greets me, and I wish we could move beyond these basic niceties and start to become friends. But she carries on to her spot on the big flat rock. I turn back to the mill. Today, I plan to start painting.

I wonder whether to visit the mayor's office to find out if there is any news on my visa, but I asked when I went into the *mairie* for directions to the local dump to get rid of the rubbish.

'Non,' the woman on Reception had flatly replied. They would email when they had an answer for me. There wasn't much more of a discussion to be had.

I decide to get stuck in here. I'm sure my visa will be sorted soon, and I want to be trading as quickly as possible with the height of summer on its way and all the walkers and families coming to the area. As long as I have my visa in place by the end of the month, I'll be able to open.

I turn on my phone's radio and lay out a couple of dustsheets I've brought in preparation for giving the main room a lick of white paint. I turn the radio up louder and pull a baseball cap over my hair, just as a knock at the door makes me jump.

If it's Laurent, with some lame excuse to come in and nose around, then I'm ready for him. I take a deep breath, turn off the radio, unbolt and pull back the heavy door, fully prepared to send him on his way.

The sunshine piles in and for a moment I'm taken aback. 'Oh, it's you,' I say, smiling. It's Claude, the baker from the vending machine with the very attractive smile.

'Hi.' He holds out a hand to shake mine, then pulls me closer to kiss me on each cheek, making me feel just as he did the other day in the village square: slightly shy, attractive, *seen*.

'I came to see how your plans are happening,' he says.

'Well, I'm getting there,' I say, quickly pulling off my baseball cap, keen not to look too scruffy. 'The place is getting cleaner by the minute.'

'It looks great!'

I discreetly run my fingers through my hair, shaking out the soft curls.

He spots the paint pot and points. 'So, you've got a real vision for this place?'

'I do, yes! Would you like to look around?' I say. 'See what I've planned?'

'That would be great!'

I stand back to let him in. And, bizarrely, I feel like a young woman with something close to attraction to this man. Maddie's words come back to me, encouraging me to meet someone new, like Pete seems to be doing, spending time with Mandy. I shut the thought down quickly. I can feel colour in my cheeks and a tightness in my throat. Something about the way Claude looks at me as he steps into the big room makes me feel like the years are rolling slowly back. This is a new me, in a new life. I'm just making friends. But it feels quite exciting. I give a little cough and clear my throat.

'This is the main room. I'm about to start painting,' I say. 'I want it all clean and fresh. I'll get rid of the traces of whatever has been going on here while it's been empty.'

He seems interested, which makes me feel good. I'm delighted to be sharing my ideas and dreams for this place.

'Let me show you upstairs.' I lead the way to the staircase in the big main room and upstairs to the large attic space overlooking the lake. I think that this was once used to store the grain. 'There is so much potential to do rooms up here, if I divided this space up. A *chambre d'hôte* maybe. And the *salon de thé* downstairs and outside.' He follows me to the big open room. Clean, swept and the floor washed, but still with scribbles on the walls.

'And you are doing this on your own?' he asks.

I turn to face him. The sun on his face is making him look even more handsome. 'Yes, I am,' I say, lifting my chin a little. I find myself caught in his gaze and looking back at him, not immediately whipping my eyes away. I don't know when I last found a man attractive. It hasn't crossed my mind in years that I might find someone I fancied or, even more unlikely, that the feeling might be mutual. It's like a whole new world opening up before me and it feels very strange, but good – more than good, in fact.

It's as if I've just boarded a rollercoaster at the fairground and am about to start the ride of my life, thrilling and exciting. Me, Juliet, at forty-eight. I'm standing in a sunshine-filled room in France, with this man smiling at me as if something special is happening. We stare at each other, small dust particles dancing like fairies in the shaft of light shining through the open window. I look away first. I'm not sure how these things work. He's attractive, yes, but I have no idea how people go about starting the ball rolling. The closest I've been to a date in years is Sunday-morning coffee at the garden centre.

'Let's go down,' I say quickly, waving at the stairs.

'Of course. I'd be delighted.' I can feel him watching me as I head downstairs from the large, cavernous attic space, back to the main room of the mill. Although we've met only once before, he's here, interested in the mill, my plans, and possibly, dare I think, me. And it really is a very long time since I've been looked at like that. I give a little shiver, despite the sunshine outside.

'This is the kitchen. It's all kitted out. Just a bit old, neglected. But all the parts are working.' I'm rambling. 'And this is . . .' I pull back the curtain.

'Ah,' he chuckles, 'the bedroom.'

'Oh, yes, sorry.' I pull the curtain back to my small living quarters, the little living area with the wood-burning stove, and the wooden steps up to the mezzanine and my bedroom area. 'I didn't . . .' *Stop talking, Juliet*. 'It needs painting too. Lots of old markings on the wall, from the past. Messages of love, unreciprocated by the look of it. There's a broken heart, and a name . . . Bijounette, on the wall here in the bedroom. It needs freshening, brightening up . . .' *Stop talking, Juliet!* 'Just some tender loving care, really.' *Stop!*

He's staring at me with an amused smile. *Don't look at his lips.* I'm suddenly hot. What is wrong with me? I'm acting like an infatuated schoolgirl.

'Would you,' I clear my throat, 'like some coffee?'

'*Merci.* That would be excellent,' he says. 'And I brought you a baguette. I didn't know if you had had time to get out and I want you to like my bread enough to buy it for your *salon de thé.*' He points to a baguette he's placed on the counter.

'Thank you. I hadn't planned on serving baguettes. It will be mostly cakes, sausage rolls, that kind of thing,' I say.

'But a baguette, it is the sign of being in France, *non*? You are not in the UK now. You are here in France. You need to be a little more French. Not so nervous. Enjoy what we have.'

He's right. That's why I'm here, isn't it? To enjoy what France has to offer. I chew my bottom lip.

He turns back to the big room, taking it all in.

'*Oui,*' I say. I'm not feeling like the teenage girl now, more of a woman who has lived life and knows what she wants. A confidence I have never experienced before. A need to feel wanted and to be desired. 'I'll make coffee. Have a look around.' I hold out a hand to the room, then turn back to the kitchen work surfaces and put on the kettle. I catch a glimpse of Claude as I pull out small coffee cups and saucers from the shelf under the worktop.

His hands are behind his back as he paces around the room. I find myself snatching glances at him and, to my delight, he's doing the same to me. I have a strange giddy feeling inside me. But it's pleasant. I like it. Like a holiday that's just begun with endless possibilities for relaxation and laughter.

'You've done a lot already. I hardly recognise it. This place holds lots of memories.'

'So I'm told,' I say, thinking of Laurent's words, pushing the irritation of his visit to the back of my mind, determined not to give him head space.

'We used to come here as teenagers.' He runs his hand along the clean wall. 'This was where we would hang out . . . come to the lake, when the mill was quiet. And now, it looks like it's got a whole new lease of life.' He flashes me another of his smiles and my stomach does the flip I remember from years ago, but which seems refreshingly new.

When I first went on holiday with my friends, I developed a huge crush on the barman at the resort in Spain for the way he looked at me. By the time our coach was pulling away from the hotel, the next was pulling in and Juan was making his move on another young woman who fell for his charms. His promises to stay in touch and visit were as fanciful as he was fanciable. It was soon after that I met Pete. Safe and reliable Pete. And that's just what he's been. We had seen each other at school, but only became acquainted when we were pushed together by friends. And it's been a wonderful twenty-five years of marriage. Dependable. We made all the right moves along the way, hit all the right notes. Marriage, house, kids, sliding into early retirement. I just wasn't ready for that bit. Right now I need some excitement, to feel alive.

It's like I've been eating vanilla ice cream all these years and suddenly discovered salted caramel. Different, exciting, more layered.

'I'm planning to keep the walls plain,' I say, with rising conviction for my vision, 'but with lots of bunting, greenery and cushions.' I spoon coffee into the cafetière.

'And the mill's workings?' He points to the large flat millstones and cogs.

Although I've started to clean them, there is still a lot to be done. 'I'm not sure. I was thinking of making a feature of them. On the other hand, I could get a lot more tables in if they were taken out.'

'I agree. There is little sense in keeping them. They're not even attractive.' He smiles. 'Unlike present company, of course.'

My stomach does a triple somersault.

I left the UK aware that something was waiting for me. The excitement of not knowing what tomorrow would bring. I came out here for fun, to feel alive, to prove to myself that I could do anything I set my mind to. I came for an adventure and that's what I'm going to have! I'm not a young woman any more. Who knows when I might feel desired again? This is fun. The way he says my name, it's as if I'm the only woman he's ever spoken to like this. I know I'm not but, right now, it's wonderful to feel so . . . seen.

Claude walks towards me as I reach for the coffee pot. He puts his hand over mine, and I stop. I hadn't thought about taking this any further than some flirtatious banter. He draws my hand away from the coffee and holds it. 'How about we forget coffee? Let's have wine . . .'

he says, and indicates the bottle I have on the sideboard –
I bought it from a local vineyard on my day out at the
brocantes.

I smile and even laugh. 'Well, as long as that's all it is!'
I joke. This is going a little quicker than I'm comfortable with.

'But of course. New friends and neighbours getting to
know each other. Should they not?' He plants a kiss on
the back of my hand. It doesn't excite me like his earlier
interest had. But he's right. We are just getting to know
each other and that's nice. It's been a long time since I've
made new friends and enjoyed a drink with someone
who wants to talk to me. It's just a glass of wine, I tell
myself. It's just making friends.

'Why not?' I say, feeling bolder again. Isn't this what
I wanted? 'And how about lunch?' I hold up the baguette.
'I have cheese.'

'*Du vin, du pain, du fromage? Parfait!*' he says, and we
load a tray with bread, cheese and tomatoes and take it
outside onto the lawn, where I spread a blanket from
my bed.

It isn't long before I discover that sitting on a blanket
on the ground isn't half as comfortable as I thought it
would be. In fact, it's not comfy at all! So we move to sit
on the fallen tree trunk, throwing the blanket over it and
putting the tray on a chair from inside. And there we sit,
beside the lake. It feels so nice to be with someone who
actually wants to know about me.

'So here you are, in France, starting a new life. Are
there things you wish you'd done differently, before
now?' he asks, sipping the wine.

I look out across the lake. 'I suppose I wish I'd been more spontaneous. Done what excited me sooner. Not left it until now. I wish I'd said yes more in life and not been nervous. Life's short.' I turn to look at him, his face closer to mine.

'You are a very beautiful woman,' he says suddenly. And, like the kiss on my hand, it doesn't quite land where I want it to. It feels a little forced.

Despite the wine, the sunshine and my *joie de vivre*, I'm not sure that this is how I wanted the conversation to go. Flirting is uncharted territory and seems to be heading in a direction I'm not sure I'm ready for.

'You have very beautiful eyes,' he says, taking my wine glass from me and putting it on the ground. I think he's expecting me to respond to this in some way, but I don't move. He reaches up and touches my curls, which grew back after I lost my hair. He clearly has a practised routine. He moves his face a little closer to mine and I can't decide if I want to kiss him or not. I wonder what it would feel like to kiss another man after all these years of only kissing Pete.

'Beautiful lips too. Like they are made for kissing,' he says, and I suddenly get an urge to giggle and tell him his chat-up lines are pretty cheesy. But on the other hand, why shouldn't I kiss a man I find attractive? Isn't that what people do, these days? Hook up? But I'm not sure I find him attractive any more.

I pull back and pick up my glass. 'Erm, look . . . I don't usually . . .'

He raises an eyebrow, along with a little corner of his

mouth. 'You don't usually sleep with men who come visiting bringing baguettes?'

And this time I laugh. The thought of sleeping with a stranger is a long way from where I'm at. I was flattered by the flirtation, but I'm not going to jump into bed with him. It's been a while. And, of course, I have a scar.

'You are embarrassed?' he asks. 'It is just making the most of life.'

'Well . . .' I say, sipping my wine. I'm reminded of a line from Shirley Valentine. Intimacy for Pete and me was Saturday night after *Britain's Got Talent* and birthdays. In the comfort of our bed.

'You do not find me attractive?' he asks matter-of-factly.

'Well, yes. You're very attractive.'

'Then why should we not do this?' he says, and kisses me. For a second or two, I let his lips sit on mine, just to know how it feels.

Chapter 10

I pull back. 'I wasn't expecting that,' I say, not feeling any excitement or thrill. It was more of a disappointment, like kissing a wet rag. Would it improve with practice?

'And tell me, did you like it?' He smiles confidently.

'Well, it was different from what I'm used to.'

'Different?' He tilts his head, not impressed with my assessment of his kiss.

'You will feel more when I kiss every part of your body, in your bed.' He stands, holding out a hand. 'We will embrace one of life's real pleasures.'

'It's a lovely offer,' I laugh, wondering if he's joking, but I don't think he is, 'but I'm a bit old school. I'd need to be taken out for a nice meal and get to know you better before taking things any further.'

He sighs and lets his hand drop. 'Very well, we will have dinner,' he says, as if it's an annoyance. Suddenly I'm not feeling half as attracted to him. In fact, hardly at all.

He seems to realise it and puts on one of his smiles, while I have an overwhelming urge to wipe my lips.

'Dinner will be lovely. We will talk more about using my bread for your *salon de thé*, but I'm afraid now I have to go.'

I'm not sure what I was thinking, imagining that this man was actually interested in me, when clearly all he was after was a little afternoon delight before going back to work. I try to bring things to just-friends. 'It must be hard, being a baker, working all hours.'

He shrugs, smoothing his hair and finishing his wine. 'It's not so bad. My wife helps out so we take it in turns to do morning and evening shifts.'

'Your wife?' I sit bolt upright, as if someone has just thrown a bucket of cold water over me. I'm shocked and suddenly shivering. 'Your wife?'

He gives me a smug smile, which makes me feel sick. 'It is the French way, *non*? Think about it. We could get together again some time. It might be lots of fun.' He raises an eyebrow.

Fury and embarrassment swirl in my head and stomach, replacing any remnants of the desire I was feeling not so long ago. 'I didn't expect . . . I thought you . . . You kissed me!'

'You thought I wouldn't be married?' His face crumples as he laughs. 'It was pleasant enough kissing you, but you could do with some practice! I can help, if you like, when I have another free couple of hours.'

It's as if I've been slapped, hard. Worse than feeling invisible, I feel like a very obvious moving target, standing out like a sore thumb. The woman who walked out on her marriage, with a pocket full of stupid dreams. A stupid, middle-aged woman who thought she could come to France and find herself again.

'You clearly wanted me to. I could feel you were coming on to me. Don't worry, it happens all the time. My wife understands that women find her husband attractive.'

'Get out!' I say, my face burning at the very recent memory of his lips on mine. I'm not sure who I'm crosser with, myself or him. 'Just get your things, and go!'

He's adjusting his watch and smoothing his hair again. 'Sure. But first I need to find what is mine while I'm here.' I'm surprised he doesn't pull out a mirror and check his appearance. He's more in love with himself than anyone else, and I can't help but feel for his wife. If she knows about his flirtations, though, she's mad to stay with him.

'You need to find what?'

'What I came for. As lovely as the welcome was, it was a shame you didn't follow through on the promises your body language was making.'

'Get out!' I say furiously, my cheeks burning and my eyeballs stinging with rage at his behaviour.

'Like I say, when I get what I came for. The cellar, it is still accessed by the trapdoor?'

And the penny drops. Really loudly. I put my palm to my forehead.

He's here for the tin.

I'm on my feet and storming towards the mill, into the cool of the big room and to the kitchen area where I emptied the contents of the little bags into the sink. I grab the tin out of the bin and march back to him, fury powering my jelly-like legs.

'Is this what you're looking for?' I hold it out to him, anger making my hands shake and the lid rattle.

'Ah, yes, thank you!' He reaches towards me. I can't bear even to have his fingers touch mine. I hesitate, handing it over. 'I know you own the place now, but would you mind if I still meet my business clients here? It's always been a convenient, out-of-the-way place to see them, but close enough to town.'

'*Mind?*' I grip the tin so tightly I think I might dent it. 'Would I *mind?*' I can barely speak I'm so furious. What kind of fool does he take me for? Clearly the sort I've just shown him I am – the kind who was flattered by a few generous words and flirtatious looks. 'Yes, I mind very much!'

He goes to take the tin and I throw it at his feet. The lid opens, and nothing falls out.

He turns and stares at me. 'I think you may have something else of mine.'

And I turn very cold.

He just took something of mine – my dignity. What was I thinking? I'm not here to meet someone new. I'm here to find me. Now I feel used. Grubby. Angry. I run my forearm across my lips.

I could cry. But I won't. That was for the younger me. I could run away. But that's what yesterday's me might have done. This is today me. This me is staying exactly where she is and standing firm. I hold his steely stare, evenly. 'I don't know what you're talking about,' I say.

'This tin contained something belonging to me.'

'Like what?'

'A little security, that's all.'

This place, deserted and taken up by the local drug scene. No wonder no one wanted it. I look out on the beautiful lake, and hear a car door close as the attractive fisherwoman arrives. The beautiful view is now tainted as raindrops begin to fall into the water. The fisherwoman passes us, bids us good day and continues to her flat rock, setting up her fishing rod under an umbrella. She doesn't move, as if weathering the storm, literally.

'I have nothing of yours,' I say, as evenly as I can. 'And, just for the record, where I come from, if you're married, you don't kiss other women.'

'It's a very old-fashioned way of thinking. And it was you who kissed me,' he says, fuelling my fury.

'Come near my property again and I'll call the *gendarmes*. I presume that still works in the old-fashioned way around here? You get caught supplying drugs, you get charged?'

He swears under his breath as he turns on his heel and stalks away.

Chapter 11

I hear his car drive off. I'm standing in the rain as fat drops slide down my hair and face, making me even more miserable if that were possible. I don't think I could feel any worse. Part of me wants to run inside, pack up my belongings and go home, with my tail between my legs. But then I see the fisherwoman look at me and raise a hand. She may be checking I'm okay. With all the effort I can muster, I raise a hand back, also checking with her that she's okay in the rain. But I bet she doesn't feel as wretched as I do. I feel stupid, falling for his charm in the first place.

But another part of me wants to stand tall, not be driven out by a stupid move and a shark taking advantage of me. I want to stand up to him for all the other women who've been made to feel foolish, when really we should feel strong, with the scars we wear, the families we've raised and our bravery in finding ourselves. I turn and walk into the mill.

I go to the back of the big room, to my computer on the work surface, keen to connect with my old life. I message Annie and tell her how stupid I've been. It's just seconds before I get a reply, telling me he sounds like an idiot, and to move on. Life's too short. And she's right. I may have made a fool of myself, but there are far worse things and so much more to look forward to.

I open my inbox and see an email from the mayor's office, titled 'visa application'. My heart quickens.

I open it and stare at the screen.

'DECLINED.'

Chapter 12

I try to read the email properly, but the words keep jumbling as tears spring to my eyes. If I thought I couldn't feel any worse, any more stupid, well, now I do. I slam down the lid of the laptop. What does it matter what it says? I can read the word 'declined' clearly enough. And, all of a sudden, I can feel self-pity piling in on me. Could things not have gone my way, just this once?

I stand up and feel drawn to head outside where the rain seems to be passing. I grab my zip-up fleece from the hook beside the door, pull it on over my dress, wind a scarf around my neck and walk slowly to the lake's edge. I stand with my arms wrapped around myself. The fisherwoman is still there. I scan the water's edge for the kingfishers but can't see them. I go to the corner of the lake where the canoe is, then walk onto the path, pulling the fleece tighter around me. The sun is starting to push away the clouds but there's still damp in the air, raindrops hanging on branches and leaves. I walk along the worn path, over the big rocks, with no idea where it leads. I can see the big flat stone where the fisherwomen meet. Beyond that, the path peters out. It's more rocky and, on the other side of the lake, dense with trees. I decide to turn back, not wanting to interrupt her fishing or her thoughts, but she turns to me with a smile.

'*Bonjour*,' she says, as she does every time she sees me. There is something very comforting about the routine of it, even if we don't know each other.

'*Bonjour*,' I reply, with a smile. 'You're still here,' I find myself saying. 'Even with the rain.'

'I am,' she replies, in English, as I watch a tug on her fishing line.

'Grab that.' She points to the purple plastic bucket next to her fishing bag.

I bend and hold it out as she reaches down for a net beside her. I watch as she pulls the fish from the water, hands me the net and, without saying a word, I catch the creature in it, laughing with delight, as does she. I'm still laughing as she puts down her rod and removes the hook, before dropping the fish into the bucket of water.

'Do you eat them?' I ask.

'Yes. But we only take what we will eat. Just enough.' She tilts her head. 'Would you like coffee? Or something stronger?'

'Coffee would be lovely,' I say, 'if you're sure I'm not interrupting you.'

'Not at all. I am Geneviève,' says the woman, holding out her hand, and I smile as I take it. She nods, prompting me.

'I'm Juliet,' I reply.

'*Enchantée*.' She pours me coffee from her flask and some for herself.

'Have a seat.' She offers the camping chair, which I accept. I sip the coffee, looking out over the lake to the trees beyond. It's as if time has stood still. Nothing else matters.

Beside us there is a little waterfall, clearly from a river feeding into the lake from the rocks above. A stream flows from it too.

'The brown trout like it here,' she tells me. 'There are beehives in the woods,' she adds, sipping from her cup and pointing across the water with her free hand. 'On hot days you can hear the buzzing. And further up the lake, you have to go up,' she points to a rocky outcrop, where the water is tumbling down, 'climb over it and back down the other side,' she says about the waterfall. 'It's not too hard and beyond that is a place perfect for swimming.'

We lull back into silence and then I say, 'You spend a lot of time here.' I'm watching two dragonflies dancing across the water in the sunshine.

'I like to be here. The peace,' she says. 'I started fishing when I was ill. I had cancer. It kept me . . . in the moment.'

I take a deep breath. 'I've been through the same thing,' I say.

She nods. 'If you want to join us, you'd be welcome.'

'*Merci.*' I smile. 'I found the same kind of peace in baking. I just felt centred. Like nothing else that had happened or might happen was in my mind, just the baking. I would be awake in the night, feeling the dread of it spreading or coming back, and find myself thinking about buttercream icing, Christmas flavours for muffins or what to do with the jars of marmalade I'd made.'

We stare out over the water.

'It's whatever brings you peace. This place is very peaceful.'

'It is,' I say, looking back at the mill, loving seeing it from this new perspective.

'Some of the women who come here have had the illness. Others have been touched by it, by their loved ones, family members having it, maybe caring for them, or losing someone to it. Coming here, learning to fish, it is a rest from it. It's somewhere we can relax, focus, eat and laugh.'

'That's perfect,' I say.

She holds the fishing rod, gently moving her hand and the line in the water.

'And so you are living here now. How do you like it?'

I let out a long sigh. 'My visa has just been declined.'

'Oh. And that makes things difficult now with you staying?'

I nod. 'Yes. Without it, I have just four weeks before I'll have to return to the UK. I wanted to open a *salon de thé* here at the mill but it seems I've got a lot of things wrong already since I've been here. Put my faith in the wrong people.'

She reloads her hook with bait and then, with a flick of her wrist, launches the line into the air. It lands with softness, precision and a tiny plop.

'Sometimes you need to stand in the rain,' she says, 'to see things more clearly. The best catch comes after the rain.'

I sip the last of my coffee. I've made a proper mess of all this, I think, looking out at the dragonflies finally meeting and flying together.

Geneviève sips the last of hers. 'I have wine if you would like some, or a sandwich.' She points at the baguette sticking out from her bag. '*Jambon, beurre?*'

I raise a hand. '*Merci. Très gentille,*' I say. 'It's kind of you, but . . .' I look at the baguette again. 'Where do you buy your baguette from?' I ask.

'From the vending machine, these days. It's a shame. The *boulangerie* was very good but there weren't enough people here to make it pay. Then the owner, he shut very suddenly and left. And it never reopened. A couple of people tried, but it didn't last. They left very quickly. We wonder what it will be next, if anything. There is nothing left in the village. Laurent tries hard to keep the *tabac* going but numbers in the village are low. He's a good man, but I wonder how much longer he will manage.'

Laurent, the man I'd more or less accused of hiding drugs in the mill. My cheeks flame. Another mistake in my rush to feel I was at home and had life here sussed. My toes curl. It wasn't Laurent after the drugs, but Claude.

'I may owe him an apology,' I say quietly, and she doesn't reply, just watches her line, gently tugging at it.

Then she says, 'It can take time to see how things work,' she says, and although I turned down her offer, she adds, 'Let's eat.' She lights a small gas burner, sits on a nearby rock and prepares the fish she's caught on a small wooden board with a sharp knife.

I watch, intrigued, as she fillets it and prepares it for

the pan, with bubbling butter, the scent of garlic rising. Then she covers it in a spritz of lemon juice and showers it with freshly chopped herbs, tears off chunks of bread and puts one on each plate. She takes the cork from a bottle of white wine and pours me a glass.

I thank her, and am given a small plate of the freshly cooked fish with the hunk of baguette on the side. It smells amazing. I take a sip of the cold white wine, then put the little stubby plastic glass down next to me and use the bread to scoop up a mouthful of the buttery fried fish. She brings out a tomato from her bag, slices it on the chopping board, then does the same with a pink onion. After drizzling them in oil, she offers the board to me to help myself. I have the fish, the tomato salad and bread on my plate and it feels like a feast. Something so simple yet so perfect.

'It's delicious,' I tell her as the steam fills my nostrils.

'You must savour food and wine . . . like life,' she says, and I couldn't agree more.

I wanted to enjoy life. To love what I was doing. Life, I'd come to realise, was precious, and short. It wasn't that my life was awful. It wasn't. But I wanted more. I wanted to feel alive. Things had changed in me. *I* had changed. I had my appetite back, and not just for food and wine or cakes. I had a dream. Why not go for it? A silly little dream, some might say, but it was *my* dream. And now, just like that, it's been taken from me.

'And there, after the rain, comes sunshine,' she says, and points. It's the kingfishers. They've come out from their hiding places and we watch the flashes of blue darting to and from the lake.

'You know,' she says, sipping her wine, 'it's said seeing a kingfisher brings luck and positivity, like Nature's way of saying, "Good things are coming!" A sign of peace and prosperity. Seeing a kingfisher means it is time to leap into something new, especially if fear has been holding you back. Or so I read,' she says, looking straight ahead, holding her glass of wine.

I sip mine. 'You may be right. I needed to stand in the rain for a while. I think I know what I have to do.'

'Then that is a good thing,' she says with a smile.

'Life had become very routine,' I find myself saying. She says nothing but I know she's listening. 'A series of routines. Contented ones. Only I wasn't content. But my husband was. And that's fine. Then, with the treatment,' and I run my hand over my wavy hair, 'there were more routines. Doctors, hospitals, nurses, down days. Once I was in remission, he wanted life to go back to how it was before. But I needed something different, something new. I needed to take a risk, go on an adventure. I had to do this for me. After all the treatment, I am in control of my day . . .'

She nods in understanding and tops up our glasses.

'Getting the all-clear has lit a fire in me. To do the thing I've always dreamt of, and if I fail . . . I fail. It's better than the alternative.'

'It really is,' she says, and I know she understands, because she has been there too.

I finish the wine and stand up from the camping chair. 'I have no idea if I can, or if it'll work, but . . .' Suddenly the fire in my stomach is fanned by my humiliation and frustration.

She sees another tug on her line and I pick up the net. She pulls in another fish, I catch it, and we put it into the bucket.

'You have to be patient sometimes to get what you want. Change your bait. Take them by surprise. Just wait, bide your time. Stand in the rain.' She smiles at me.

Something inside me rises up and rages. I'm angry with the illness, angry for what a young woman like Annie is going through. And I'm determined not to let it ruin everything. Feeling the heat now, I pull the scarf from around my neck. I've promised Annie she's coming out here and I'm going to make that happen.

Chapter 13

The following morning I don't wait to ask the receptionist if the mayor is free to see me: his office door is open behind her desk. I walk straight past her as she squeaks, '*Non, Madame, non*, not possible today! This is not how things are done here. *Non!*' She jumps up to follow me. '*Ce n'est pas possible! Vous ne comprenez pas!*'

'*Oui!*' I say, over my shoulder, and carry on walking. Old habits die hard here. *Oui . . . C'est possible!* I'm ready to take on anybody who stands in my way today. I'm fired up as I march into the mayor's office, take a deep breath, put my hands on his desk, lean over and announce, 'Okay, I'll do it!'

He looks up at me, then says slowly, in French, as if to remind me of where we are, '*Bonjour, Madame.*'

'What? Oh, yes, *bonjour*, sorry, *désolée.*' I look down at his proffered hand and shake it.

'Take a seat,' he says, again in French, and then, having made his point, switches to English. 'How are you? How is your work coming on at *le moulin*?'

I sigh. Clearly we are doing things his way. The slow way. 'Fine, thank you.'

There's a pause. And I realise I'm expected to respond. '*Et comment allez vous?*'

'*Très bien, merci.*'

Now that the courtesies are out of the way, I continue: 'So, although work is coming on fine at the mill, my visa was declined. Surprisingly quickly.'

'Ah, that is a shame.' He shrugs.

'Clearly someone didn't want me to stay to set up my new business there.'

'As I say, a shame. That place has a lot of history and is important to the community.'

His hands are on the desk, his fingers intertwined, and I'm sure he's leaning on my file of paperwork.

And then I remember sitting beside the lake with Geneviève, after the rain, and pulling in the huge fish. How we laughed, the triumph and the delicious taste of the meal, simple, with butter, lemon, the bread, oh, the bread. The crisp exterior, breaking it to reveal the soft white inside. And the tomato salad, the slices of pink sweet onion, all drizzled with olive oil, reminding me why I'm here.

'I can do this. I know I can. I can make a difference here, at the mill. But I can't set up my own business unless I have my visa.'

The mayor says nothing.

'So, the *boulangerie*, is that what you're saying it'll take, for me to get my visa here? Is it? Because, okay, I'll do it.'

He raises his eyebrows. 'You will?'

'The bakery, the *boulangerie*, yes, I'll set it up again, get it going. So you'll have bread baked in the town.'

He looks at me, a glint in his eye. 'Without a visa you have no right to stay . . .'

'But I'm sure you could help with that, for someone prepared to open the *boulangerie* here,' I say slowly. 'To give something back to the community.'

He sighs. 'I feel I may have been too, how do you say, hasty.' He wavers. 'As you said yourself, you aren't a baker. You are just a cook, who makes cakes. English cakes.'

'British,' I correct him.

'You are British. You are not a professional baker of French bread. I may have misjudged things. How can a home cook bring back our *boulangerie*?'

'But I'm willing to give it a go and make it work.'

'Give it a go? Madame, we are talking about one of the most prestigious professions in our country. We take great pride in our bread-making. You cannot just *give it a go*. You know nothing about our ways. You know about tea! We drink coffee, lots of coffee, and wine. And we eat bread. With every meal! When you said you were setting up a *salon de thé*, I thought you had skills in this area. But I understand now I was wrong.'

I lift my head higher. I'm not going to let him run me out of town with my tail between my legs. I came here to get a taste of a new life. A second chance. I'm not going let him stop me before I've begun. I take a deep breath. 'I promise I will do my very best. I know about baking, and I'm passionate about it. I will be just as dedicated to learning about bread-making.'

At first he says nothing, so I continue. 'I will work

hard to get the *boulangerie* up and running. I know how important it is to you. And, as you say, how much more will shut down here if you don't let strangers in? Is this what you want for the town? All that will be left is a bread-vending machine and maybe a coffee machine next to it. Or what about the road that could go through the middle of the town, making sure the town is no more, just a road to somewhere else?'

He gazes at me and I wonder if I've gone too far, but I can't stop now. 'You said you wanted the bakery open again. I'll do it! I'll get it open and running, and then I'll open my *salon de thé*.'

'I want it open . . . but an Englishwoman with no experience in baking. We could be a laughing stock!'

'Do you want your *boulangerie* open, *oui ou non*?'

'*Mais oui!* Yes!'

'Then I'll do it. And you'll sort out my visa. I'll be as French as I need to be to make this happen,' I say, frustrated.

'You will become French?' he asks, bemused.

'Whatever it takes. I'll learn the language, the etiquette, the history. I'll throw myself into it.'

He nods. 'That's good to hear.'

Never underestimate the determination of a pissed-off middle-aged woman, I growl in my head, but he seems to have got the message.

'You will open the *boulangerie* and sell daily bread?'

'I will. If that's what it takes to get my visa, then yes. And in time I'll set up my *salon de thé* at the mill.'

He peers down at the file under his hands.

'But I need the agreement that I'll get a visa to stay if

I do it.' And I barely know myself, sounding firm and businesslike. But this is business and it's about me, taking my chance with both hands and not being treated like I'm as green as I am cabbage-looking. Even if I may have behaved like that. This is not a movie, or a holiday, and I'm certainly not here to find a man. That was never what this new chapter in my life was about. I need to focus on what I *do* want.

'A temporary visa could be arranged, a short-stay one,' he says, 'which will give you the right to work. And then, say, once the *boulangerie* is taking money, a more permanent visa could be arranged for you to reside here.'

We're talking the same language now. I just needed to take my time. 'How long will the short-stay visa cover?'

'You have three months to get the *boulangerie* up and running. By the beginning of September, you must be making a profit. If you are, you will get your longer visa to stay and work. If not, you will return home to the UK.'

'That would be agreeable,' I say. 'Three months from today.'

Suddenly he beams. 'The *boulangerie*, back in the village! It will stop us disappearing into oblivion. Becoming a ghost village, abandoned and knocked down to make way for some road. A celebration!'

He opens his drawer and pulls out two glasses, then one of many bottles of whisky. He pours two large measures. He hands me a glass and I take it. 'I wonder what got my visa declined the first time,' I say.

'Maybe you were missing some important paperwork. We can help with that. You just bring us our daily baguettes. *Bon profitez!*' he says.

'Yes, to profit,' I toast, misunderstanding the expression but feeling it's appropriate anyway.

'Yes, to profit, or I'm afraid your visa won't be approved, and I suspect the mill will need to be sold . . . if a buyer can be found . . . at the right price,' he says, making sure I understand what he's saying, and I realise this is not a done deal. Selling the mill will be hard. Who else would want it? It was on the market for so long that I'd probably have to sell it for much less than I bought it. This long-term visa isn't in the bag, not by a long shot. I think about Laurent at the *tabac*, shouting that the mill had been promised to him and I wonder if this is part of a plan to get me out. I need to put everything into this to make it happen.

'Here's to bringing back the *boulangerie* and our daily bread.' He holds up his glass and tips back his whisky. 'You'll need to meet your new landlord,' he says, then opens his desk drawer, takes out a key and puts it in front of me.

'Where do I meet them?'

'Here, now. It is me.' He smiles at his little joke. 'I'll have your tenancy agreement drawn up immediately.'

You can't fault his game-playing. Like a chess master. Get the *boulangerie* in profit, or lose your right to a visa and sell the mill to the person I promised it to originally, but for a much lower price. Well, it looks like I'm in the game, and I want to win. I tip back the whisky and feel it burn all the way down my throat, as if I'd just made a pact with the devil. I put the glass on the table and take the key.

I step out into the village square and see a cat is lying

out in the shade of the plane trees, just in front of the *boulangerie*. So, that's it, I think. I'm getting a temporary visa. I can stay until 5 September. I'm not running home. I'm here for the adventure and to prove to myself I can do this. I'm going to stay and make my mark here. I deserve this chance to find my own happiness. And if this is the only way to do it, so be it. A bit like when I first found out I was ill – I couldn't run or hide from it. I had to face it and fight it, no matter how unpleasant it got. And that is exactly what I intend to do now. Sometimes you just have to close your eyes and take a leap of faith . . . because going back isn't an option.

Chapter 14

I don't know what compels me to do it. I just know that if I'm going to open a *boulangerie*, I need to see how it all works. Not just pop in for a baguette, but watch and understand. And there is only one *boulangerie* I know of around here. It's in the neighbouring town and it's Claude's. I'm not going to run away and hide. I want him to know I'm here to stay, that I'm not just a tourist whose feelings he can toy with.

I get into my car — it's hot, hot, hot — and turn the blower on full blast, but it's throwing hot air at me. I open the windows and drive out of the square towards the bigger town.

As I head into the roundabout, the traffic is building on the way. It's market day and people are parking along the main road and walking. There are tourists in straw hats and shorts, sauntering along, sellers hoping they'll stop and buy from their stalls. It's surprising that so many people are visiting the town, yet in the Village du Grand Lac, there is no one. Maybe I'll be able to persuade them to come to the *salon de thé* when I open. But first I need to do some *boulangerie* research.

I drive into town and park near the *chambre d'hôte* where I stayed. I get out, put on my sunglasses and follow the narrow streets towards the main square, past stalls selling jewellery, baskets and scarves. Closer to the centre there are stalls selling seafood on piles of cold ice, cheeses, cider from family-run orchards with samples being handed out, and the smell of crêpes hangs in the air. And then I see Claude's bakery. A smart light grey exterior, white writing on the window, and a sheaf of wheat underlining the family name: Guiomar.

Claude Guiomar. The man who made a fool of me.

I stroll towards the bakery, keeping my eyes on it, moving around the shoppers and holidaymakers enjoying the Breton sunshine, stopping and tasting from producers. At the *boulangerie*, a steady stream of people are going in and leaving with baguettes and croissants. I step into the long, narrow shop. The baking kitchen is nowhere to be seen. There are rows of loaves in tall baskets, croissants fat and flaking under the glass counter, like I remember from the first day I arrived back in France, when I pulled over and ate the baguette with coffee. I intend to do the same now.

I stand and wait. Eventually, a woman at the far end of the shop turns to me. And then I hear his voice, barking instructions from a concealed kitchen. The tall, slight woman turns to him and says something back, nodding to a trolley containing trays of croissants and baguettes. He steps out into the shop and, although I've prepared myself for this, my insides lurch – and not in a good way.

At first he doesn't see me, or maybe doesn't recognise me. But I recognise him.

He does a double-take.

'Ah, the lady from *le moulin*,' he says. He turns to the woman and says, in French, 'She has bought the old mill. The one I told you about. Wants to make it into a *salon de thé*. She found me a very attractive man. I had to tell her, "*Désolé*, I am married."' He's entertained by his own version of events.

I squirm but am determined not to be deterred. 'I have come to try your bread. *Une baguette, s'il vous plaît*, and a croissant,' I say, keeping things polite and professional.

'You're welcome,' he says. 'My wife will serve you. I have to take the van out.'

She stands at the till. Not smiling, not at all.

'*Bonjour*,' I say to her, remembering my manners.

For a moment she says nothing, then, '*Bonjour*,' barely moving her lips. She moves to the till and stands poised over it and I wonder what Claude has told her about me. I bristle and my cheeks burn at the thought of him telling her I was practically coming on to him and how disappointed I was that he was married! When in fact, it was very much the other way around, him coming on strongly to me!

'*Je voudrais*,' I say, in clear, correct French, '*une baguette et un croissant, s'il vous plaît.*'

'*Une baguette*, which?' She waves a hand at the rows of bread and I feel she's making this difficult for me.

'As you recommend, Madame,' I say, trying to get her to guide me. She takes a baguette, rolls it in a square of

· 116 ·

paper and puts it down firmly on the counter, clearly bored of my custom. So, one thing I need to offer at the *boulangerie* is service with a smile. I make a mental note.

'*Et un croissant*,' I repeat, pointing to the fat, shiny croissants under the glass counter. She steps towards them, looks up at me, goes to the back of the shop and the trolley of trays there. I'm hoping they're fresh out of the oven. My mouth is actually watering.

She puts one into a paper bag and hands it to me, then types it into the till and says the amount too quickly for me to understand.

'*Pardon?*' I say. She sighs and shows me the amount on the card machine. I tap my card, and before I've even put it back into my purse, she has turned away and is wheeling the trolley of trays to the kitchen.

I leave the shop and head to the café on the other side of the square, not wanting to be close to the bakery. I've seen what I needed to see. Where the bread comes from around here. What a local bakery offers. Now for the bread itself . . .

I order a *café crème* and a glass of water from the waiter with the tray. While I wait, I tear off some bread and try it. It's nice, just bread. The waiter comes out with my hot, frothy, milky coffee and the water. I thank him, then take the croissant from its bag, waiting for the smell to hit me. But nothing does. I pull off the end and touch the inside. It's solid, cold. I take a bite. Disappointment is all I can taste. It's dry. Not crunchy outside, not soft and buttery within. I put it down and dust off my hands. She's sold me yesterday's pastry. She's letting me know I'm not welcome.

Part of me wants to go back and ask for a fresh one. But the bigger part of me wants to get back to the Village du Grand Lac and start getting ready to open the *boulangerie*, in the hope I never have to come here again.

I have been put in my place. Served the insult. I didn't deserve fresh croissants — I am a tourist and wouldn't know the difference.

Well, I do. And I'm about to *make* a difference. Claude needs to learn to treat people with respect: me, his wife and any other unsuspecting woman who momentarily falls for his fake charm. It was a moment of weakness. But now I know where I will find my self-respect — on the baking battlefield.

Chapter 15

What on earth have I agreed to?

It's the following morning, and I'm standing outside the disused *boulangerie*, with the peeling maroon paint on the wood around the big window, covered from the inside with yellowing netting. I'm looking at the '*Fermé*' sign through the glass door with the sun-bleached blind pulled down. I give myself a good talking-to and remind myself I'm doing this to get my visa, and to set up the *salon de thé* where I will live a lovely quiet life on the banks of the lake with the kingfishers, making cakes for people to enjoy. I pull out the key from my bag and slot it into the lock. I turn it and push the door but it doesn't open. After giving it a shove with my shoulder, it still doesn't budge. It's stuck at the bottom. I kick it once, and then again, harder this time. It flies open, sending the bell above the door into a frenzy. I hear the bang of a window opening above and a dog barking furiously.

'*Allô?*'

I step back from the door to look up.

'*Qu'est-ce qui se passe?*' a sharp voice says.

'Hello? *Bonjour?*' I shade my eyes from the sun with my hand.

'*Qu'est-ce qui se passe?*' a white-haired woman repeats. She has a cigarette in one hand and leans out of the window, a silk scarf tied around her neck. 'I will call the *gendarmes!*' She points at me with bright red nails, cigarette smoke swirling.

'Oh, I'm not breaking in. I have the key. *La clé.*' I hold it up. She says something quickly in French.

'I'm sorry, I didn't understand. Could you repeat that, please? Do you speak English?'

The woman sighs deeply. 'Why, Madame, would you have the key to the *boulangerie?*'

'I'm reopening it.' I remember my manners. 'I'm Juliet. I own the old mill. I'm opening the *boulangerie*. People will have fresh bread every day again.'

'*Oh, mon dieu!*' She waves the hand with the cigarette. '*C'est pas vrai!*' she rolls her eyes upwards.

I'm confused. 'But this has always been a bakery, hasn't it?'

'A noisy one at that! Much better now it has closed. I should know.'

'But the town wants a bakery.'

'The obsession with bread. There is a machine they can use. Why must we be so obsessed with bread in this country?'

'Well, it does appear on every meal table here,' I reply, trying to be jovial.

She looks at me and I look back at her, her short white hair curled neatly into a soft quiff at the front. 'Are you a chef?' she asks sharply.

I shake my head.

'Are you French?'

I shake my head again.

'Phffff!!' She throws up a hand. 'If a French baker can't make it work, how will you? A British woman! I will speak to the mayor. A ridiculous idea!'

The window slams, startling me, and then I feel my backbone stiffen.

I stare at the shop front again, the peeling paint and old leaves gathered in the doorway. Behind me, smartly dressed women carrying baskets are arriving in the square. It's mid-morning and there are a few stalls at the foot of the church steps. One man is selling oysters, another langoustines from the back of a van. A chap with an old 2CV is selling vegetables off the bonnet and a woman with a table is offering goat's cheese and home-made wine from large plastic bottles. Two women kiss each other briefly in greeting before picking up their oysters and vegetables, then walk over to the fully stocked baguette machine. I can't help but wonder what this place might have been like when the *boulangerie* was open, if the market was busier. It feels flat. Not like the market I've just come from in the neighbouring town. Or others I've visited when I waited for the purchase of the mill to go through. This village seems almost deserted, waiting for someone to close it for good.

The women just stare at me as they pass by. Then, once a safe distance away, lean into each other, shoulder to shoulder, clearly discussing me. I raise a friendly hand and get a stiff nod back as they bustle towards the vending machine and buy their bread. It's a small but consistent customer base. The women glance at me again, then turn to walk briskly away in their smart, low-heeled shoes, baskets at their sides, baguettes in hand, ready to prepare lunch.

And then I'm on my own in the square in the shade of the plane trees. The few stall holders are still packing up, and then there is just the sound of *pétanque* from the older men as ball hits ball.

I kick away the leaves outside the *boulangerie*. I step into the small shop area, running my hand along the worn wooden counter, then walk behind it to the kitchen at the back. I stand and stare. I have no idea what all this equipment does.

I get a flashback to my days at the hospital, arriving terrified and without a clue how anything worked. I watched, week by week, as people came in, how we became accustomed to the machinery, the nurses and each other. Some were helped slowly until they were well enough to be signed off treatment. I think about the scar on my left breast. Others, like Annie, were not so lucky.

I hold up my phone, take a photograph and send it to Annie.

You'll never guess what I've gone and agreed to. I smile as I type.

Tell me! she messages back, and I explain how I've come to have the keys to the local bakery.

Then I text the family WhatsApp group.

Wow! says Pete.

Cool! says Jake.

Woohooo! says Maddie. *Can you bake bread?*

Working on it, I say.

Bit like my DJing! says Jake.

All okay, Jake?

Yeah, he replies. *Bit like you, I'm working on it.*

Every journey starts with the first step. Keep going, I type.

I will, he says.

I send kisses, then leave the shop for the supermarket out of town to buy yet more cleaning products and flour. All I seem to have done so far is clean! The three old men playing *pétanque* watch me go with interest. A day at a time, I repeat. But there's one more thing I need to do before I start cleaning the *boulangerie*, something I need to put right.

Chapter 16

I return from the supermarket, having enjoyed pushing the trolley up and down the aisles. The shop is much the same as back home, just smaller and with different products. I can negotiate this, I tell myself. I've been navigating all of this new life since I got here. I found driving on the other side of the road strange at first, but I'm getting used to it. On the journey back from the supermarket, I felt the beginning of familiarity about the route, just as I do now, parking under the shade of the plane trees in the square beside the baguette machine.

I pick up the cake tin next to me on the seat, which I went to the mill to collect on my way back from the supermarket, and get out of the car. The back seat is packed with cleaning products to leave at the *boulangerie*, a brush, mop and different bags of flour for testing. I look at the *tabac* and take a deep breath. The three old men are now sitting outside at a round table with cups of coffee in front of them. I lock the car and walk slowly towards the *tabac*, nodding to them as I approach. *'Bonjour,'* I say politely as I pass. They incline their heads and stare at me as I go inside, clearly wondering what I'm doing here.

Inside, not only is it dark and cool, it's also empty. There's no one here at all. There are a small number of café-style tables with chairs, a couple of tables for two, one for four, and a large barrel for standing at to drink coffee or a lunchtime *pastis*.

'*Bonjour?*' I call, a little nervously.

'*J'arrive,*' I hear, and then Laurent appears in the doorway that leads to the back room, practically filling it. He stops, then slowly approaches the other side of the counter. His long dark hair appears to have been recently washed; he has a thick beard and brown eyes the colour of conkers, with eyebrows to match. He frowns when he sees me and puts his large hands on the counter, silver rings on his thumb and other fingers. For a moment neither of us speaks, and then he says, '*Bonjour,*' and nods politely but cautiously. 'How can I help you?' He holds a hand to the coffee machine, '*Café* or a beer maybe? Or have you come to hit me on the head again with whatever you might have in your basket?'

He may be joking – his dark eyes are sparkling.

I take a deep breath and put my basket on the counter. 'I think I may owe you an apology.'

He allows a moment to pass without speaking, the awkward silence making me squirm. But, I tell myself, I've been through worse than a large rugby-playing type making me work at an apology.

He opens the dishwasher and steam pours out, like a dragon waking from its long winter slumber.

'You think,' he says, picking up a cup from the

dishwasher and inspecting it, then looking at me with his dark eyes, 'or you know?' He lifts one eyebrow.

'I . . .' I clear my throat and hold his stare. 'I'm sorry. *Désolée*,' I add.

'For what? Seeing me off your land like a bad smell?'

I chew my bottom lip. 'I'm sorry for both. Either . . .'

He carries on drying the cups. 'Was it the long hair or the tattoos that made you assume I was bad news? Or maybe you'd been listening to local gossip?'

'I don't know anything about you. But I did assume . . . Look, I brought you something, to say sorry.' I try to move this on.

He raises both eyebrows now. 'You brought me something?'

I reach into my pocket, pull out a euro and hold it up.

'I owe you one euro,' I say, and I slide it across the shiny polished bar. 'For the bread machine.'

He smiles and reaches out, his fingertips just touching mine as he takes it and drops it into the till with a dramatic gesture.

'*Merci*,' he says, then looks back at me.

Am I forgiven? Will I be able to work here, opposite the man I practically accused of drug-dealing and assaulted?

'You've paid your debt. It's fine.' He starts to wipe down the already clean bar.

'And I made you this. Well, I was baking, back at the mill . . .' I pull the cake tin from my basket and push it over the counter. The old men wander in from outside and up to the counter to see what's going on. 'I thought you might like it.'

Laurent stops wiping the bar and looks at it, then at one of the old men, who says, '*Qu'est-ce que c'est?*'

For a moment I think it was a terrible idea, but I've come this far.

Laurent smiles. 'He wants to know what it is,' he translates.

'Yes, I got that, thank you.' I lift my chin and look at the men staring at the cake tin.

'A Victoria Sandwich.'

'*Un quoi?*' says one, cupping a hand over his ear.

'*Un gâteau*. A Victoria Sandwich,' says Laurent.

I lift the lid, take it out of the tin and put it on the bar.

The three old men frown at it. 'An English cake!'

'British,' I correct.

They eye it suspiciously.

'It's made with eggs, flour, sugar, homemade strawberry jam,' I say, pulling out a knife from my basket – a favourite I always took, rolled up in a tea-towel, when we went on family picnics. I cut the cake into twelve slices, then push it towards Laurent and the gathered men.

They raise their eyebrows.

I see one reach out and take a slice. He bites into it, crumbs tumbling over the counter.

Laurent nods slowly. 'I see.'

There's an uncomfortable silence that is interrupted by surprised 'nom nom' sounds coming from the elderly man eating the cake. The other two reach for slices themselves.

Laurent chuckles. 'That is a good reaction,' he says. And I feel a little relieved. Someone is eating what I made and likes it. I can bake, I remind myself.

'So, is that it? You came to bring me a euro and cake?'

I can tell we're still on sticky ground. 'I did. And, as I said, I came to apologise. And to say . . .' I take a deep breath and a run at it '. . . I'm opening the *boulangerie* opposite. I hope you'll want to come and buy bread.'

He stares at me. 'The *boulangerie* in the village?'

'Yes, so that people will have fresh bread instead of relying on the vending machine,' I say.

'My wife swears by Claude's bread,' says one of the old men, helping himself to another piece of cake. 'Says it stays fresh longer than others.'

Laurent slaps the counter, his rings clattering. 'But it shouldn't stay fresh. That's the point!' he says crossly, in French, and I get the feeling this is a regular topic of conversation at this bar. 'No one ever bought French bread for its shelf life. They buy it for the crunch, the soft middle to soak up the juices on the plate, not for how long it can hang around in the kitchen. If it's hanging around, it isn't good bread!'

'She probably said that because she fancies him,' says the third old man, already eating a second slice.

'Or maybe she is one of his lovers!' jokes the first, helping himself to more cake.

'Who *hasn't* he slept with?' says the second.

My cheeks burn at the memory of his lips on mine. 'Anyway.' I clear my throat and Laurent looks back at me. 'I hope you'll come and try my bread.' I say it confidently, even though secretly I am wondering how on earth I am going to compete with the local baker when I know barely anything about bread. As the woman above the *boulangerie* remarked, I'm British and I'm not a professional baker.

'You won't be the first to try,' says one of the men at the bar, and the others nod in agreement.

I clasp my hands together and turn to leave.

'Madame,' I hear Laurent say as I reach the door. I turn back with one hand on the cool handle. 'Madame, wait,' he repeats, and beckons to me.

'Juliet. I'm Juliet,' I say, trying not to feel I've made a fool of myself by bringing him a cake.

'Juliet,' he says, as he takes a bite of cake. 'It's good,' he says slowly, taking another bite and raising the piece in my direction. 'If you make decent bread, I'm sure people will come. You just have to offer them something different from what's already available.' He shrugs one shoulder. 'If it's as tasty as your cake,' he smiles lazily, and holds up the piece he's eating, 'I'm sure you will have no worries. *Bonne chance et bon profitez.*'

'*Merci.* And apologies again.'

'Wait,' he says as I turn to leave. 'I have a gift for you.' He reaches into the till and then slides a euro across the counter. 'You never know when it will come in useful. A good-luck gift for your new venture.'

I smile at the gesture and walk back over to the counter to take the coin. '*Merci,*' I say, and put it back in my pocket.

He smiles as I leave the café, and I find myself smiling too, my head high as I walk back to the *boulangerie*, push open the door and the bell rings – followed by knocking on the floor above.

'*Arrêt!*' comes a complaining shout, presumably from my neighbour upstairs.

I lean against the door, my back to the *tabac*, ears burning. I remember his words: 'the crunch, the soft middle to soak up the juices . . . If you make decent bread, I'm sure people will come.'

I hope so, because it's the only way I have of getting the mill up and running. I head to the scullery, just beyond the bakery, and turn on the taps over the sink, which splutter and spurt. Once the water starts pouring, I run a cloth under it and start to clean as if my life depends on it . . . because life as I know it actually does.

Chapter 17

I spend the next week cleaning at the *boulangerie*, getting up early, drinking my coffee and looking out over the lake. Most days, Geneviève arrives to fish. We greet each other, share a coffee as she sets up her seat for the day, and I leave with my bucket of cleaning products and drive the short distance to the village square. As I get out of the car each morning, I raise a tentative hand to Laurent as he sets tables and chairs outside the *tabac*, which I'm pretty sure will stay fairly unused, apart from the three *pétanque* players, ushered out of their houses for the day by their wives. I also make a point of bending to stroke the little cat that wanders over to greet me from the direction of the *mairie* every morning.

I open the door to the *boulangerie* and the bell above it rings. Already my neighbour upstairs is banging on her floor, telling me to keep the noise down.

I sigh. 'I'm going to have to take you down if I'm to get any peace,' I say to the bell. I look around for something to stand on. A chair or a table. It's been a long time since I've done something like this.

I see one in the scullery, a square, dark wood table, and haul it towards the door, half lifting, half dragging it across the polished tiles, so as not to incur any more complaints from the woman upstairs, followed by a volley of barks from her small dog.

I stare at the table. Years ago, I would have climbed onto it and got on with the job, like the time Christmas dinner set off the smoke alarms, scaring the living daylights out of the children and my mother. Pete's mother tutted and Pete asked if he should call the fire brigade. I said no, and handed him a tea-towel, one each to the children, and told them to waft it at the smoke alarm. I grabbed a chair from the dining room, climbed onto it and removed the battery. Everything went immediately silent, and the children ran around waving their tea-towels above their heads for the next half-hour while Pete's mother told him how brilliant he'd been to sort out the problem.

Just like back then, I'm dealing with this problem solo. I get a chair and put it against the table. I'm more cautious than I would have been at home. I step onto the chair first – it wobbles and I grip the back, then slowly lift my left foot to join the right. I'm crouched unsteadily on the chair, wondering whether to get down and leave it or keep going.

I glance out and see Laurent watching me from the other side of the square. He's standing, a chair in hand, putting them out in the sunshine. I may be crouched on a chair, but my pride is refusing to let me get down. I straighten and step up to the table. One foot, and then I have to take the leap of faith to get both feet on the table. I straighten and am face to face with the little brass bell.

I unhook it from over the door. Hopefully, now, there will be less banging from the neighbour.

I look at Laurent who has carried on setting out his tables and chairs. I did it. I didn't need help. I'm doing this on my own. Little victories, I tell myself. One day at a time. I can do this.

I look down at the floor and my head swims. That's new. I've never felt that before. I peer up at the door frame and pretend I'm checking for cleanliness while I try to work out how to get down . . . or at least wait until Laurent has gone back inside and I can do it as clumsily as I like. And I do. Once he goes back into the little bar, I crouch on the table, grab the back of the chair and sit down heavily, then shimmy off the table and onto the floor, jarring my knees. Not so much the woman I used to be, but the one I am today. And that'll do me.

I pull the table and chair into the window bay, in front of the old oven that's just for decoration now, and in front of the net curtains I've washed and rehung across the window.

I put the bell next to the till. The shop and kitchen are spotless, and I can't put it off any more. I have to bake bread and make sure it's good. Laurent's words ring in my head: if you make decent bread, I'm sure people will come.

I look at the ovens in the bakery behind the counter.

With the kitchen clean and sparkling and work at the mill on hold, today is the day. I need to actually start baking.

It's just four ingredients: flour, water, yeast and salt.

I can do this.

I prop my phone against the bag of flour I bought at the out-of-town supermarket and follow the YouTube video.

Maybe I can't, a voice says in my head.

And then I think of Claude. *Oh yes I can.* I think of Jake, me telling him about every journey starting with the first step. I think of Annie and her determination to get well enough to visit me here. I can do this, and I'm going to! I get out the ingredients, begin weighing them, then remember why I'm doing this. I'm doing it because of Claude, because of Annie. And because I can.

I measure everything carefully, following the instructions on my screen to the letter. 'Every journey starts with the first step,' I repeat, as I bring the ingredients together and start to work the dough, ready to bake the next day. I'm in my own world, enjoying the peace in the privacy of the kitchen. Maybe there's something to be said for being invisible after all, left to enjoy yourself, finding your purpose.

Chapter 18

It's early in the morning, not yet light. I want to be at the *boulangerie* without anyone watching me from the *tabac* and while my neighbour is still asleep, not banging on the ceiling. I need to get in as much practice as I can if I'm to have this business up and running.

The ovens are on.

I've shaped the loaves into long cylinders and re-proved them. I've followed the instructions from You-Tube and what I could remember from all the googling I could do. They look like baguettes. I admire them lined up on the baking sheet, each in its little hammock, ready for the oven.

I stand back and photograph them, ready to send pictures to everyone back home. Then I slide them in and shut the door, before I dust off my hands and set a timer. Once that's done, I go to the scullery and make a coffee, then walk back through the shop and open the front door quietly. I stare out over the empty square. Dawn is breaking. I breathe in, taking time to be in the moment.

The little cat strolls over to me, rubbing against my

legs. I bend and stroke him, his purring making me smile. I go inside, fetch a bowl of water and put it down, stroking the cat some more and enjoying the peace of the early-morning light, the company of my new feline friend and the coffee. My thoughts turn to the mill and the work I've got to do there. I share pictures I've taken recently with the family WhatsApp group and Annie. I haven't heard from her for a few days, which is unusual, but I send the pictures of the *boulangerie* and the unbaked baguettes, waiting to be turned into golden wonders. I hope that news from my business venture will make her smile. I wait to hear back from her.

The smell of burning catapults me from my thoughts. I run back in through the shop, around the high wooden counter and to the kitchen beyond. Smoke tumbles from the oven as I throw open the door and cough. The smoke alarm starts its incessant beeping and the banging starts from upstairs.

'*Arrêt! Mon dieu!* I'm dying from smoke up here!' she yells in French. She's talking very quickly, but I get the gist of what she's saying.

I open all the doors and windows and wave a tea-towel in front of the smoke alarms.

'Is everything okay?' I hear a shout from across the square. It's Laurent. And I'm not sure why, but I don't want him to think I'm not up to this. It's like I have something to prove, after misjudging him so badly. I want to prove I can get something right.

'*Absolument!*' I try to smile and give a thumbs-up. 'All good!' I wave the smoke out, as if it was completely normal, and hear the window open upstairs.

'I could suffocate up here! What are you doing down there, Madame?'

'Sorry, Madame. I'm sorting it out now.'

'*Vite!* Quickly!' she says, and bangs the window shut.

With the burnt baguettes in the bin, and the smoke alarm finally off, I examine the oven and realise there's a problem with the temperature-control button. While the casing moves, the mechanism inside is stuck on the highest setting. Try as I might, I can't shift it.

I grab my bag, lock the *boulangerie* door and head to the mayor's office. Instead of waiting to be told '*Non*' by the receptionist, I stalk straight to the mayor's desk as the woman throws up her hands, and I catch a flash of red from her long, painted nails. I can feel her scowl as I pass.

'Madame Juliet!' He smiles. 'How are things going at the *boulangerie*? Will we soon have our own bread made here in the village?'

I let out a long sigh and shake my head. 'Not unless I can get the oven working properly and my neighbour stops complaining by banging on the floor above.'

'Ah, Madame Bertou.' He nods. 'She has been a little tricky as a tenant since the bakery shut.'

'Difficult is one word.'

'She is set in her ways. She stays in her apartment. The *boulangerie* closed years ago, as you know, and the space has been empty since. It will be an adjustment.'

'For her or for me? Oh, and the oven isn't working properly,' I say, keen to get on. 'Do you know who I can call to fix it? I've tried googling someone to do oven repairs but I can't find anyone.'

He smiles. 'Of course. You need Laurent.'

My heart sinks. 'Laurent?'

'He runs the *tabac* across the street. He is the best engineer around here. Unless it's cars. That was Gilles, but he closed his garage some years ago too. He plays *pétanque* with his companions in the village. But for this, it's Laurent you need.'

Of course it is, I think, and I have no doubt he'll be amused by the cliché of me, the British woman, setting herself up as a baker and burning her bread.

'He is your best hope around here for a quick fix.'

I leave the *mairie* and wish I didn't have to, but make for the *tabac* all the same.

'It's the knob,' I assert, after saying *bonjour* to Laurent and greeting the three regular customers in French.

Laurent raises his eyebrows.

'On the oven,' I say quickly. 'The knob is loose and the oven is stuck at the highest temperature.'

'Ah,' he says, understanding.

He translates for the three men at the bar.

'Ah . . .' they say.

A conversation breaks out quickly between the four, and I don't understand most of it. There are hand gestures and demonstrations of what I think are nuts and bolts and screws, and where the problem lies.

My eyes ping to and fro between Laurent and one man in particular in a light beige jacket and cap to match, as they discuss mechanisms and remedies. I'm assuming that's Gilles. Lots of shrugging and waving at the *boulangerie* seem to bring the conversation to a close.

'I'll come now,' says Laurent, going out to the back room and returning with a bag of tools. The same rough-around-the-edges bag of tools I put outside the cellar door at the mill.

'*Merci*,' I say, a little contrite.

I head out of the door, wishing the three men a good day, and Laurent follows me out into the summer sunshine.

'Wait – the *tabac*? Who will look after it?'

He smiles. 'My customers.' He glances back at the three men propped against the bar, watching us. 'I don't think we'll have a rush on any time soon.' Despite his relaxed smile, I can see that's not a good thing. How much money can he be making if he's only selling three cups of coffee in the whole morning?

We head over to the *boulangerie* and I push open the door. He glances up, clearly expecting the bell, but it doesn't ring. And somehow that seems sad. Like the life has gone from the place.

I watch as he puts his bag down, extracts a tool and goes straight to work. In the meantime, I busy myself, sweeping the already very clean floor. In no time at all, he stands up straight and throws his tools back into the open bag on the floor.

'It should work fine now,' he says, standing back from the oven and washing his hands in the sink.

'*Merci*,' I say, wishing I could have repaired this for myself. 'How much do I owe you?'

He considers, then gives me one of his lazy smiles. 'Call it a favour. A new beginning between business neighbours.'

'No.' I reach for my purse. 'Really, I need to pay you.'

He looks at me with a tilt of the head, as if amused. 'It was just an adjustment,' he says, before he adds with devilment, 'It was a good job I had my tools.'

I blush at the memory of hitting him on the head and tossing out his bag. 'I need to do something to pay you back.'

'Bring me some bread when you have made some . . .' – he looks at the cremated articles in the bin – '. . . that is edible.'

A laugh ripples through me. And he laughs too, his chest rising and falling, his dark hair cascading over his shoulders, which judder with mirth.

'It's a deal!' I say.

'Well, *bonne journée*,' he says, as he picks up his tool-bag and heads out of the door, into the sunshine, and back across the road towards the *tabac*. The three elderly men are waiting to debate the mechanics of the oven knob and whose solution was the best, I presume: they're animatedly holding up their hands and making a point to each other, which may be the same point, but it seems to have caused great discussion.

'Come on, now. I can do this. I can make something edible,' I say, and find myself laughing again as I turn back to the oven.

Chapter 19

The following morning, I follow the YouTube video to the letter, just as before. Making sure I do everything correctly and miss nothing. The weather outside is a near-perfect summer's day. No breeze, just warm sunshine. I turn on the oven and weigh out the ingredients for the dough. I need seven kilos of dough for twenty baguettes. I halve the amount of flour I need for the mix.

I pour the flour and water into the kneading machine and set the timer on my watch, then check the instructions, adding the yeast and the salt.

The dough is starting to come together and I can smell the warm, soft mixture filling the early-morning air — and as it does, my spirits lift.

When the timer sounds, I switch off the kneading machine and add the dough to the cutting machine. It delivers sausage shapes, all the same weight, out of the chute. I stretch each piece of dough, then put them into rows, ready for proving. This next fermentation takes two hours. I make another batch, just to be sure I'm doing it right, whilst I'm waiting. I wait and I wait . . .

until finally, my first batch are plumped up and ready for baking. I cut straight diagonal lines down each one so that the air can escape and, using the wooden palette knife, I put each piece of dough onto the baking tray. Then I spray each with water and slide them into the oven. While I'm at it, I make a batch of shortbread just to keep my hands busy. I step out into the morning light to see Laurent outside the *tabac*.

'*Bonjour, Juliet*,' he calls across the square, and waves politely, before unlocking the door.

'*Bonjour, Laurent*.' I raise a hand, then turn back inside, anxious not to be away from my bread for too long.

After exactly fourteen minutes, I pull it out.

I stare at the loaves on the work surface. They look like baguettes. Golden and crisp on the outside. I pick one up. It smells like a baguette. I break it in two. It cracks. Steam spirals upwards from the soft inside. And suddenly a wide smile breaks out on my face. I've done it. I've made French bread!

I breathe in deeply, tear off a piece, and the white, fluffy crumb pulls away like cotton wool. I smell it again, before popping the warm bread into my mouth. First the crunch from the shiny crust, then my teeth sinking into the soft white inside. I'm euphoric.

I gather up the loaves in my arms, put them into a basket, alongside my tin of shortbread, and head out of the bakery door. I look nervously at the *tabac*. I'll pop across later to see Laurent, but I have to know first of all how I've done. And I know just the people who will tell me. I jump into the car and head to the mill, where the cars are parked along the driveway. The fisherwomen are there.

'Geneviève!' I call, and wave. She raises a hand and smiles. I hurry around the side of the lake towards the flat rock where the women are fishing in the morning sun.

'I've done it! I've made bread!' I tell them, indicating the five loaves I'm carrying. 'Here, for your lunch! To go with your fish!' I beam.

Geneviève takes them in her arms. *'Bonjour, Juliet.'* Then she kisses my cheeks gently. 'You were at the *boulangerie* early again this morning. I miss our morning coffees!' She laughs.

'Oh, yes, sorry, *bonjour.*' I kiss her cheeks and feel the baguettes' warmth between us. 'I picked the best ones, but I think I still need to work on them all looking the same.'

'Well done!' she says. And hearing her say that, I could burst with pride.

'Bravo!' say the other women, and give a little clap. 'Bravo!' Although I've only just met them, their support means everything. I hope they know that.

'Let me know what you think! I have another to deliver to see if I can spread the word.' I beam even wider, if that was possible, and turn to leave.

'Bonne chance,' Geneviève says, and the other women join in and wave as I pick my way along the edge of the lake, down the slope and back to my car. I drive back to the village square and park. I look at the *boulangerie* and there, in the window above, Madame Bertou is staring at me, dog under her arm, drawing long and hard on her cigarette.

It has to be worth a try. I go into my shop, grab another baguette, then hurry up the stairs to the front door of the flat above.

'Madame Bertou,' I say, as she opens the door. '*Bonjour.*'

'Madame.' She nods with downturned mouth and a cigarette between her fingernails. She's wearing a silk scarf around her neck, as always, a blue-and-cream-striped top, smart, dark blue jeans and Gucci-style slip-on shoes with the gold horse-bit across the top.

I hold out the loaf, like a runner handing the baton to the next in a relay. She looks down at it but doesn't take it. She draws on her cigarette. 'What is this? I thought you would have given up this ridiculous notion of trying to make bread after the burning. Oh, *mon dieu*, it was disgusting. Why are you still persisting?'

'I have to,' I say, still holding out the baguette.

She waves her cigarette at it. 'We have bread here already from a *French* baker. From the machine. And it's a lot quieter!'

'I'm not trying to be a French baker . . .' I say, feeling as if a weight has been lifted off my shoulders. I'm not trying to be anyone else: I'm just me, Juliet, falling in love with this new adventure. A journey I couldn't have imagined being on a few months ago. Just being me.

She looks down at the baguette again. 'The shine is good,' she says, the corners of her mouth still turned down. 'It smells . . . not bad.' And finally: 'I will try it. As long as it isn't going to poison me like your last bread did, with its terrible burning.'

I could try to argue that it wasn't my bread's fault but the oven's, but decide not to.

She takes the baguette.

'*Merci,*' I say.

'*Bon après-midi,*' she says and looks at me.

'*Bon après-midi.*'

I nod to her, but she doesn't acknowledge me so I go down the stairs and walk towards the *tabac*.

'*Du pain!*' I announce, as I walk through the glass door into the *tabac*, holding two loaves to my chest.

Laurent looks up from behind the bar where he is drying glasses again. '*Bonjour,*' he says.

'I did it! I made bread! *Bonjour!*'

He looks at me in surprise, his hair dark and shiny in the sunlight, beard neatly trimmed above his jawline. He nods slowly. 'We already said good morning, Juliet. Remember? Or am I so forgettable?' He smiles. 'Some people in France would take offence. You're lucky I'm not some people!'

'What? Oh, sorry!' I wave a hand. 'Anyway, I did it! I made bread!' I am unable to keep the grin from my face. 'Here!'

I place the two baguettes on the counter.

Laurent puts down his tea-towel and bends over to study them. He lifts one and smells it.

'Let me know what you think,' I say, practically giddy with excitement, putting a tin of the shortbread I made on the counter. I'm watching him carefully and, I have no idea why, my stomach does a nervous flip as he looks at me with an interested and amused smile. 'I'm going to be opening the shop next week, now that I'm making bread.'

He frowns. 'Next week? It can take years to become a professional *boulanger*.'

'Well, it seems I've got the hang of it, so with any luck I'll be up and running sooner than that,' I say, with a confidence I can't quite feel — but time isn't on my side.

He looks at the baguettes, as do the three older men standing and leaning against the bar. He turns down the corners of his mouth. 'It looks like bread.'

'Try it,' I say, ridiculously eager.

He pulls off the end, bites and chews. I hold my breath. Then he passes it to the next man at the bar. 'Gilles,' he says. Gilles tears off a bit, bites and chews, then turns down the corners of his mouth and passes the baguette to the two men next to him.

'*Du sel*,' says Gilles, shaking his head. 'Needs more salt. The salt has killed off the yeast. You add the salt before the yeast.' I concentrate hard on what Gilles is saying.

'Too soft,' says the next. 'Needs longer cooking time.'

'More steam,' says the other, with a flourish of his hand.

And I look between them, all pulling the corners of their mouths down, shaking their heads one after the other and putting the bread back on the counter.

'I like it white. But not soft,' I manage to translate.

'My wife prefers it darker, crunchier.'

Suddenly I realise there is a woman at the end of the bar, with bright red lipstick. She doesn't speak, but seems to be hanging on Laurent's every word as he tries the bread again and agrees with practically all the comments made, putting the half-eaten piece back on the counter and dusting off his hands. He shakes his head. It takes me a moment to recognise the woman, clearly enjoying every moment. It's the receptionist from the *mairie*.

'It needs work, lots more work,' says Laurent.

'But it's bread!' I say.

'But it's not a traditional baguette.' Gilles and the others agree. 'It's an imitation. An interloper.' And they laugh.

'*C'est dégueulasse.*'

'*Oui.* How you say?' Gilles says.

'Disgusting,' says another.

My bubble has burst. I'm crushed. I hurry out of the bar. And just as I do, I see the white van pulling up at the vending machine and a small queue of older women gathering beside it, waiting for their lunchtime loaves. Claude steps out: short legs, shorter than I remember, with a round belly over his belt. Why on earth did I find him so attractive in that moment of madness?

'*Bonjour, Juliet!*' He waves in some kind of polite pretence and rage fires up inside me. I'm furious.

He opens the doors at the back of the van and starts to fill the machine. I look at his bread, all the same size and colour.

'Let's meet again soon,' he calls, and I blush as the women look at me.

I hurry back to the mill as fast as I can and make my way round the side of the building to see the women on the rock, laughing and joking. For a moment their joy fills me, and makes me feel better. It was a mistake. Now I need to move on, I tell myself. Not run away. Just move on. I step towards the edge of the lake and the women, who haven't seen me. I'm curious to know what's making them laugh so much. And then I see it: they are tossing what looks to be bits of baguette into the lake. *My* baguette.

They're using my bread as bait!

I fling myself through the big green door into the mill and go straight to my living area, and my bedroom at the back of the building. I lie on my bed and give in to exhausted sobs.

Chapter 20

As I hear the women leaving for the day, I stay put in my bedroom until the final car has driven off.

I came here to reinvent myself, to stop feeling invisible, and all I've done is make myself stick out like a sore thumb. I climb down the few steps from my bedroom and look at some of the pencil drawings here; drawings on the wall of Punch and Judy faces and, like in the cellar, lists of orders, clearly for sacks of flour, but tucked in a corner is a broken heart, with a name next to it on the crumbling plaster. I can't quite decipher what it says, but make out the word *'bijou'*, meaning jewel, a term of endearment. There was clearly a love story here at one time, and I wish I knew more of it.

I go to the kitchen, make a cup of tea, then walk outside and watch the goldfinches on the lawn. There are dandelion seeds, like fairies, floating on the breeze, and I walk around the edge of the lake in the setting sun. Something about this place keeps drawing me back, making me want to stay, and to try harder rather than just chucking it all in. And just when I need them, the kingfishers turn up.

The following morning, before daybreak, I'm up and out of bed and heading back to the *boulangerie*. The little white, brown and black cat is there to greet me, purring as I bend to stroke him. It's nice to feel welcomed, even if it's just by a friendly feline.

I let myself in with the key and turn on the lights. A strong wind is blowing this morning and the door slams behind me. I wait to hear banging from the apartment above. And it comes.

Thump, thump, thump! 'Be quiet! People are trying to sleep!'

I sigh, head to the kitchen and turn on the ovens. Then I go back outside and put down some more water in a dish for the cat, making sure the door doesn't bang this time. Back in the kitchen, I make up the dough, but this time with some adjustments, maybe more salt, more proving time . . . I'm determined to get it right.

Hours later, I've tried to make it lighter, darker, added more salt before the yeast, more water . . . but every batch has been a disaster. I'm not even going to bother getting someone to taste them. I throw them all straight into the bin and stare at the mound of burnt, under-cooked, floppy baguettes.

I go to the table in the window and sit. I wipe my hands over my forehead and realise I'm covered in flour. I wipe my hands on a tea-towel and decide to take a breather outside. I make coffee in the scullery from the kettle there and walk out of the front door, clutching my mug.

I couldn't have timed it better, or worse, as I watch the short queue of women buying bread from the vending machine, then bidding each other goodbye and hurrying home. No one is waiting to chat, just putting their coins into the machine, picking up their baguettes and leaving. The little cat weaves itself around my legs, purring. And once again I'm grateful for the uncomplicated company.

Above me, Edith Piaf's voice is floating out from what sounds like a vinyl record player. I hum along to the song as I wander back to the *boulangerie* and put down my empty cup. A thought occurs to me. I go back outside and put a foot on the steps of the staircase to the side of the building, then another and another. I climb to the apartment above and stand in front of the door. Then, with a deep breath, I knock.

Nothing. Just Edith Piaf singing.

I should go. It was a ridiculous idea. But I've come this far, I think. I might as well try once more.

I knock again.

Still nothing.

I turn to leave when the music stops. I knock again. This time, the dog barks and very slowly the door opens. The aroma of Gauloises cigarettes and strong coffee pours out to meet me, mixed with very pungent perfume.

'*Bonjour, Madame,*' I say, knowing I have to get the etiquette right.

'*Madame, bonjour.* Have you a problem? Why are you

knocking on my door? Is this an unarranged visit or is there an emergency that cannot wait?'

'I need to know more about the *boulangerie*. About the bread.'

She stares at me. 'I cannot help you.'

'But you've lived here for years, I gather. You must have an opinion, like everyone else around here, on what type of bread to make. Dark, light, salty?'

'Why? People always go on about bread . . . bread, bread, bread . . .' She waves her spare hand around, the one that's not holding the dog. 'There is a reason no one wants that *boulangerie* . . . It will bring you no luck. A big, strong man worked here, making perfect baguettes. But it didn't bring any happiness to anyone. Leave the bread to people who know. Stay away from the *boulangerie*. It's better that way.'

'Or maybe someone doesn't want it to work?' I think about Claude and his bread machines. She doesn't respond. 'Like a bread racket?'

She says nothing and shrugs. 'You have to offer something different if you want these women to buy from you and not Claude. It's like changing your doctor . . . someone you trust. They need to know you will turn up. You need to impress them. Why would they choose bread made by a British woman, who isn't even a trained baker?'

I look past her and see the small table and chair where she must normally sit, overlooking the square. I can tell the conversation is over – her tone indicates as much – but I cautiously proceed. 'You said I needed to offer something different. What did you mean? I need to find out how to make the bread they want to buy. Do you know who can help me? Please.'

'I'm sorry, I can't help.'

The dog is squirming under her arm. She goes to shut the door.

'Okay,' I say. I'm not going to get any further. 'I suppose I just wanted to leave my mark. Feel I've done something I can be proud of.' I'm searching for the words about how I feel. How I needed to step outside my comfort zone, take the risk, live the good life.

The door opens again. 'If you want advice, Madame, try the *tabac*.' She juts out her chin and I've been dismissed.

The door shuts and I walk down the stairs in the brisk wind, having wasted my time. The three men at the bar have already given me their opinions and none of it has helped. My beginner's luck with the first loaves has run out on me and I have no idea how to get this *boulangerie* up and running if I can't make bread. And judging by the disasters in the bin, I can't.

Chapter 21

When I go to close the *boulangerie*, I find, on the front doorstep, a baguette. It's upside down, bottom side up. I frown and pick it up. Who would have left a baguette there for me? Is someone offering me some kind of advice on how to make a good one? Or perhaps they've left it there to taunt me, laughing at my efforts.

I close the shop, lock it and walk across the square, feeling as if I'm being watched. I probably am. Edith Piaf has started up again and I imagine Madame B, as I like to think of her, back in her window seat.

I walk into the cool of the *tabac* and put the baguette on the counter while I climb onto a stool.

'*Bonjour*,' says Laurent, sounding surprised.

'*Bonjour. Un café, s'il vous plaît*,' I say.

He nods politely. 'Of course.' He pours the coffee and puts it on the counter.

I rummage in my bag and can't find what I'm looking for – I must have left my purse back at the mill. But then

I remember. I put my hand on the euro in my top pocket and hand it back to Laurent.

He gives a smile of satisfaction.

'*Bonjour*,' I say to the three old men, ready for their daily *pétanque*, and they reply politely and formally.

I sip the coffee. The steam fills my senses before I take a sip. Hot, earthy and strong.

Laurent looks sideways at the baguette on the counter while polishing glasses. He nods at it. 'Is this one you made earlier?'

I sip the coffee again, making the tip of my tongue tingle as I shake my head. 'It was on the doorstep of the *boulangerie*. Perhaps someone is telling me how I should be making bread properly. But there was no note, just the bread.'

He narrows his eyes. 'Which way up was the bread?'

'Sorry?' I ask, confused.

'The baguette, which way was it lying?' He demonstrates by turning it one way and then the other.

'This way, upside down.' I shrug, 'Why?'

'A baguette can be a delicious meal, with cheese and tomatoes . . . or it can be a symbol of bad luck.'

'Bad luck?'

'Yes.'

'It's just a baguette!' I say, reaching for it.

'Maybe someone doesn't want you here, making bread,' he says. Gilles and the other men are watching with interest, nodding and frowning at the loaf.

I pick it up, ignoring them. I rip off the rounded end. It's starting to go a little stale. The outside is not crunchy; the inside is white. I taste it. It's pleasant, but not amazing. Not like the baguette I had on the first day I arrived in France on my own – that first taste of my new life.

I offer a piece to Laurent, but he shakes his head. He takes the loaf from me. 'In order to keep the bad luck at bay, you have to do this.' He pulls out a penknife from his pocket, marks a cross in the back of the baguette and puts it back on the counter.

I shrug. I've faced worse than a disgruntled neighbour wanting me to leave. The way things are going, it looks as if Madame B will get her wish sooner rather than later if I can't make a satisfactory baguette. He puts away his penknife, picks up a tea-towel and dries a coffee cup. I sip the hot strong coffee, which revives my flagging spirits. I say to Laurent, without much thought, 'Why were you at the mill that day?' I hold the little coffee cup in both hands, enjoying the warmth, despite the hot day.

'The day you hit me over the head?'

'You were in my property,' I challenge him.

He makes a conciliatory moue, as if to say, 'Fair enough.' Then, a little more seriously, 'I came for my tools. I really did. It's the truth. The ones in the cellar I used on your oven. Nothing else you might have thought! I'm many things, a hothead at times, yes, but I am not the local drug-dealer.'

'Did you spend a lot of time at the mill?'

He looks at me, mulling over the question, and then he nods. 'Yes, I did.'

I sip my coffee.

'They say that if you throw yourself into what you love doing, you'll end up finding yourself there.'

'And did you?'

'Yes, I did,' he repeats, and we lapse into our own thoughts.

Then, 'There are drawings on the wall, in the mill,' I say.

He focuses further on what he's doing, still drying the coffee cup until it can't be any drier. 'The drawings?'

'You know the ones I mean . . . in the old store room, which is now my living room, and down in the cellar.'

'There are old orders on the walls,' he said, 'from local businesses wanting flour.'

'Yes, but other messages too. Love notes, I think.'

He says nothing and puts the cups onto the shelves.

'I'm about to start painting it, but maybe I shouldn't. Maybe the drawings mean something to somebody.'

'You painted over them?'

'Not yet. Like I say, I wonder if they'd mean something to someone.'

'Maybe they do. The mill holds secrets for many people.'

'Not just the local drug-dealer,' I say, and there is a moment of connection in which, if we weren't being quite so guarded with each other, we might have laughed.

'So why were your tools at the mill?' I ask.

He shrugs again and says casually, 'I was doing some repairs. Keeping the workings in order. It is a mill, not a bed and breakfast or café.'

I think I'm being told he's not happy with my plans for the mill. Despite his best efforts not to, he's looking at me.

'Do those drawings, the pencil marks on the wall, do they mean something to you?'

He nods slowly. 'Yes.'

'It's you, isn't it? The mayor said there could be another buyer for the mill, if I wanted to sell, if I had to go home because I couldn't get a visa. It's you, isn't it? I saw you at the mayor's office that first day.'

He takes a deep breath, still drying and polishing cups and glasses, putting them on the shelf above his head. 'As I say, it's a mill. It should stay a mill. *Le moulin* is a very special place.'

'I know that. So can I assume you know something about the drawings, then? There's a heart. A name . . .'

He stops polishing and stares at me. 'My grandparents,' he says. 'My grandfather was the last miller there.'

'Then you know how the bread here was made . . .' I say tentatively.

'I have been around bread all my life,' he replies, 'but I am not a baker.'

'But if you have been around bread, then . . . you can help me?'

He laughs. 'And why would I want to do that? Help out someone who has arrived in a town they know nothing about, with plans to change everything about the old mill that has been at the heart of this village for decades and who now thinks they can just live a new life, making bread?' He throws up a hand as if in despair.

His words hit hard and I feel backed into a corner. 'Or maybe you have a chip on your shoulder about people buying houses in France for cheap prices?' I ask evenly.

'*Non*,' he says crossly, 'not any property.'

'Just the mill?'

'The mill should be kept for the community. It should at least be remembered for the building it was, the part it played in the area's history.'

And I can't help batting back a home truth. 'But without the *boulangerie*, you don't have a community.'

'And soon without a *tabac* too,' puts in Gilles, sitting at the bar. 'Sorry, Laurent. But you have no customers. You can't keep this place going for ever without more people,' he says, in French.

Laurent frowns at him. 'All the time I'm here, you still have somewhere to go when your wife shoos you out of the house for the day.'

They all nod in agreement.

'And we only come here because there is nowhere else to go,' says Gilles. He and the other two men sip their mid-morning *pastis*.

'Look,' I say, hoping to get this back on friendlier terms, 'I'm sure you could help me if you wanted to. If it's about money, I don't have any at the moment but—'

'It's not about money.'

'What is it about?'

He takes a beat before he replies, with feeling, 'It's about the passion. Without passion, there is no good bread.'

A ripple of excitement runs through my body, surprising me. 'I have passion,' I say.

'Do you?' He raises one dark eyebrow.

'Yes!' I say firmly.

He resumes his glass polishing. 'For bread?'

'For baking. I love to bake. Baking has got me through some very difficult times in my life, and this challenge is no greater than others I have faced. I need to get the *boulangerie* up and running, or I can't get my visa to open my *salon de thé* at the mill. And without that, the mill will stand empty again, unless you're in a position to buy it. Which I presume you're not, or you would have done so by now.' I stare at him as if no one else is in the room as we cross swords. 'What about you?' I narrow my eyes. 'What's your passion?'

He looks at me steadily. And sighs. 'It's the flour. Your flour is bad. Without good flour, the bread is worthless. Without good flour, you will not make good bread. That, and the *savoir faire*.'

The flour! That's why my bread is bad – and the other thing he said.

'The *savoir faire*?' I ask.

He nods. 'The know-how. People have trained for years to learn how to work with the dough. Without good flour and the *savoir faire*, then . . . phfffff.'

I nod slowly. 'So, you can help me?' I ask. 'If you can tell me where to get good flour, I can make good bread . . . with passion!' I attempt a laugh.

He shakes his head and says flatly, '*Non*.'

Chapter 22

'But why? I can help you! We can help each other. If people come for bread, they may come for coffee. By the sound of it, you need the money to keep your *tabac* going just as much as I need customers so that I can stay here.'

He says nothing. I can see he's not going to change his mind, but add: 'I just feel I owe it to them, the names sketched on the walls, the etching of *"bijou"*, not to give up on the place. For it to be left to rot.'

He stops polishing again and I realise I may really have hit a nerve. 'Don't worry. I know you said you can't help.' I slide off the bar stool and pick up my bag, turning to leave.

'And you?' he says to my back. 'What do you need from being here? An Instagram account, living the French dream? In an old watermill?'

My face darkens. I turn slowly to face him. 'You know nothing about me, or why I'm here. I'm asking you to help me and in return I will help by trying to stop this whole village being shut up. I'm trying to keep the mill going, to keep it alive. I didn't ask for insults.'

'I apologise.'

A lump forms in my throat and I swallow. 'I just need to make good bread.'

The three men look at Laurent, who clears his throat and says evenly, 'The mill is important to me. It is my grandfather's legacy. I want to see it kept for the community.'

'Well, if I can't get a visa, I'll have to leave and that mill will be sold to anyone who can pay – not just to you, to *anyone* who can pay. It could become a holiday let, a second home. At least I was trying to bring it back to life for people to enjoy. I mean, look at this place.' I gesture to the empty square, the silent *pétanque* pitch under the shady plane trees. 'It's empty. Sounds to me like you're so busy thinking about the mill, you're not making the most of what you've got.'

The three men seem not only to understand what I'm saying, but nod and agree, looking at Laurent.

'You help me, show me how to make the bread, and I'll give you bread for your customers. You could offer sandwiches, *jambon-beurre, salade.*'

'*Rillette* sandwich,' says one of the old men.

'*Poulet . . .*'

'*Avec moutarde . . .*'

Laurent holds up his hands.

'Okay, okay . . . If you want people to buy your bread, it needs to be different. Special. It needs that extra bit of love. You have to put in the right ingredients and follow your instincts, listen to what your heart is telling you.'

He looks at me. 'But a bakery can't operate without good flour. You need clear spring water – the water is very important. As are the salt and the yeast. But most importantly good flour. The right blend of grains.'

'So how do I get it? Where?'

He shrugs. 'There are flour mills, of course, most a little distance from here.'

'What about *le moulin*? What about the flour that used to come from there?'

Laurent looks at me and it seems he may just have let down a barrier. 'I came back here for the mill, to try to keep it open for the community, for my grandfather's memory. But I left it too late. I should have returned earlier, when he was still alive. It was my intention to buy it. But not everyone around here was pleased to see me back . . .'

'Claude?'

He nods. 'We have history. Our family dispute goes back to my grandparents. I can't forgive what his grandfather did to us. I won't. But if you are to become associated with me, if I help you, he will see it as a battle, a *war* even. He won't like his customers being taken from him.'

I consider this. Right now, I can't think of anything I'd like more than Claude being hit where it hurts. 'You came back here for the mill,' I say evenly. 'And I need flour from the mill. That's all. I don't have to know what you mean by leaving things too late, or the family dispute you have with Claude. I'm here for a fresh start. And what I need to make that happen, is flour. Looks like maybe you have something to prove, too. Maybe this is the chance you needed as well – a chance to lay any ghosts to rest.'

He narrows his eyes and the three men watch with interest. Then he says, 'Are you serious?'

My pride may be bigger than my bank account, but I have no desire to go back to the UK. Not yet. This is beginning to feel like home. 'Never more so. I'm not giving up yet.' I stare at him, challenging him again – this time to say yes.

'You are suggesting that we work together to get the mill up and running?' he clarifies.

'Yes,' I say firmly.

A small smile creeps onto his lips and he laughs as if he can't quite believe what I'm saying.

'Just one thing,' I jump in, determined not to make any more mistakes. 'I'm not interested in you ... romantically.'

He laughs again and I squirm. 'Really, I'm not looking for anything like that,' he says.

I joke back: 'You don't need to have a middle-aged woman fawning over you and your good looks.'

He raises his eyebrows. 'You think I'm good-looking?'

I laugh. 'You don't need me to tell you that. But just so we're clear, I'm here to find my passion in baking. We both want the *boulangerie* to work, you for the mill and the *tabac*, me for my visa. Understood?'

'Understood,' he says.

'So?'

He shakes his head again. 'I wish I could say yes but, I'm sorry, I don't think it can happen.'

I throw my hands up in frustration. 'You just said you understood!'

'I do, but I am sorry, I don't think it can happen.'

I let out a long sigh of disappointment and leave. As I do, I look towards Madame B sitting in the window and understand that she wasn't dismissing me: she was directing me, telling me what I needed to know, that the answer is in the mill. If only Laurent had agreed to help. But now I'm out of options.

Chapter 23

I'm sat outside the big door to the mill, on the tree trunk there, which must have fallen in a storm. I'm holding my cup in my hands, clutching it to me as I watch the morning light, promising a warm day to come. I wish the kingfishers would appear and show me some kind of sign about what I should do. I lift my face and breathe in the freshness of the morning air.

I message the family WhatsApp group, then Annie, telling her I'm waiting for the kingfishers, who are being shy. I describe the colours of the dragonflies darting over the water and the hum of the bees, hard at work. She sends a thumbs-up – at least it's a reply, but her messages are less frequent, even though I know she's enjoying hearing about life at the mill. I have to keep going to have more news for her. She is pushing me on. I hope my promise of getting her to the mill is doing the same for her.

I shut my eyes. In the background, I can hear the cars pulling up, doors slamming, the fisherwomen greeting each other. They will take time to kiss each other lightly on the cheeks. It's a routine, a formality, one they won't miss out. It is considered, not rushed. It's what keeps life ticking over in France. Routine, formality, and taking time to enjoy the good, simple things, like fishing together. It's a simple pastime where they come together and quietly support each other. Life here seems to be much more about actions than words. It's a way of showing understanding, of saying, 'I know what you're going through and I'm there for you,' without having to use words. Everyone needs support, just as I've needed Annie's and I think she's appreciated mine. My photographs and updates have given her something else to think about. We all need to lean on others who know how we're feeling. I have no idea why I thought I could do this on my own. I can't. I realise that now. I need support too. If only Laurent had wanted us to do it together.

I hear the women walking up the side of the mill towards the lake. I open my eyes, nod as they each raise a hand to me and wish me *bonjour*. Clearly not as embarrassed as I am about them using my bread as bait and laughing at the British woman wanting to open a *boulangerie*. Because they're right. I don't know what I'm doing. I'm just winging it badly.

I shut my eyes again, listening to the good-natured conversation as they make their way around the lake and set up for their Saturday fishing day. As for me, I will have to make an appointment to see the mayor. Tell him I tried, but it can't be done. No one wants to eat my bread. And I can't improve it without the right flour and the . . . What was it Laurent said? The *savoir faire*.

Even if I could produce a decent baguette, the villagers

aren't likely to break their habits. Everything has a place in France and, no matter how much energy I put into the bread, I won't be able to compete with Claude and his vending machine. They won't buy from me. I'm not French and I'm not a *boulanger* . . . and I can't get anyone to help me.

Not unless you offer something different, or special. I hear Laurent's words in my head. But I have no idea what else I can offer with the four ingredients used in making bread.

'Okay, I'll help you.' I hear his voice.

'If only that was the case,' I say.

'I will. I'll get the mill running and we'll make the flour. Something different. Something special.'

I spin round to see him standing there, tossing a euro up and over in his hand. 'But you said it couldn't be done.'

'I didn't say it couldn't be done. I said it couldn't happen.'

'Well, yes, but if it can't happen . . .' I gaze at him standing on the grass beside the lake in jeans and a rugby shirt.

'That doesn't mean it can't be done.' He walks towards me.

I shield my eyes against the sun with a hand, looking up at him. 'What made you change your mind?'

He steps forward. 'You. And the writing on the walls.' He comes to sit on the fallen tree beside me. 'As I said, whatever went on here, they were my grandparents.'

'Yes.' I blush. 'And I'm sure you didn't need me to lecture you about honouring their legacy.'

'No. But it was nice to find someone else who feels as I do, that doesn't want the past to be forgotten. Even if it wasn't all good. It's part of the journey to the here and now.' He takes a moment. 'I should have come back earlier. I left it too late. I could have helped my grandfather before he died. I could have taken this place on.' His voice is low and rasping, full of regret. 'I made a mistake in not returning sooner, one that I'm not sure I'll ever get over. I was full of guilt. I'd already let him down once, and I did it again. I was foolish to think that one day I might be able to buy this place to make amends. I was trying to put right the mistake I made by not being here when he died. He raised me when others who cared about me couldn't.' He takes a breath. 'I owed him everything.'

'What happened to your parents?'

He looks out across the lake. 'I never knew my father. And my mother died in a car accident when I was eight so I lived here with my grandparents.'

I hesitate, wondering if I'm being too intrusive, but gently ask, 'And your grandmother?'

He turns the euro in his hand between his fingers. 'She left for quite some time. Left me and my grandfather. She came back eventually, and my grandfather forgave her for leaving, but I never could. I couldn't be that big.'

'And now?'

'Now, I try to put it behind me. But it still upsets me that she left my grandfather for another man. And left me. But more than that, my biggest regret was not returning here when my grandfather needed me before he died.'

· 169 ·

His long dark hair falls away from his face as he turns to me. 'But I think you may be right. Being here, doing this, it may be the way to lay the ghosts to rest.'

'So? You're going to help me?' A smile is creeping onto my lips.

He lets out a long sigh. 'Here in France, we do things with a little more subtlety,' he says. 'Let the answer come to you.' A smile is pulling at the corners of his mouth, too. 'But, yes, I'll help you. Maybe I needed to be reminded of what I was doing here and why it was important. It's not just about the building, it's about the flour, and the taste, which is unique to this place, to this village. The bread now is nondescript. It could be from anywhere. I wanted to keep the mill as a building. When I heard you had bought it, I thought you would rip the heart out of it. I wanted to hold onto it, preserve it. But what good is the building if it's not producing flour?'

'But where do we start? I'm just a home cook. A cake-maker. Who clearly makes dreadful bread.'

'The bread wasn't dreadful.'

I raise a questioning eyebrow. '*Dégueulasse!* That's what they called it.'

'Disgusting? *Non.*' He shakes his head, then tilts it from side to side. 'Bland, maybe.'

He laughs, deep and rich. A nice laugh.

'But seriously,' he says, 'this is about honour. Getting the mill back up and running and the *boulangerie* in the heart of the town. This is about saying, "We're still here." We might be a small village, but we should not be forgotten or overtaken by a bakery from a neighbouring town whose owner sees what he wants and takes it, in business and in life.' I see his nostrils flare, presumably directed at Claude, which is something we have in common – although I'm not sure why he hates him, other than that he owns the baguette-vending machines. But there is clearly no love lost between them. 'We should not be invisible. We should be seen, because our village is worth it. My grandfather's work here is worth it. It is time we remember to celebrate what and who we are.'

'I couldn't agree more.' I smile. 'So, where do we start?'

He hands me the euro. 'With a euro to seal the deal. Remember, you never know when you might need it.'

As he places it in the palm of my hand, I get a shiver of excitement about everything that is to come. Maybe this will work out after all.

Chapter 24

*B*ang, bang, bang . . .

The banging is going right through my head. I push back the cotton sheet on my bed and climb down the wooden steps and head into the kitchen. It's early Monday morning. The only other sound is the dawn chorus in full voice. The banging noise I can hear is coming from the cellar.

I lean into the sideboard with effort and push it away from the trapdoor, open it, and take the steps. The cellar door to the outside is open, letting in the early-morning light.

'*Bonjour, Juliet!*' Laurent says, smiling, though we are hesitant on how to greet each other. For a country that has such set ways and etiquette for greetings, we're lost for a moment.

'Oh, um, *bonjour, Laurent.*' He raises a hand, evidently uncertain, as do I. We know we aren't enemies – we want the same things: the mill to work, the *boulangerie* to open, the village to thrive – but we aren't friends either.

Friendship is based on trust, and I'm not sure either of us is there yet.

I need him to help me get the mill working, to bake bread, to get my visa. I know for a fact that Laurent wants the mill, and I'm just a spoke in his wheel. But we need each other, friends or not.

'Did I wake you?' he asks.

'It's certainly early,' I say, pulling my dressing-gown around me.

'I wanted to come here before I open the *tabac*,' he says.

I look at the hammer in his hand. 'What are you doing anyway?'

He lets it swing by his side and pushes back his hair, shiny in the sunshine. 'Well, the mill isn't that far from being ready to try. I need to fix the last of the paddles on the wheel. Come and see.'

I follow him outside, up the slope on one side of the mill, across the lawn to the other side of the building where the wheel is mounted on the wall there. He's carrying what looks like a wooden paddle. 'This is one that was broken. I'll get it in place. Then . . .' – he looks up at the wheel as if it lived and breathed, with affection and a hint of excitement – '. . . we will be ready to give her a test run.' He pats the wheel. 'Once she is turning, we test all the joints to make sure they are moving smoothly and that the wheat can be ground. Then we can make the flour, as long as we have the right ingredients.'

'But I thought you knew how to make flour. You're a miller!'

'I know how to work a mill, and how to grind the

grains, but we want the recipe for flour that was ground here. Let's hope we can find it somewhere on the walls inside. Another reason I should have returned sooner than I did – I would have been able to get my grandfather's recipe, which wheat to use and in what quantities.'

I'm staring at the wheel too. 'You really think it could be working soon?'

He jumps down into the dry pit where the wheel sits off the ground, attached to the wall and the workings inside, ready to replace the rotten paddle. 'It's not far off. I've been working on it for nearly a year. And then the mayor told me it had been sold.'

'When was the last time the wheel turned?'

'Five years ago, just before my grandfather died. I should have come back and helped him way before then. Instead, I thought I was doing the right thing in staying away. I thought I'd brought shame to the village.'

'I'm sure that's not the case,' I say, feeling his hurt.

'But I realise now I should have been here. It's what he would have wanted.'

The next week I don't go to the *boulangerie*. There's no point until we have the flour. While Laurent works on the wheel and checks the mechanisms, I take delivery of the tables and chairs I've bought from the *brocante* and put them in the cellar out of the way. I tidy any junk into one corner and carefully stack all the furniture, the crockery and cutlery I've bought in boxes in the middle. With that done, I begin to paint the walls in the big room, a clean, crisp white. Together we work on giving the mill a new lease on life. Laurent works early in the morning, then goes to open the *tabac*, returning after lunch for a couple more hours.

This morning I make coffee and take it outside along with some cherry Bakewell tarts I made that morning. I lay the tray on a table and sit on one of two mismatched chairs I've put there, next to the fallen tree trunk, then call Laurent from his work on the wheel. He vaults out of the water pit and joins me, looking out over the lake, forearms resting on his long thighs, holding the small cup in his big hands. It has become a little routine in our new working relationship. Coffee and cake before he heads off to the *tabac*. I hand him a tart and we're happy to sit here without talking, just gazing at the lake. I wonder what it was like when Laurent's grandparents were here.

'Tell me about your grandparents,' I ask, as we watch the kingfishers, entranced by their flitting this way and that.

He sighs, puts down his cup and sits back. 'My grandparents were here for some years, but in the end, as I said, my grandfather was running this place on his own, after my grandmother, Jeanne, died. Some years before that, she had left. My grandfather stayed here and kept the mill going, me with it. I was raised here in these woods, with the swimming hole further down the lake. I had the best childhood.'

'Where did your grandmother go?'

'To the next town,' he swigs his coffee, 'to be with her lover there. She left the family, me and my grandfather, for him. She gave up everything, as if we hadn't been through enough when my mother died. Then, when her lover moved on to someone new, she came home. The villagers thought my grandfather was mad to take her back . . . but he loved her. Nevertheless, it tore through the heart of the family. I couldn't move on from it like he did. He was a big man with a big heart. He forgave her. I couldn't.'

'I can imagine . . . I mean, what kind of person would do that, just leave their husband and grandson to be with another man? Sorry, I didn't mean . . .'

'It's fine. My grandfather was a strong man. He just kept going. Brought me up and ran this place.'

'So why did you leave?'

He sighs. 'I played rugby. My grandfather was very proud. But I had a temper, a hot head. I was angry about losing my mother, angry that she was foolish enough to drive intoxicated. And when my grandmother left my grandfather like that, I was away, in the South, playing for my team. He was almost broken and I hated that he was alone here. I blamed her and her lover for causing him so much heartache. I was told I was a good player, could've been great, but I lost it once too often on and off the pitch and was eventually dropped by my team. I just . . . felt I'd let him down. The village was proud of me, until I blew it. So I stayed away. I didn't want him to be embarrassed by me. I wanted to save him from that. I carried on as if this place didn't exist.'

We sit in silence for a moment or two.

'But you're back now.'

He nods. 'Yes, but it's too late. My grandmother died first. I came back to see my grandfather before he died, but I should have been here. He was running this place on his own. I should have helped him. He always told me to go and make the most of my life, but I should have stayed. Instead I was working vineyards, getting into more trouble with other workers. I missed rugby, the physicality of it. I missed being proud of myself. Eventually, I retrained as an engineer . . . tried to become respectable, but none of it brought me joy. I realised I wanted to be here, to bring the mill back to life.'

'And the writing on the wall?'

He chuckles. 'As a youngster I wrote most of those orders there when I couldn't be bothered to find the order pad! Other than that, I don't know. I guess someone declaring their feelings, venting their fury about a lost love. Maybe someone who came here to find peace when it was quiet.'

'Ah . . .' I smile. 'So not you or anyone you know, then?'

He shakes his head.

'I've photographed them all on my phone. Just in case they mean something to someone.'

'And you, Juliet? Have you found anything relating to the recipe, the flour? We need to work out exactly what the quantities were and mix the flour to the same blend.'

'Nothing I can find yet.'

'My grandfather knew it all by heart,' says Laurent. 'I should have learnt it when he was still alive.'

The sky seems to be getting darker.

'It can't be gone for ever,' I say.

A few drops of rain fall, so we pick up our cups and head inside. I shiver. 'When the sun goes in, it's cold in here,' I say.

Laurent looks around the freshly painted big room. 'Where's your wood?' he asks.

'Wood?'

'For the fire.' He points to the grate in the stone fireplace, blackened around the edges.

'I didn't expect to need it in summer.'

He looks surprised. 'You haven't been to collect some?'

'No,' I say. 'I didn't know I had to.'

'You need to stay warm, and so does the building. She's an old girl. She needs looking after.' He pats the walls.

I think of his grandfather here, working the mill, bringing up Laurent, while his wife was philandering. The fire in my stomach starts to build. 'Well, we'd better get some!' I say. 'Tell me where to go.'

He smiles. 'I know all the best places. My grandfather taught me from an early age.'

'Okaay . . .' I say. 'I'll get my handbag.'

'You won't need that. Just yourself.'

We go out of the big doors, which are open. There are no fisherwomen at the lake today: it's Monday, market day.

The dark clouds are building in the sky.

'Come on, I'll show you how we collect wood. No need to buy it from the supermarket.'

He heads for the corner of the lake, at the start of the worn footpath around the edge. Once he reaches the open canoe, he steps down into it, wobbling slightly, and holds out a hand to me.

'You want me to get in there?' I look at the weatherworn craft in the corner of the lake. Light droplets of rain sprinkle over the water, causing little ripples.

'*Oui*, it is the best way,' he says. 'Come.'

'Oh, no . . . I'm not good on water. I love looking at it, but I've never been that good a swimmer.'

'You're not going to swim, you're going to paddle, up there.' He points to where the lake becomes more shaded under the boughs of the trees. 'You can't live in a watermill and not use the lake. It's here to help you! It's your friend!'

'You've got to be joking!' I laugh.

'*Non*,' he says, still holding out his hand.

I stare at it.

'Come on, Juliet! You want to be warm, don't you?' He is standing in the gently swaying boat.

'I really don't think I can,' I say. 'Like I say, I'm not good on water.'

I never have been, not since I went on a fishing trip with Pete in our early dating days. The weather was so bad that I spent the whole time hanging over the side being ill. I haven't been back on the water since.

'It'll be fine,' he says, and I wish I could believe him. But isn't this what we're trying to do here, build trust? I look at his hand. 'Really, it's the way we do this around here.'

He holds my stare and I don't know whether to trust him or not. The last time I looked into a man's eyes, I ended up letting him kiss me and making a complete fool of myself. And, I remind myself, I'm doing this to prove I'm not a fool. I'm doing this to get the mill running, and to make bread. Yesterday's Juliet would have stayed firmly on dry land, worried about what might happen. Now that I have a second chance, I'm prepared to take the risk.

Slowly I reach out my hand, and he holds it. He tugs encouragingly and a ripple of excitement runs through me, making me feel half my age, as if anything is possible. I see a flash of blue from the kingfishers, like some sort of sign. And suddenly, with a burst of courage, I take a huge stride, hoping I land in the canoe and not the lake. As beautiful as it is, I do not want to end up in it.

I land, wobble, and reach out for something to hold on to. I find myself right up against Laurent's firm chest. I can smell him, cologne and wood from his work in the mill that morning. I look up and he's right there, looking down at me. I glance away and try to take a step back, nearly toppling. He catches my elbow. I don't want him to think I'm attracted to him. I'm not, I tell myself. I'm not going down that route again. I am not Shirley Valentine.

'Now, take a seat here,' he says, and I do as I'm told and sit facing him. 'The other way round,' he adds. 'You'll need to paddle.'

'What? Oh, yes . . .' I spin around on the small seat, making the boat wobble again. I grip the sides and shut my eyes, thinking this has been a terrible mistake. I feel the boat move as he lowers himself onto the seat behind me.

'Now, take this,' he says, and I open my eyes to feel a paddle being lifted from the floor and slid in beside me. I follow his instructions and balance it across the sides of the boat in front of me. My heart is racing.

I watch as Laurent expertly flips the rope from its mooring stake and tosses it into the boat. There's a bit more wobbling, but then I hear and see, out of the corner of my eye, his paddle dipping into the water.

'Put your paddle in and just keep paddling,' he says. 'I will steer from behind,' he says. 'Now, you take the left side, I'll take the right. You just have to keep paddling. It's when you stop, that's when boats become unsteady, especially in choppy waters; that's when boats capsize. You have to keep paddling.' I'm not sure if he's talking about the canoeing or life itself. Maybe both.

He pushes the boat away from the shore and I start to panic. 'Just paddle. I will steer,' he says.

Within seconds we're away from the bank. I dip my paddle into the water, and when I've pulled it as far back as it can go, I lift it, put it back into the water and pull again, like Laurent does. I'm smiling as we move quietly through the lily pads, the dragonflies darting out of our way. I wish Maddie and Jake could see me, Pete too! He'd never believe it. This is beautiful. If I wasn't so nervous, I'd get out my phone to prove what I'm doing here. But I just keep paddling. We glide across the water, rhythmically, knowing the fish are feeding below us. The odd duck quacks from the bank as we pass the little waterfall just beyond the fisherwomen's spot, and rivulets run from the main lake into the wooded area.

Laurent paddles behind me, and we're travelling slowly through the water. I catch a flash of blue. The kingfishers are there and now I'm even closer to them, watching as they sit at the edge of the lake, waiting for the right moment to dive and come up with dinner.

Suddenly one plunges into the water. I hold my breath.

'Keep paddling,' I hear Laurent say softly as we float up the lake into a much more shaded area, where trees meet trees and their branches entwine. I keep dipping the blade in the water and pulling it back in a gentle rhythm, when suddenly a kingfisher appears, a small fish in its beak, and I'm delighted.

'Success,' Laurent says. 'You just have to keep trying.'

We carry on until he guides us to the shore and grasps an exposed root on the bank. 'This is where we come for wood. You can only get to it by boat,' he says, 'so there's always plenty.' The rain is dripping onto the leaves above us, which are creating a canopy. 'Put your paddle into the boat,' he instructs, and I do so, entranced by the beautiful woodland glade we're in. 'And this is where to swim.' He points to a part of the lake just beyond, where the trees dip low into the water. It's like a natural swimming pool, with a waterfall over the rocks above it and more rocks as the water flows out on the other side.

'There is nothing like it. This is where I come when I need to think, to be alone. When I need to take a moment, I come and swim.'

'It's beautiful,' I say.

'You should try it. It's very private.'

'I'm not sure I'm confident enough in the water.'

'Give it time,' he says.

I draw my eyes from the swimming hole to where the weeping willows drape their long branches in the water. 'Maybe I'll get brave enough at some point,' I respond. I would like that very much.

'Now, take my hand,' Laurent instructs, and suddenly all the fear has returned.

I slowly stand and the boat starts to wobble. In a panic, I launch myself at the lakeside bank, clinging to it for safety. The front end of the canoe shoots into the air.

'Woah!' he says, steadying the canoe and himself, then moving to the centre of the boat.

'Sorry!' I say, grimacing.

'Slow and steady. That's how we do it. Not in the heat of the moment.' He passes me the rope.

When I offer a hand to him, he accepts it. He pulls himself from the canoe and secures it. 'Now,' he says, 'over here, this is where we manage the woodland space and help ourselves to wood from the piles when we need it.' He starts walking, then bends over and hands a log to me. We load ourselves with an armful each, then pack them into the canoe. 'We should be quick. The weather isn't good.'

But I have to spend some time photographing the glade and the swimming hole to share it with my family and Annie, to give them an insight into what they can expect when they get here. I make a video of the area and send it so they hear the sounds of the raindrops on the leaves. I tell them I wish they could know how it smells here, so fresh.

The journey back to the mill is slower. The boat is lower in the water and I don't want to make any waves. Slow and steady. 'One more run and that should do you for now,' Laurent says, as we paddle back up the lake, the rain heavier than before and starting to soak through my clothes. I put my paddle into the water and pull back hard, remembering what Laurent said: all the time we're paddling, we're stable. It's when we stop, we're not.

He steers the boat to the side, under a tree.

'The rain's heavier. Let's wait here a bit,' he says, and points for me to get out. He follows and holds the rope as we stand under the boughs of the trees and wait. The sky is getting darker and more threatening. The wind whips up and the trees sway. Suddenly there is an almighty clap of thunder, and lightning illuminates the sky. And then the heavens really open. Huge raindrops, like I've never seen before. I stand looking at the lake as the rain hammers down on it. And it keeps coming, raining harder and harder.

'The lake is filling,' Laurent shouts, over the noise of nature. 'It doesn't look like it's going to stop. We need to head back, before the mill starts to—' He pauses.

'Starts to what?'

He seems hesitant.

'Laurent, before the mill starts to what?' I shout back.

'Nobody mentioned it to you?'

'Mentioned what?' I'm getting jittery. 'What are you talking about?'

'The mill, when it rains and the water level rises.'

The rain is pouring down his face, and his shirt is soaked.

'What about the mill?' I shout over the downpour, and I can feel the cold rain sticking my top to me, making me shiver. I wrap my arms around myself for warmth.

He throws up his hands. 'This is why people shouldn't be allowed to buy mills without knowing about them!' he says, against the noise of the rain on the overhanging boughs and leaves.

And I suddenly understand what he's talking about.

Chapter 25

Laurent pushes off from the bank and the rain is pelting into my face, as if it's punishing me.

I plunge the paddle into the water, deeper this time, and drag it back as we battle on, eyes screwed up. I dig deep and pull on the paddle, and so does Laurent. The canoe moves through the water, though not as quickly as I'd like. We have to get back to the mill, or everything I've worked for so far, all the effort I've put into painting and clearing and sourcing furniture, will be for nothing. It's like we're fighting against the clock when every pull on the paddle counts.

What am I doing in a small boat, on a lake, collecting firewood in the hope that a watermill can be repaired so I can make flour for bread? I could be at home, watching reruns of *All Creatures Great and Small* and doing a jigsaw instead of battling across a filling lake to save my belongings and my investment from flooding. I knew I didn't like being in boats!

But something in me keeps the tears at bay. At least, I think they are – I can't tell with raindrops sliding down my face. I can feel the pull on my shoulders and the ache in my wrists as we keep paddling towards the mill, and then I see it. The water has burst the banks of the lake and is flooding the lawn, which means it must be tumbling down the front steps into the mill. Everything I have is in there. Everything will be ruined.

I put my head down and keep paddling, as Laurent told me to do.

Suddenly there's a bump and we're at the bank. I don't wait to be told what I need to do next. I just do it.

'Juliet, wait!' I hear Laurent say, but I can't. I have to get to the mill, try to stop the water coming in.

I launch myself from the canoe onto the wet, soggy bank. I cling to the sodden grass, my nails embedded in the soil, like my life depends on it. My fingers plunge into the earth and grip, allowing me to pull myself to my feet. And still the rain comes, pouring down.

I run around the lake to the lawn in front of the mill where, as I suspected, the water is pouring over the grass and under the green door into the main room. I open the doors to see water seeping across the floor, pushing its way deeper and further into the building. I run outside to Laurent, who is in the middle of the lake, the canoe upended with him at the rear, trying to get his weight forward to stop the thing sinking.

'Shit!' I say. 'Laurent!'

I see my paddle floating towards the other side of the lake. I feel utterly useless. I wave my arms at him, although I have no idea why. 'It's flooding! The mill is flooding!'

He leans forward with all his strength and grabs the

middle section where I had been sitting, then climbs up the canoe, putting his weight into the centre. Slowly the bow lowers and he stands up straight. But as he does, his paddles slides overboard. He reaches for it, grappling and stretching, but it quickly drifts from his grasp. He's stranded in the middle of the lake, and shouts something at me.

'What?' I yell back. 'It's coming in!'

He stands up tall and puts his hands either side of his mouth.

'I can't hear you!' I shout.

He points. I turn around, then back to him.

'OPEN THE SLUICE GATE!' I hear him shout, clearly this time. 'The gate, to the wheel! Let the water in!' and I understand exactly what he's telling me to do. I need to divert the water, let it run into the pit where the wheel is.

I run over to the gate. There is a round wheel at the top. I take hold of it and turn the handle, as fast as I can. It spins, but nothing happens. I turn it the other way, but still it doesn't do anything. I try again, but the gate doesn't move.

I look at the square bolt head in the middle of the wheel that should be catching and turning, but it's worn and loose in its setting, spinning and slipping. The gate won't move. And as my sodden arms drop, I realise something. I reach into my wet pocket and pull out the single euro. I drop it into the hole where the worn bolt sits.

I twist the wheel again. This time it doesn't turn at all. I'm exhausted.

I look back at Laurent and see him raise his hands

into the air. And then, in one swift movement, he dives from the canoe into the water. He takes a few long strokes to the lakeside and pulls himself onto the bank, the muscles in his arms showing through the wet shirt that is clinging to his chest and shoulders.

You just have to keep paddling.

I turn back to the handle, give it one more twist and, suddenly, I feel resistance. Then I feel it catch, the loose bolt not loose any more. With the euro coin in there, it bites and starts to move. My heart lurches. I twist it again, much harder, and hear the bolts start to move the mechanism, the sluice gate starting to shift. I carry on turning the wheel, hard.

Really hard.

The sluice gate moves upwards and I turn until, with effort, the gate is up and I hear a whoosh, followed by splashing. Water gushes, tumbling through the sluice gate into the dry pond, there to feed the wheel.

'What's happening?' I hear Laurent call. It seems to have taken ages for him to get here. But, then, he did have to swim out from the lake where I abandoned him.

'It's open! The water's flowing!' I shout, but he can't hear me.

He runs barefoot over the lawn, splashing across the wet grass – the lawn is struggling to cope with all of this water. Laurent's clothes are soaking: his jeans are clinging to his thighs, and his T-shirt to his chest. He comes to stand behind me, making me shiver with delight.

'You did it!' He squeezes my shoulders.

'I did!' I beam as we stare at the water filling the pit. His body is against mine and, despite the rain, I can feel its heat. We stare at the pool as the water from the lake spills into it, rushing and gushing over the edge. Together, we hold our breath and wait. I am shivering, cold, but hot with excitement. And then it happens. A gentle creak, so quiet I don't know if I've heard it. And then again. I turn to look at Laurent's face, close to mine over my shoulder. A smile spreads as he runs his hand over his long hair and pushes it off his face – his attractive, kind face.

Oh. I do fancy him. I really do.

There is another creak and I drag my eyes away from his because my heart is racing faster than I know it should. I look back at the wheel. There is a longer creak and a groan and, suddenly, it begins to move. I can feel Laurent's breath on my neck as he exhales with relief.

There is a squeak, then a louder one, and another creak. A wobble. As the excitement in me grows, the wheel groans and moans as it starts to turn, like someone getting up out of an armchair they've been sitting in for too long. But once it's turning, it gathers pace, and the water pushes it harder and harder.

'*Ça marche,*' he says quietly.

'It's working,' I whisper.

And then we watch as it stutters, stops and starts again. Then, like a toddler finding their feet, it begins to turn, slowly and steadily, discovering its rhythm.

'It's really working,' I shout with elation, as I jump up and down and turn to Laurent.

'*Oui! Ça marche!*' He grins and I'm alive with excitement. He grabs my hand and, like teenagers racing from school for the long summer break, we run towards the mill door. There, we stop and stare as the recently oiled cogs begin to turn and the old mill comes back to life.

Suddenly, behind us, we hear clapping and cheering. We step back onto the flooded lawn. The rain has eased and the fisherwomen have clearly been waiting in their cars for it to pass.

'*Ça marche!*' Laurent shouts to them.

The women clap and cheer and shout, 'Bravo! Bravo!' clearly delighted to see the wheel turning again. And it's not just the mill that has come back to life. I have too! I've never felt more alive – and Laurent is still holding my hand. I don't want him to let go.

'*Ça marche!*' I shout, standing in the rain.

'*Allez, allez, allez!*' shout the fisherwomen.

Laurent turns to me, soaked to the skin, water running down his face, just as it is on mine. Behind us we can hear the gentle whoosh as water is scooped up and sends the wheel turning. We are beaming, staring at each other.

'You did it!' I say.

'*We* did it,' he says. And we fall into a huge hug. When we release each other, he looks as if he's about to kiss me, and I am drawn closer to his lips, but before I lose my head again, I pull away. And he follows. There is no way I can ruin this by going somewhere I shouldn't.

We give a little cough.

'This is great!' I say, feeling I've shattered the moment, which is good.

'It is, it is,' he says, and there's a hint of awkwardness between us.

'Now we can start making flour!' I say. 'We can bake great bread!'

He nods sagely.

'What is it?'

He runs his hand over his beard, where droplets of rain have gathered, like diamonds. 'If only we had that recipe.'

And my heart plummets like a stone to the bottom of the lake.

Chapter 26

'Quantities. We need to work out the right quantities. I wish I'd learnt the recipe when he was still alive. But if I know my grandfather,' he looks up at the mill, 'the answer is in the building somewhere.'

We walk towards the doors of the mill, where the water has run in and I can still hear the drip, drip, drip, where it has seeped through the floorboards and into the cellar.

'Well, we should find some dry clothes and start work,' he says.

And the cosy bubble we shared when the wheel began to turn has burst. I can still hear the wheel turning, though, which feels comforting and is driving me to keep moving forward.

Keep paddling.

Laurent leaves, barefoot, his shoes still floating, cut adrift on the lake. 'We'll wait for it to make its way to shore,' he says, of the canoe. 'It'll head back to the bank when it's ready.'

'Can I lend you something? Some shoes?' I ask.

He peers at his feet, which must be at least a size eleven or twelve. And then looks at my size sixes. And we laugh. 'I'll be fine. I have the car.'

He leaves the mill, picking his way down the bank at the side of the building and carefully dodging random stones. I can't help but feel there was a moment back there when I could have taken a different route, but I'm glad I didn't. I've made that mistake once since I've been here and I'm determined not to repeat it.

'Shall we?' In dry clothes and wellington boots, Laurent has returned to the mill and I'm trying not to think about how nice he smells straight from the shower.

We push back the sideboard covering the trapdoor to the cellar. Drops of water are still falling into the ankle-high pond that has gathered there. All my boxes of napkins and tablecloths are soaked. I could cry. But I don't. That wouldn't help anyone. They can be laundered. With them are the boxes of detritus I cleared from the shelves, ready to be taken to the dump. But what's important now is looking for the recipe for Laurent's grandfather's flour. We have the mill, the wheel is working. Now all we need is the final piece of the puzzle.

'It seems as good a place to start as any,' says Laurent, and as he looks at me, a little flame reignites in my stomach that I try to douse.

'Let's get the doors open and help the water out,' he says matter-of-factly. 'Then we can start to work out what's in here.' He looks around at boxes of my belongings and the ones full of detritus.

Laurent pushes open the door to the outside and the

water starts to find its way out, curling and twisting. He hands me a broom and together we cajole and corral the water out of the door, with long sweeps. By the time the sun is dipping in the sky, we've rediscovered the concrete floor and are swishing the stragglers outside, like bouncers in a nightclub, keen to close for the night.

Laurent leans on his broom. 'At least tomorrow we can sort through what's here and try to find what we need for the flour.' He props the broom against the wall. 'Don't forget to close up down here before you go to bed,' he says. 'And put the sideboard over the trapdoor.'

'I won't forget,' I say, exhausted.

He turns to me, his expression soft. '*Bonsoir, Juliet.*'

'*Bonsoir, Laurent,*' I say, with a faint smile, my joints aching in every single part of my body. 'I'll see you tomorrow.'

'*À demain.*'

'Actually, Laurent, would you like a drink? A glass of wine or a beer? I think we've earned one today.'

'That would be very nice, thank you,' he says, smiling. He comes back into the cellar and goes to shut the door.

'Leave it open for a bit,' I say. 'Help it dry out.' I make my way stiffly up the wooden steps.

In the kitchen, I pour a large glass of wine for myself and open a bottle of beer for Laurent, then head outside to the front lawn where the rain has finally stopped. We wave at Geneviève, who is packing up for the night, then stare out at the lake and listen to the wheel turning as the sun sets. 'It's a lovely sound,' I say.

'It is,' he replies. 'It reminds me . . .'

'Go on,' I say.

'It reminds me of the good things in my life. Like the beating heart of it.'

I wonder if he's going to say anything more when I hear a shuffle behind us. I am just about to invite Geneviève to join us when I hear, 'Well, this looks very pleasant. Room for one more?'

And my heart lurches into my mouth.

Chapter 27

It's Claude, popping the atmosphere like a malicious child stamping on a birthday balloon. I feel angry and sick. He must have come in through the open cellar door and out through the front door, cutting off the corner of the house. He probably wanted to see what's been going on in the place without having to ask!

For a moment, Laurent doesn't say anything.

'*Laurent, bonsoir,*' says Claude.

'Claude,' Laurent says, taking a swig from his beer.

'I didn't know you two were friends,' says Claude, with an interested smile.

'Actually, I was just leaving,' says Laurent, his softness gone and his guard fully up. He swallows some beer and goes to stand.

'Oh, no, stay,' I say, looking up at him. 'Finish your drink.' I lift my chin. 'We have things to discuss,' I tell Claude.

'As do we.' He looks at me pointedly. Laurent narrows his eyes. 'I heard you were planning to open the *boulangerie* in the village?'

I say nothing.

'Just a reminder, the village already has a baker providing bread for them.'

'Not a good one,' says Laurent.

'The locals seem quite happy with how things are, and wouldn't want to change for a person who is here today and will be gone tomorrow. If I take away my vending machine, they will be left with nothing. And that will be down to you. You won't be welcome after that.'

He's threatening me.

'*Allez vous en!*' growls Laurent, telling Claude to go away.

And there's a pause, unpleasantness filling the air.

'I'll leave you to your evening. Laurent.' He nods again, bidding us goodbye. This time Laurent doesn't bother to reply, just takes a long sip of his beer.

'Claude,' I call.

He turns back, surprised.

'Use the path around the house, like everyone else,' I say firmly. 'This is my property now.' And he's not going to intimidate me in it.

He turns back and marches off to the path by the side of the mill.

I hear his car leave.

'Another beer?' I say to Laurent and, without waiting for a response, I hurry inside, down the wooden steps and slam the cellar door. I hurry back up the steps and push the heavy sideboard over the trapdoor, grab a beer from the fridge, an opener and the bottle of red wine, and head back outside to where Laurent is.

'It's none of my business, of course, but with Claude,

just be careful.' For a moment Laurent is quiet and I feel uneasy. Then he says, 'He and his family like to get what they want. As I say, be careful. They mean business.'

'You clearly have quite a history between you,' I say, and sip my wine.

'It was his grandfather, Charles, who became my grandmother's lover. He seduced her, made her promises of a better life, and she left my grandfather for him.' He chews his bottom lip. 'Then when he decided he no longer wanted her in his life, he threw her out. The whole village knew about it. She was left with nothing, not even her dignity. But my grandfather wouldn't see her like that and brought her home.' He taps the side of his beer bottle with one of his silver rings. 'Just don't get too close. That family have a way of getting what they want. Using people and spitting them out. He could make life very difficult. Just be careful.'

My cheeks burn with indignation. It seems that Claude and his family have a habit of ruining everything for everyone. 'I will. *Merci*.'

I'm wishing that the earlier atmosphere hadn't disappeared. I want to go back to where we were, talking about happy times, here at the mill, making me smile.

'I should go,' he says, standing. '*Bonsoir*.' As he leans in and kisses me on both cheeks, I feel I've finally made a friend in Laurent. A very attractive one. And it feels good. Whatever happens, he must never know that Claude kissed me. I don't want to lose our new-found respect for each other. I like our friendship the way it is. Without Claude causing any complications. And that's how it's going to stay.

Chapter 28

The following morning, I'm determined to find the recipe for the flour. After my coffee, I let the family and Annie know the adventures of yesterday: the mill flooding, opening the sluice gate by using a euro coin and the wheel starting to turn. I don't tell them about Claude, the baker/drug-dealer whose product I flushed away and who I let kiss me. And who is now very unhappy about me opening the *boulangerie*. I finish my messages when Laurent arrives around the corner of the mill, as I'm watching the early-morning mist.

'*Bonjour*,' he says, and leans in to kiss me on each cheek, making me smile.

'*Bonjour*,' I reply. 'Coffee?'

We start the day gathering our thoughts, our eyes on the trailing weeping willows dipping their branches into the water and the blue flashes of the kingfishers, as we listen to the quack of the ducks and the low hum of bees, moving from one flower to another.

We finish our coffee and start going through the boxes in the cellar. We find an old photograph of the mill from when Laurent was a boy. He is clearly touched by it and tries to dry it out in the warm, bright sunshine. There's also a tool he remembers his grandfather using, which brings tears to his eyes, and some kitchen equipment, but nothing helps us with the flour recipe.

Before long, Laurent has to get back to the *tabac*. 'I'm sorry we haven't found anything,' he says.

'Me too,' I say.

After he's gone, I go to the old store room, my living quarters, and decide to clean in here. I have to do something. But I have no idea what we can do about the missing flour recipe. If we don't find it, I'll have to admit defeat and tell the mayor that I can't do it.

I sweep and wash down the walls in my bedroom, at the back of the building behind the kitchen, thinking of what this place must have been like as a busy working mill, sacks of flour packed up and ready to be delivered. And for Laurent as a boy, his place of safety and happiness.

Then I begin to paint the one wall with none of the writing on it. I'm hesitant to paint over any of the drawings on the wall, especially the picture of the heart with *'bijou'* written within it. I take more photographs of the drawings and work around them. The room is clean and fresh, ready for a new beginning, but I don't want to erase its entire history. I wonder whether to frame the drawings and the writing. But perhaps I won't get that far, because if we don't find the flour recipe, I'll have to put the place up for sale. At least it will look better than it did when I arrived. It looks loved again.

*

In bed that night, my mind is whirring. The answer to the flour recipe has to be somewhere. Someone must know. With the window open, letting the smell of paint out and a warm breeze in, I'm listening to the owl in the trees, coming from the direction where we went to collect wood. I think about the pretty glade there and the swimming hole I'm yet to try. There is so much more I want to explore and find out about this place. *And Laurent*, a voice says in my head. And I think about the *boulangerie*, waiting to be brought back to life, despite the grumpy neighbour. Who pointed me towards Laurent. She's always smartly turned out – white hair cropped short and blow-dried into a wavy quiff, red nails, Gucci shoes, her little dog completing the look. I turn over and fall asleep to the sound of the owl.

The next morning I let myself into the *boulangerie*, make coffee and some cake, and try to imagine what this place will look like once it's open again. When I finally hear Madame B moving around upstairs, I take a deep breath and go up to her apartment. I knock on the door and the dog barks.

'*Arrêt! Bibi!*' I hear her say crossly from behind the door. I may be a grown woman, but every part of me wants to run. I can't. We're out of options.

The door opens a fraction. 'Madame! What do you want now?!"

'*Bonjour, Madame Bertou.*'

'Yes, *oui, bonjour*,' she says, decidedly irritated. 'What are you doing knocking on my door at this time of day, or at any time of day?'

It's now or never. I'm taking a risk, but I think my instincts are right. 'What do you know about bakery? The mill, too, for that matter?' I know there's something she's not telling me.

'You're talking nonsense. I can't help you. I haven't been to the mill in years.'

At her mention of the mill, I know she's hiding something.

'Don't go interfering in things you know nothing about. Now, leave me alone and keep the noise down. *Au revoir, Madame*.' She tries to close the door on me.

'That's why you don't want anyone in the bakery, isn't it? It's something to do with the mill.' I don't know what it is, but I've clearly hit a nerve.

'I've told you to leave me alone. If you knock on my door again, I will call the *gendarmes*. I have been to see the mayor, Bertrand. The fool! I have told him about the noise. Now, go away!'

'That's really not fair, I'm not making any more noise than any other bakery. The ovens have to be turned on to bake the bread.'

'Well, you must have a very clumsy way of doing it. You make more noise than anyone I've known. Now, leave me, *s'il vous plaît*!' she says angrily.

And this time she shuts the door firmly on me, telling her dog, '*Tais toi!*' Be quiet. But the dog continues to bark.

I go downstairs, furious. I know it's her. I know she can help. What is her problem?

Instead of going into the bakery, I head over to the *tabac* and climb onto a stool at the bar.

Laurent is there, behind the coffee machine.

'Any luck?' Laurent enquires, and I know he's asking about the flour recipe.

I shake my head.

'I'll come over when I close up here,' he says.

'What's the point? We can't find it. I made these, by the way, while I was in the *boulangerie* this morning. Lemon drizzle traybake.' I put the little rectangular fingers on the counter. 'Just something to do with my time, while I was waiting . . .'

'Another British classic for your *salon de thé*?' I hear the tease in his voice.

'I'm not sure that's ever going to happen now,' I say, my positivity exhausted.

He picks up a spongy finger, admires its icing, and bites into it, catching the crumbs as they fall. 'These are good,' he says. 'Don't give up yet. The answer is in the mill, I know it.'

'But what if it isn't?'

'My grandfather didn't want to give up on the place. I won't either.'

He pours me some coffee and I slide a euro to him. He slides it back. 'For the cake,' he says, and we smile.

I stir the coffee thoughtfully and he says nothing while he eats the lemon drizzle. Then, with a little laugh in his voice: 'I'm beginning to think that maybe British cakes are needed here in rural France.'

Suddenly I laugh too. When he says it like that, it sounds ridiculous. Why would they need British cakes here in rural France when they have shops and markets in other towns all around them? I don't know what I was thinking.

'Madame Bertou was right. Me, British, not even a qualified baker. I wasn't thinking at all. I just had the idea in my head, another life to lead. On the other side of the rainstorm.'

I wish I hadn't mention rainstorms, reminding me of how he looked in the rain. How it felt, him standing close to me as the sluice gate began to work.

'You can't control what life throws at you. You can only choose how you deal with it. And it seems to me that learning to bake cakes was a very good idea,' he says with a smile.

Laurent's three regulars arrive in the café. *'Bonjour, Messieurs,'* I say.

'Bonjour, Madame,' they reply, with a nod and a smile.

'Ah, gâteaux!' says one, grinning, and I offer the plate to them.

'Help yourselves,' I say, and this time they are far less hesitant, taking one each as Laurent serves their coffee and grins at me . . . making me tingle and smile back. *It's how you choose to deal with it,* I say to myself. I look back at the *boulangerie*. Right now, bread is how I'm trying to deal with this. But unless we can find the flour recipe, I can't see why people would choose to come to the shop rather than the vending machine. As Laurent says, it's like changing your doctor. To get someone to shift their loyalties, you have to give them a good reason to do so.

Suddenly, there's a shout. *'Arrêt! Arrêt! Bibi!'*

I turn on the bar stool to see Madame B at the top of the stairs from her apartment above the *boulangerie*.

'Non! Viens! Arrêt!'

But little Bibi, her little dog by the sounds of it, isn't listening and is already at the bottom of the steps and careering across the square after the cat.

'Oh, no,' says Laurent. 'This isn't good. Not for the cat or Bibi.'

I'm already off my stool and heading for the door with a piece of lemon drizzle in my hand. Madame B is making her way down the steps, nimbly but not fast enough to catch up with the dog.

Bertrand, the mayor, is out in the square now shouting at the dog and the cat, which appears to be his from the way he's calling affectionately to it and threatening the dog. The cat runs across the road and up the nearest plane tree outside the *tabac*, with Bibi in hot pursuit, just about to fling himself into the road.

'Bibi,' I say, and wave the cake at him. 'Bibi!' I bend over and hold out the cake. Bibi slows. I creep forwards, holding out the crumbling slice.

Bibi stops, and looks at me as an approaching turquoise car comes into view. It's Monsieur Martin, in his electric vehicle. The dog turns back towards the cat across the road.

'Bibi!' I try again, just as the cat hisses and spits and waves a taunting paw at him. Bibi looks back at me, then barks and launches himself towards the cat, racing out into the road as Monsieur Martin is hurtling up it.

I lunge and grab Bibi, scooping him up just before he throws himself in front of the car. Monsieur Martin toots and raises a hand to me, cigarette dangling from his lower lip, oblivious to the near miss.

'Oh, Bibi!' Madame B is nearly with me now, holding

out her hands for her dog. 'Oh, Bibi,' she says again as I give him to her, and he licks her face excitedly. She pushes her face into his furry body. '*Bijou*,' she says. 'My *bijounette*,' she repeats, telling him she doesn't know what she would do if anything happened to him. I stand and stare at Madame B.

'Bijounette,' I repeat, the name triggering something in me. Then I remember the wording on the walls of the mill. Bijou and the heart. I look at Madame Bertou. Suddenly, I have a gut feeling that there is more to that name than it just being a pet's name. It seems to mean everything to her. It's as if she's carrying everything she cares about in her hands, in that name. I take a deep breath. I may be wrong . . . but then again, I may be right. I have to try. 'It's you, isn't it?' I say simply.

For a moment she says nothing and then, 'I don't know what you're talking about.'

'You're Bijou – the name with the heart by it, on the old mill wall!'

She says nothing.

'I'm right, aren't I? It's your name on the old mill wall. You have a past with that place.'

She looks up slowly from hugging the dog and takes a deep breath. '*Merci*,' she says, stiffly but meaningfully, 'for saving Bibi. I am very grateful to you.'

Laurent joins us. 'Bravo, Juliet, you were very brave. Especially as it was Monsieur Martin driving. I feel you may need a Calvados right now.'

I smile at him, but I can't let this go. I turn back to Madame B. 'Madame, it's you, isn't it? You wrote those words on the walls of the mill, didn't you?'

She holds my stare. 'Yes, it's me. I'm Bijounette.'

'You're Bijounette?'

She nods. 'I was young, well, younger . . . and in love.'

'Madame Bertou?' says Laurent.

She looks at him with tears in her eyes. 'I loved your grandfather very much. After your grandmother, Jeanne, left, and you were away, I had hoped there was going to be a chance for us. I used to visit him at the mill, help where I could.'

Laurent is clearly in complete shock.

'I think we could all do with a Calvados,' I say, and gesture to the table and chairs outside the bar. Madame B dips her head, as if a huge weight has been taken off her shoulders, and lets me guide her to the table. Laurent goes into the bar and brings out three glasses and a bottle of golden liquid.

Just then the church bells chime, and the three men check their watches, clearly desperate to stay but knowing lunch will be on the table. They get up to leave, telling each other they'll return soon, but barely able to keep their eyes off us. As they make their way out of the *tabac*, their heads swivel back to try to keep up with what's going on.

I take a sip of the strong liquor; it burns as it slips down my throat, making me cough a little. Madame B and Laurent do the same.

Chapter 29

'I loved him. I had always been in love with him. And I thought maybe, when your grandmother left, there was a chance for us. And there nearly was. He used to call me Bijou, his jewel, Bijounette, a small trinket. It was a term of affection. It's why I gave it to Bibi. Because she is my jewel . . . and also to remind me of that time.'

'I could see the hurt that Claude's grandfather had caused, stealing Jeanne from your grandfather, but hoped he would come to love me. I drew on the walls in pencil. But,' she swallows, clearly finding the memory hard, 'when your grandmother wanted to return, he came to speak to me. Told me his plan to take her back. It was for the best.' She sips her drink. 'I begged him not to. I even begged him to keep me in his life if he did take her back – keep me a secret – but Raoul was an honourable man and wouldn't do that. He kissed my cheek and wished me love and happiness. I never went near the mill again. Instead I would sit and watch from my window, waiting for market day to catch a glimpse of him. He inspired me to take on the *boulangerie*. I trained and took over from the last baker, just to be close to him. But after Raoul died I closed the *boulangerie* for good.'

'*You* were the baker?' says Laurent, surprised.

She nods. 'I did my apprenticeship before you came to live with your grandparents. I went away for two years and spent even longer training in different parts of France to learn how to make bread, hoping it would help me stay close to Raoul.'

'You . . .' I'm still flummoxed '. . . you know how to make bread.'

She sniffs and gives a little laugh. 'Yes. Of course it was seen as a man's profession, but I was determined. Got up earlier than everyone else, worked harder. When I took the place on, I hired an assistant, swore him to secrecy, and we pretended he made the bread, when in fact it was me,' she says, stroking Bibi. 'But once the mill closed, after your grandfather died, there was no point in continuing. Customers were fewer and fewer and, of course, with Raoul gone, the mill silent, there seemed little point in going on.'

'I never knew any of this,' says Laurent. 'I didn't even know you were a baker.'

'It was easier that way. People can be very distrustful. A woman baker! Nothing much changes. A British woman trying to bake French bread?' She looks at me and I know what she means. 'Like I say,' she sniffs again, 'I employed Davide and said he was the baker. But he was my assistant. When I decided to close, he moved away and set up a café in the Dordogne.'

'I remember Davide. And everyone thought it was him leaving that closed the *boulangerie*,' says Laurent.

'Didn't that make you cross? Didn't you want people to know it was you?' I ask, enraged on her behalf.

She shakes her white head. 'I just wanted to shut myself away. Live with my memories and play out in my mind what might have been. You see, unrequited love, it's the love that never dies.'

She looks at me and then at Laurent. We glance at each other and quickly away. *That's not us*, I think. *It won't be*. I'm not in love with this man. I just . . . like being with him. That's all. Nothing more than that.

'Will you come to the mill?' I ask Madame B. 'I think you could help us.'

'No,' she says firmly.

'What? Sleep on it, please?'

She finishes her drink and we watch as she carries Bibi back up to her apartment, shutting the door firmly behind her.

Chapter 30

The following day, Laurent's sole focus is on making the sluice gate work smoothly – rubbing down the cog and replacing the fitting on the top, then checking and rechecking it. Waiting.

I do what I've always done when I need to focus on something other than my worries: I bake.

As the sun starts to set, casting beautiful oranges and yellows over the lake, I step outside onto the lawn. 'She's not coming, is she?' I say, as Laurent walks out of the mill to stand beside me, handing me a glass of wine, and holding a bottle of beer for himself. I have come to love this little ritual of a drink at the end of the day, looking out over the lake as the sun begins to set.

'No, I don't think she is,' he says, and tips his beer bottle towards my glass. '*Santé*,' he says. Which means an awful lot more than he knows.

'To good health,' I say back, catching his eye. I immediately snatch away my gaze and scan the water for my familiar friends, the kingfishers, wishing they would show themselves and give a sign of what to do next.

I go to speak, but as I do, there's movement behind us and I hope it's not Claude again. I turn slowly to see Madame B, Bibi under her arm, steadying herself by leaning against the mill wall.

'Madame Bertou,' I say, and Laurent stands up to greet her.

'Sit, sit,' she says to him, waving a hand and brushing aside her usual insistence on formalities. She's a little out of breath.

I walk towards her and hold out a hand. She takes it and I lead her over the lawn to the edge of the lake where Laurent and I are sitting. She's entranced. Neither of us says a word, letting her take the lead. 'It was love,' she says. 'I just fell in love.' She turns back to the mill and looks up at it. 'And for a moment I thought he might love me back, but if he did, he didn't admit to it. He was waiting for your grandmother. He wasted so much time and love, waiting for her to return.'

'So you spent time here,' I ask tentatively.

'Whenever I could, I'd offer to help.'

'We want to get the mill up and running, make the same flour,' I tell her, hoping I haven't mistimed this, but she seems to be listening. 'I've looked everywhere . . . I can't find the recipe. It has to be here somewhere.'

She points to the front door. 'May I?' she asks.

'Of course!' I say, and follow her.

She goes down the two stone steps into the big room and looks around, drinking in the memories and taking in the changes.

'I wanted to keep it as authentic as possible,' I say. 'But it needed renovating. I'm keeping the mill workings,' I say, nodding to the dormant wheels and the millstones. 'I made that decision without any real thought, but it would feel wrong to take out the heart of the mill.' Laurent nods and smiles back, understanding.

Madame B puts Bibi on the floor and he scampers around, sniffing and exploring, and carries on to my living quarters, with my mezzanine bedroom, at the back of the building. My bedroom . . . where I've been painting.

She pulls back the curtain and steps into the once store room where the pencil marks covered the walls, just like in the cellar.

'I've taken photographs of the drawings,' I say. 'But I thought I'd frame them on the walls. If that's okay with you? I want to keep the history of this place here.'

She doesn't say a word, running her hand over the walls, as if reconnecting to the words that were once written there, to the past and her one true love.

'This place isn't about one person. It's about all of you. A community. A lifelong love affair.'

She touches the wall. 'I remember everything as if it was yesterday,' says Madame B, and her face lights up with the memories, playing it over in her head.

'What do you remember?'

'How happy I felt here,' she turns and smiles, 'and the pencil drawings . . . as if I'd just done them!' She runs her hands over the walls and she is smiling, but I can see tears rolling down her cheeks. 'He would be proud of you, doing this,' she says. 'Very proud. He was a lot of things and stupid wasn't one of them. Not one to wear his heart on his sleeve or show his feelings. But he did show me how to make the T55 flour for the baguettes. He didn't write it down, I suppose, because he found writing hard, but also, he didn't want anyone else finding it. He didn't want any other bakers using his recipe. No one could rival his flour and he wasn't going to let Claude's family take anything else from him.'

She gazes at Laurent and me, then laughs. 'Yes, I remember, now that I am here, as if it were yesterday. Would you like me to show you?'

We nod.

'Yes, it's been a long time since I saw the mill in action,' says Laurent.

'The thing is to get the wheat fine enough. We want T55 flour. This will make for a light loaf and whiter than the T65. And, of course, you must use the right farmer for your wheat. Your grandfather liked to use a combination of different wheat from different farmers.'

She looks at us. '*Demain matin*, tomorrow morning, we will visit the wheat farmers. It's all in the wheat . . . and the *savoir faire*, the know-how. Baguettes may take only four ingredients, but a good loaf is all about the know-how, the chemistry.'

'But what were the ratios of different wheat?'

'I think I can remember,' she says. 'Near enough.'

'But if you can't, then we can't make the same flour . . .' Laurent says.

'So there is a space for you to put your own mark in it. A piece of the past, the present and the future. Follow your instincts, Laurent. Put your mark on this place. Choose the wheat closest to what you remember, by the *terroir*, how it feels. When we cook with it, how will it taste? Like you remember?'

Over the next week, we tour the French countryside, Madame B sitting in my Fiat Panda, with Bibi on her lap, guiding me by memory to the family farms she knew in the past.

'No, not left, straight ahead – oh, no, left here,' she would say, sending me up small, uneven roads, not signposted, with Laurent squeezed into the back seat, his knees up around his chest.

'I used to love visiting the farms with Raoul. It's been a long time since I've been to these places.' Her smile fades. 'It's been a long time since I've been anywhere.'

'Do you leave the apartment?' I ask, looking straight ahead on the dusty roads.

'Of course I do! Once, maybe twice a week. For groceries, and cigarettes, and of course I take Bibi to stretch his little legs. But we were happy in our own company,' she says, 'until an irritating British cook kept knocking on my door!' I see the corners of her mouth lift into a small smile. Something tells me she might be quite enjoying being out and in company. As is Bibi, sitting up tall and proud, looking out of the front window and watching the countryside go by.

At each of the farms, Madame B explains we are from the *moulin*, and introduces Laurent as Raoul's grandson. He is greeted warmly. Some of the farms have older members still there, who remember Raoul and want to share a glass of wine with Laurent to talk about his grandfather, his skill and the respect he won from farmers for his choice of wheat, his prompt payment and his commitment to quality over profit.

By the end of the week, June has slipped into early July and we are sitting under the shade of the weeping willow by the lake.

'So, we have the ingredients for the flour,' I say, to Laurent and Madame B.

'We need water,' she says. 'Water is one of the most important ingredients.'

'A friend of mine has a spring. His water is tested and excellent quality. He will deliver it to you at the bakery,' Laurent tells me.

'Good, good!' Madame B nods.

'And yeast?'

'And yeast, yes. I have spoken to a supplier,' I say. 'It's not cheap, but it will be good. I think your grandfather would agree on quality over profit,' I say, and Laurent nods and smiles.

'Now all we need is salt ... from the coast,' says Madame B, and with that we all get back into the car and drive out to the Brittany coast for a day by the sea, locating a salt producer and eating small, sweet mussels, in white wine and garlic sauce, with crunchy *frites*, creamy homemade mayonnaise and a carafe of cold rosé wine, eating in the salty, sunny air.

The next day Madame B watches Laurent open the sluice gate, far more smoothly this time than when I did it, and we watch the water fill the pit below the wheel and listen as it starts turning. Under Madame B's watchful eye, Laurent starts to grind the blend of soft and hard wheat, testing and testing.

'For the granulation,' Madame B tells me, when I ask what he's doing.

She and Laurent stand over the flour, shaking their heads and starting again. And I think about us in the lake: *Keep paddling*.

And we do keep paddling. We keep going until, later that week, '*Tiens*,' she says. 'There.'

'That's it?' I look at the little pile of white flour.

'Really?' asks Laurent. 'You think?'

'I do.' She nods firmly.

I look at the pyramid of flour, the foundation on which this place was built.

'He made me promise never to tell anyone, in those years I helped here, unless they deserved to know. You, both of you, deserve to know.'

'We did it!' I say rapturously.

'We have the flour recipe!' Laurent kisses Madame B excitedly and firmly on each cheek, then hugs me. 'Now we have the flour, all we really need is someone who knows how to make bread.'

I look at Madame B, who narrows her eyes.

Laurent lets me go and I feel as if I've been wrapped in a soft blanket. Then, in a gentle tone, he says to Madame B, 'I'm sorry you didn't get to spend your lives together. I would have liked to see him with someone who made him happy. He was loyal. And maybe he should have taken his chance at happiness.'

'You made him happy,' she said, with a watery smile,

holding her hand to his cheek, as if he were a little boy. 'And this, wherever he is,' she points to the sky, 'will make him happy. But love is something to be celebrated, wherever you find it. Hold on to it.'

Somehow I find myself staring at Laurent and him at me, and I don't want to stop.

'There was a moment, when I thought maybe something might happen – that Raoul might feel about me as I felt about him. But he never got over losing Jeanne to Claude's grandfather. And I suppose, I never got over him.'

'When I wasn't hiding in the kitchen at the *boulangerie*, I would sit and watch life from my window, wait for market day when we still had a proper market. I'd watch Raoul arrive in town proudly showing off his grandchild. He loved you more than anything, Laurent. Grief can do strange things to people, he told me, when he explained his wife had come back. Losing their daughter, your mother, in that awful car accident. Neither of them ever got over it. It turned their lives upside down. But he carried on, pulling his grandson tighter to him. He just wanted to keep you safe.'

He kept on paddling, I think, tears pricking my eyes.

'After she left, as I said, I thought there might be hope, but I don't think he could ever let anyone else in. I loved him. And I think he cared about me, but only as Little Bijounette. A precious friendship. He was older than me, by fifteen years, and I think that mattered to him. Besides, he was still married. But I couldn't stop hoping that one day . . .'

'Well, I see the rumours are true! The old wheel is

· 218 ·

turning again!' Claude is standing in the doorway, ruining the atmosphere, like pouring water onto a fire.

'*Bonjour*,' he says, 'Madame,' nodding to her.

She sniffs, wipes her nose with a tissue from her sleeve, sets her backbone and lifts her head. 'Monsieur,' she replies.

'May I?' he asks, and, without waiting for an answer, comes to stand next to the big grinding stones where we're gathered.

I go cold, as if I can physically feel the frostiness from the two men at either side of me.

Laurent sighs. 'You again. Like a bad smell, you keep turning up.' He walks past him towards the door.

'You leaving, Laurent? Not because of me, I hope! I came to see if the rumours were true that you were trying to get this place running again. But you must see it's a lost cause. Like your grandparents. Your grandfather should have realised . . .'

Laurent's usual easy-going manner disappears. In one or two huge strides he is standing in front of Claude. He leans in, face to face, and growls, 'Say another word about my grandparents and I will rip that head of yours off your shoulders.' He grips Claude's shirt front.

For a split second I see a flash of fear in Claude's eyes, but then his smug smile returns and he stands his ground. 'I understand you were upset about your grandmother wanting to join our family,' he says, with *faux* feeling, 'but that, a bit like this place, was a silly dream. She was only ever a pastime for my grandfather. It's sweet that you think this could be a fully working mill again. Most people aren't stuck in the past like you. Times change, things move on. This mill will never be what you hope. It's a fantasy.'

For a moment, Laurent stares at Claude, then suddenly releases him. 'You're not worth it,' he mutters.

'Laurent,' I say quickly, 'could you check if we have any more wood to come in? I may need more for the fire.'

With a curl of his lip towards Claude, he heads for the door.

Claude recovers himself, straightening his shirt. 'That's it, run along, Laurent, I have things to discuss . . .'

Laurent glares at him over his shoulder and, for a moment, I think he may turn and hit Claude. Instead, he gives a small shake of the head, then strides out into the fresh air.

We watch him go, and when I turn back, I see Madame B has brushed away any traces of the flour we've made, like a pro. Not a speck left behind.

'Like I say, Julie . . .'

'It's Juliet,' I hiss.

'This place is a fantasy. It will never happen. The village doesn't need any more bread. They have mine. It's better you give this idea up.'

He looks at me and I feel my skin crawl. How could I have been so stupid as to find this man attractive when I first met him? I pull myself together. I haven't come this far to be bullied.

'I will do what I want with my building,' I say firmly. 'I don't need your or anyone else's permission. Now, I'd like you to leave, please.'

'You heard her, Monsieur,' says Madame B, and Bibi joins in with a bark, lunging forward. Claude backs away.

He stares at Madame B and I'm impressed by the respect she commands. Then he turns to me. 'Of course.' He looks towards the open door, where Laurent is returning from the wood pile on the bank by the lake, carrying an armful of logs. The canoe finally made its way to shore, as Laurent said it would, and is retied to the marker in the ground there.

'On your way now, Monsieur,' says Madame B.

He's backing towards the door, Bibi escorting him out.

'Remember to keep me in mind for supplying your bread. I don't want anything to ruin your plans for the *salon de thé*.' He looks up at the newly painted walls and trips as he backs up the stone steps towards the big front door.

I'm seething.

'Still here?' says Laurent.

'Just leaving,' he says, but this time he isn't smirking and steps around Laurent, like a mouse – or in this case a rat. It's a good job Laurent's got an armful of logs to hold as Claude hurries out.

Suddenly I want to vent, but I can't. I can't tell them how much I've come to despise that man and why. It would make them despise me just as much.

'What was he doing here?' says Laurent. 'Was he pushing you to use his bread at the *salon de thé* again?'

'Yes. And I think he was curious about the water wheel. But I don't want him to have any idea how close we are to getting the flour right for the bread. He's the last person I want to know what we're trying to make happen.'

Madame B gives one of her derisory sniffs and heads for the front door.

'Bibi,' she calls. '*Au revoir*, you two. See you tomorrow, early, at the *boulangerie*,' she announces as she
leaves. And as I watch her go, I barely have time to think
about what she's just said. She's going to be at the *boulangerie* in the morning. This is going to happen!

Laurent, however, is still focused on Claude. 'Well,
you're better off steering well clear of him. Like his
grandfather, he takes what he can, when he can, without
a thought for anyone. And discards what he doesn't want
any more.'

'Did you hear what Madame B just said?' I try to
change the subject.

Laurent puts the logs by the fire, stands up straight
and dusts his hands. 'You had plenty of wood already . . .
I nearly hit him.'

'But you didn't,' I reply.

'I could have.'

'But you didn't,' I repeat.

'No, I didn't. He wanted me to. He wanted people to
believe the stories about me are true. That I'm here
because I have nowhere else to go. That I'm a man with
nothing. But the truth is, there is nowhere I'd rather be
than here. And I have more than he will ever have,
because I have a passion' – he puts his fist to his chest,
and my heart starts to pound – 'to make this place special
again. And,' he laughs, 'right now I can't think of anyone
I would rather share that passion with.'

A flame roars up inside me. And all at once I have a
purpose, something I'm here to do, something that will
make a difference to this community. And Laurent sets in
motion the mechanism for the grinding stone to turn.

Chapter 31

W hen I wake the next day, I look up at the dark sky. It's the silent time when night meets day, on its way in the distance. Even the neighbouring cockerel isn't awake, still tucked up and not yet announcing morning.

Under a blanket of stars, I follow the torch on my phone around the building to my car. I leave the mill and drive up towards the sleeping village, past small terraced houses, their shutters tightly shut.

I can smell the dew after the warm night, settling on the hedgerow, among the glistening cobwebs, as I drive with the windows open along the lane to the square and turn right at the end of the road. My heart skips when I see the lights on and a warm orange glow from the *boulangerie* window. I pull up and get out, feeling the welcome of the lights drawing me in, like the beating heart of the town. I smile as I open the door.

'*Bonjour, Madame*,' I say. 'You're in early.'

'*Bonjour, Juliet*,' she says, emerging from the bakery, dressed in her usual smart pressed top, a silk scarf around her neck and a white apron. She steps forward and we kiss each other lightly on each cheek. I know now that without this formality there will be no further conversation.

When I've removed my light scarf from around my neck, she hands me an apron. The ovens are already on and I can hear their hum, but no one is banging today.

'First, *café*,' she says, pointing towards the little kitchen. 'And then, we will bake bread.'

We make the coffee and I look at the dough, ready and waiting.

'The dough must be made the night before and left to rest. Like me, it needs its beauty sleep!' She laughs. Her whole face has lit up – she looks younger.

'So, the flour's going to make the difference now?'

She looks at me steadily. 'And the final ingredient.'

'But you said there were only four.'

'Four ingredients in the bowl, but the other is the most important of all. The weather. That is the *savoir faire*,' she says, with a flourish. 'How do you say? . . . The know-how. You have to work with the weather or everything will be terrible.'

She smiles again, and this time I swear she gives a little wink.

'That's where I was going wrong. The first day I made bread and it worked, it was a calm, still day. The second time, it was windy, cooler.'

She nods. 'We have to work with Mother Nature. She keeps us on our toes. Unless we listen to her, we will have nothing to eat. She is a strict teacher, but a generous provider when we adhere to her way of doing things.'

Bibi is sitting by the door, watching the world go by, or maybe keeping an eye open for the mayor's cat.

'I just wish I'd been able to do this myself.'

'But it is you who have made this happen. You have brought both of the important things together here. The flour from Laurent, and from me the *savoir faire*.'

She smiles again. 'Now, we will shape the loaves and sign them.' She waves a small knife at me. 'Don't forget, we eat with our eyes first. They must look inviting as well as smell amazing. And then we will give them another rest, before cooking them.'

We put the dough through the cutting machine. Then Madame B throws flour onto the work surface with a flourish, and side by side, we stretch out the dough and shape them, then put them on the baking cloth where they are tucked up next to each other. Madame B reshapes mine, which are not to her exacting standards. When the first lot of baguettes are proved and ready to go into the oven, she shows me how to spray them with water – just a spritz – as they go in.

'For crunch on the outside,' she tells me, shutting the ovens carefully, like closing the bedroom door on a sleeping baby. 'Usually they take around twenty minutes. But I will leave them just a little longer, to get the crust dark,' she says, setting the timer. She wipes her hands on a tea-towel. 'Now we will prepare the next batch, while these cook,' she instructs, 'and then we will have *café*.' She claps her still-floury hands.

As we line up the next batch, the smell starting to fill the bakery from the ovens is amazing. So much more enticing than when I was baking alone. It seems to fill the room and wrap around me, like a hug, as we sip our coffee by the worn wooden shop counter, which has marks and dips from the years of people leaning against it. Stopping to pass the time of day when they bought their morning baguette. Taking time to enjoy sharing a conversation, passing on news, asking after loved ones. I'm beginning to see what the mayor means. These things can't be replaced with a machine.

'It's time,' says Madame B, standing upright, away from the counter.

We walk towards the ovens where the next batch is waiting to go in. She hands me the gloves. 'You do it! I can't look! It's been years! What if I've lost my touch?'

And suddenly we're both nervous. What if they don't come out as they should? Will she be devastated? Have I unleashed feelings and emotions that should have stayed shut away?

She looks vulnerable, not the hard-faced woman I first met, shooing away the outside world, locked into her apartment with her memories.

I put on the oven gloves.

'Hurry, *vite*! You don't want them to overcook. The crust must be just so . . .' She waves at one of the big industrial ovens. 'Open it,' she says, standing right behind me.

I reach out, take the handle and pull.

Steam spirals out, enveloping us as I try to wave it away with the oven glove. The smell is fantastic. I feel as if I've entered a whole new world that fills every part of me with happiness.

As the steam dissipates, we peer forward. I take hold

of the tray and slowly slide it towards us, aware that dropping the hot sheet of metal would be a very bad thing. I am holding someone's dreams and memories in my hands.

She steps back as I pull the tray fully out and turn to the table behind us, gently lowering the tray onto it. Madame B has her manicured fingers over her eyes.

'They're fine,' I say, then, louder, 'more than fine. They look amazing!' I take her hands and lower them from her face.

She stares at the loaves. 'They're perfect!' she says quietly, and tears spring to her eyes. 'Just as they should be. As I remember.'

And it's like all the memories, the good ones, are rushing back in to greet her.

She reaches out to the baguettes, touching them gently with the tips of her fingers. She looks at me. A tear slides down her cheek. 'They remind me of him.'

And not knowing whether it's the right thing to do or not, I throw etiquette out of the window and hug her. After a few sobs, and a sniff, she straightens. I'm expecting a telling-off for not respecting tradition and manners, but instead she says quietly, '*Merci*,' pulls a tissue from her sleeve and blows her nose.

'Now, let's taste them,' I say. I'm about to rip the end off one of the baguettes but she is back to her chastising self. 'No, Juliet. We must be respectful. This loaf has taken many hours to produce. It deserves to be given respect. Let's put the next batch in and make some more coffee, lay the table.' She points to the little table in the shop window and I do as I'm told. I put the coffee on, so the air starts to fill with the intoxicating scents of baking bread and hot coffee. Could there be a better marriage? She finds a clean white apron and drapes it over the table, then puts out plates and a dish of butter. Finally, she disappears to her apartment and returns with a jar of homemade rhubarb jam.

'The baker's table,' she announces, and we pull up a chair each. I set out the cafetière with cups and a sugar bowl. We sit at either side of the table in the bakery window, just as daylight is creeping into the sky. The outline of the trees can be seen in the muted light.

I pour the coffee into two cups and pass one to Madame B. She accepts it, then offers me the loaf. I wonder what the etiquette is here. I lift my knife.

'*Non.*' She tuts and waves a finger at me. She takes the loaf back, tears off a piece and places it on her plate, then hands the loaf back to me. I follow her example, ripping off a chunk of bread. She lifts a piece to her nose and breathes in its aroma. I do the same. It smells amazing – of wheat and warmth. There is a shine on the crust, and inside, the pillowy crumb is white, soft and springy – like a deep, thick duvet I want to dive into. I can already feel the comfort I know it will bring.

'*Bon appétit,*' she says, with a nod.

'*Bon appétit,*' I reply, and watch as she tears off a bit of the crust and slowly puts it into her mouth. She lets it sit on her tongue before thoughtfully chewing, her eyes slowly closing. I watch in fascination: I can practically see the memories playing out in her mind.

Slowly she opens her eyes. 'Well, have you tasted it?'

I shake my head and follow her lead, tearing off a

piece, enjoying the crack of the shiny crust, the softness of the crumb and the saltiness that follows, filling my mouth with flavour. Finally, I swallow. 'It's the best I've ever had,' I say.

A smile creeps onto her lips. '*Merci.*'

'Really, Madame B, it is so different. And with just four ingredients?'

Her smile widens. 'It's all about the aroma, the texture and the flavour. The thick crust keeps the inside fresher for longer. A slower cook for a thick crust is how I like it. And, of course, no preservatives in the yeast. It is all in the *savoir faire*. And now I am going to teach you to do the same. But, first, we will enjoy our *café*, and this piece of bread with good butter and homemade *confiture.*' She points to the pot of jam. 'I have many jars of it!' And we laugh.

We sit and spread light yellow butter on the bread and a thin layer of jam. I bite through the not-too-sweet rhubarb, sinking my teeth through the cold butter and the pillowy dough to the crispy crunch of the crust. The mix of textures and flavours, sweet and salty, cold butter on warm bread, sweet jam on savoury butter and the salt in the bread to amplify all the flavours, is . . . heaven.

I sip my coffee and hear the beeper go for the next batch of bread. I stand up, looking out over the white netting that covers the lower half of the window.

Outside, I see one of the village women walking towards the bread-vending machine. She turns to look at the shop with interest. I raise a hand in greeting, but she doesn't wave back, or stop to show that she's at all interested, despite her snatched glances.

'It'll take time,' says Madame B, with a shrug. 'You have to earn their trust. The bread is at the heart of the dinner table. They will not turn their backs on their usual supplier.'

'Well, we'd better start by opening the doors. Let people know we're here and we've got bread to sell.'

'And in the meantime, I suggest you put that bell back over the door to tell us when the customers arrive,' she says, making us both smile.

We clear the table and pull the fresh baguettes from the oven, as warm and welcoming as the last batch.

I put them into baskets on the counter and then, as dawn turns to daylight and starlings sing in a nearby oleander bush, the sun pushes over the church spire and spills into the square. I open the bakery door and wait for the customers to come. They may not trust me, a British woman opening a bakery, but they will trust this flour and this bread.

Chapter 32

I wait and wait, rearranging the loaves periodically, wondering whether to put them on the table in the window. I place some there, then realise they'll go stale in the sun and move them back to the counter. I photograph them and send the snaps to the family WhatsApp group and Annie.

'I am going for a rest,' Madame B informs me, Bibi under her arm, as morning moves towards midday. 'I shall return later to make a fresh batch and tomorrow's dough. We'll do it together.'

'What if we don't sell any? What's the point?'

'It will take time,' she repeats. 'You should get some rest too.' She walks out of the door, and the bell tinkles behind her. I look at the unsold baguettes and sigh.

I'm clearing the bakery room and sweeping the floor, ready for our next batch, when I hear the bell over the shop door ring, telling me we have a customer. It required the same precarious process of climbing on a table to put it back up again, but I hope it's return is a good sign; the place seemed bare without it. I put the broom to one side and go into the shop. I stop.

'Bonjour,' says Laurent, smiling. *'Une baguette, s'il vous plaît.'* He looks around at the empty shop. 'I'm not too late, am I?'

His grin makes me grin regardless of the disappointment I'm feeling. 'No, we have plenty left. Take as much as you want,' I tell him, tears of tiredness prickling my eyes.

'I want to be a paying customer. Your first, maybe?' He holds up the euro from his top pocket. 'You never know when you're going to need it.'

A wave of emotions is tumbling in on me. Pride about the bread that's been made here today, the flour we used and the *savoir faire*. But also furious and frustrated that people would still rather trust the machine and the mediocre bread from Claude's bakery. A loaf made without passion, just for profit.

'Okay,' I say. 'In that case . . .' I take the euro and hand him a baguette, putting the euro into the empty till. It rattles around and eventually settles. I push the till shut and sigh.

'Now, I have bread. I also have wine, ham, tomatoes and cheese. Would you care to join me at the *tabac* for lunch? To celebrate your first day as an open *boulangerie*?'

My arms are folded, but I'm laughing. 'Even if I haven't had any customers?'

'You're here, and that's what matters,' he says.

I misjudged and misunderstood this man, who is kind and thoughtful, someone I'm really enjoying spending time with. The more I think about his respect for his grandfather, his kindness to Madame B, his loyalty in being here today, the more attractive he's becoming. He's the sort of man I would trust – and I did! I trusted him with my life on the lake! I wouldn't have done that with just anybody! The memory makes me laugh, and my retelling of the story to Annie had prompted a laughing-with-tears emoji back. I haven't heard from her for a few days, not since my last video showing the wheel in action and the stone turning. I'm beginning to worry.

Laurent interrupts my thoughts. 'What do you say? A celebration of being here?'

'That,' I say, 'sounds perfect. On the condition that you let me bring bread over and hand it out to whoever will take it.' Maybe giving out samples will help sales.

'It's a deal.' He holds the baguette, touching his forehead with it, like a salute. 'See you over there.'

I close the shop door and carry the basket of baguettes to the *tabac*, where the three regulars are sitting in the shade, out of the midday sun.

Inside the cool bar, I sit on a bar stool. Laurent has laid out tomatoes, cheese and ham on a wooden board, with a sharp knife. He pours me a glass of wine and slides it across to me.

'No company today?' I ask, remembering the mayor's receptionist who was parked here last time.

He gives a little laugh. 'What can I tell you? Not everyone is put off by the stories Claude spreads about me.' He gives a wicked smile. 'So, tell me, how was it with Madame Bertou? Did she terrify you?'

I shake my head. 'No. She's a woman who commands

respect, but actually, she's fascinating . . . and funny.' I add.

'Really?'

'Yes.' I start to tell him how I felt being in the *boulangerie* that morning, from the welcoming lights, to the smell and taste of the bread. I was privileged to be there, I thought, watching a true artisan at work. As I talk, I idly make up sandwiches from the bread and ham, cheese and tomatoes. 'It's all about the *savoir faire* apparently,' I tell him what he of course already knows. But I'm just in awe. 'She knows exactly what she's doing. And she says it's never the same two days in a row. She works with the weather, if it's hot, cold, somewhere in between. You have to learn to read the dough and what it needs. And the bread is amazing. Here, try!'

'Finally,' he says. 'I thought we were just going to keep talking about the bread! Now I actually get to taste it! To see if the flour is every bit as good as I think it is!'

I hold out a piece of bread for him and, for a moment, I wonder if I'm going to put it into his mouth, but he gently takes it from me, our fingers touching.

He chews, nodding. 'It's amazing. Just as it should be,' he says.

'I have to find a way of getting people in to buy it! If I can't, we won't need any more flour . . .' I tail off. I've made a pile of sandwiches. 'Sorry, I got carried away.'

Laurent laughs. 'We'll have to find hungry mouths,' he says, as the three old men come inside out of the heat of the day to see what's going on.

'*Messieurs!*' Laurent says, as they arrive at the bar. He lines up three glasses and fills them with *pastis*, then puts out a jug of water. The men sit at the bar and spot the pile of sandwiches I've made.

'*Jambon-beurre au tomate et fromage*,' I say, offering the plate to them.

They look at it, then back at me, unsure.

'Please, help yourselves, I made too much. You'll be doing me a favour.'

They reach out and tentatively take a sandwich each. 'Is the bread going to be as bad as last time?' I hear one ask another in French.

'I prefer her funny little cakes,' says another, thinking I don't understand and making me smile.

'My wife will kill me if I'm not back in time for dinner as usual.'

'*Bon appétit*,' I say. They look nervously at the sandwiches and at each other. But this time I am much more confident that they'll like the bread.

'*Et un cadeau*,' I say, 'a present,' and hand them all baguettes to take home with them. It's that or throw them to the ducks again.

'*Merci, très gentille*,' one says.

'No cakes today?' another asks, in English this time.

I laugh. 'I'll make some more soon,' I say. At least someone likes what I'm doing.

Laurent tops up my glass of rosé and one for himself. 'We deserve this. To the first week of the mill . . . and your first day of opening the *boulangerie*.'

But if I can't sell the bread, it'll all be for nothing, I think but don't say. I don't want to spoil this lovely gesture, and the mood here in the little *tabac*.

'*Santé*.'

The three men are clearly enjoying the sandwiches, biting into the bread, chewing big mouthfuls with joy and raising their glasses to me.

'*Magnifique!*' they say, and I beam, as if I'd made it all myself.

'*Laurent, une bouteille de vin rouge,*' one calls to Laurent.

The three take their sandwiches into the sunshine, with a bottle of red wine, sit back and enjoy lunch in the sun. After a while, I wonder if they've actually fallen into a doze.

Laurent and I enjoy our relaxed picnic, me on the stool and him behind the bar, as occasional customers come and go – a few walkers, passing through the village looking for lunch and, after a drink, moving on.

'So, how is this?' Laurent asks, as I sip my wine.

'It's lovely, thank you. Just what I hoped life would be like – not full of canoes, flooding and badly baked bread!'

'And you will stay, if you can?'

'It depends on my visa.'

'But if the mayor agrees?'

'Of course. But if I can't get my visa, where will I go?'

'What about home? Do you miss it?'

I consider his question carefully. 'I had a good life with my husband . . . but we had come to the end of the road. I wanted more. He didn't. I need to live the best life I can. I'm not sure I could go back.'

He nods. 'It was the same for me returning here. It just felt like something I needed to do.'

I find myself smiling at him. A smile I haven't felt in a long time, as if I'm sharing a special secret with someone.

'*Mais, alors!*' I hear a shout. 'This is where I find you!' I manage to make out what's being said in furious fast

French. 'I have been waiting. You were going to bring home the baguette from the machine, and here you are, eating with friends!'

It's one of the short, smart women I see waiting for bread at the vending machine in the mornings.

Then, 'Here is your lunch! Clearly you choose to be somewhere else and in someone else's company!'

She slams a plate of food onto the table. The potatoes bounce and the thin gravy shoots off the plate, taking with it a few *petit pois* and baby carrots. 'I see you have bread already, to mop up the sauce!' She turns on her heels to leave.

'No, wait!' says her husband. 'I was getting the bread. I promise! Here.' He picks up the baguette I gave him. 'Come, sit down, have a drink, try it . . .'

'I have better things to do with my time.' She turns to look at me, sitting at the bar. She doesn't smile. 'We have a baker who provides bread. We do not need to risk losing it for another stranger opening the *boulangerie* and closing it again within weeks. Better we stick with what we have.'

I blush, feeling like a temptress, enticing a man from the lunch waiting for him at home. I suffer the same embarrassment I felt at having allowed myself to be kissed by another woman's husband before I knew he was married. My cheeks burn at the memory. Is this who people think I am? Someone to be worried about? It's not like that. I just want to fit in.

'Come and sit. Enjoy a glass.' He holds up the wine bottle. 'Try the bread!' He's trying to placate her. 'It's really very good.'

She looks at me through the open glass door again, up

and down, then back at her husband. Although I wanted to be seen when I first arrived, I didn't want to be known as a woman who encouraged husbands away from their wives.

'Really,' I join in through the open glass door, 'it's the bread they're here for.'

She sniffs, folding her arms across her chest. 'What's different about the bread?' She thrusts her chin at it. 'It's always the same from the machine.'

'Trust me, it's different.'

She looks down at the table, then up at me, and for a moment, I wonder if she's going to try a sandwich. We watch her. She sniffs again and says, 'Why do I need different bread? We have been buying the same bread for years! Why the need for change? I was happy with the usual bread. Like I say, if we stop using the machine, Claude will remove it and then we will have nothing.'

She lifts her head and walks away, her little square heels clicking on the pavement. Her husband picks up his hat, finishing his glass of wine with a gulp and racing to catch up with her, his lunch plate in one hand, the baguette under his opposite arm.

The other two look at their watches, pick up their baguettes and finish their wine. '*Merci, au revoir,*' they call politely, then leave quickly before they get into similar trouble and feel the wrath of their wives.

And it's quiet.

'Well, I should be going,' I say, sliding off the bar stool, wishing I could stay. I really don't want people to think I'm here chatting up their menfolk. What if the receptionist from the *mairie* were to come in and see me sitting here alone with Laurent?

For a moment, he says nothing.

'And I'll take the rest of this bread to the fisher-women . . . they may find it useful for bait!'

'I hope not,' he says.

Suddenly I feel a sort of shyness. 'This was nice, thank you.'

'*De rien*, it was nothing,' he says.

I have no idea if he is feeling the same as me, but I think he is. That there is closeness between us, a growing friendship. But that's something I can never think about. The receptionist from the *mairie* is clearly interested in him. I'm not about to try to seduce him away from her. That would just confirm what I think of myself after the Claude scenario. I'm not doing that again, however much I may want to. We're just friends and it's going to stay that way.

I leave the bar, wishing I wasn't feeling warm and fuzzy. I leave my car where it is and walk back to the mill with the baguettes in my basket. The fisherwomen are sitting on the lakeshore, enjoying the warm summer sun.

Having delivered the bread to them, telling them to do what they want with it, I turn and walk away. I'm waiting to hear laughter, but when I reach the lawn overlooking the lake, I see that they are not throwing the bread into the water. They're eating it. Breaking off chunks, smelling it, putting pieces into their mouths, chewing and nodding. They're opening wine and raising a glass to me. My eyes prickle with unexpected tears, and my heart swells. Maybe we have found all the right ingredients.

Chapter 33

Days pass, each the same as the last. As July slips into August, I have just one month left to prove to the mayor that I'm turning a profit at the *boulangerie*, or I'll have to leave and find somewhere to go other than the house I shared with Pete.

Every morning I get up in the dark and drive from the mill to the bakery where the lights are always on, a warm orange glow in the hour before dawn. Madame B and I have fallen into a routine. Bibi sits in the doorway, watching the world go by, waiting for the mayor's cat, which comes calling, making Bibi bark. I greet Madame B with a kiss on each cheek and ask how she is, then make the coffee. When we've drunk it and the ovens are up to temperature, we begin to prepare the dough for baking, rolling it into long baguette shapes, tossing flour with a flourish – or, in my case, like a snowstorm.

'*Non, Juliet, pas comme ça!*' she chides, and tosses the flour with a practised hand, like a showman, with precision and flair. She rolls the baguettes with ease, then lets them rest, before adding her signature to them, swiftly cutting diagonal lines into the dough with a small, sharp knife, spraying them with just enough water for the 'crisp' and steam, depending on the weather, before I put them into the oven. Each day she assesses the wind, its direction, and the heat. She judges how long each batch will take to prove and bake based on these elements. I'm beginning to understand the *savoir faire* and that it will take a long time for me to acquire it, to be anything like the master baker that Madame B is.

When the first batch is cooked, we take a baguette to the table, make more coffee and eat it with butter and homemade jam. And then, with a fresh batch of bread in the ovens, we wait. I wish I knew how to get more customers in. But my photos on Facebook are only going to family and friends. And I'm not sure the housewives of the area are looking to Facebook to make their local shopping decisions.

Before the *tabac* opens, Laurent arrives with his euro to buy a baguette. I deliver it to him when I finish in the bakery at midday and buy a coffee at the *tabac*, or maybe a glass of wine. But he is the only one who ever comes. Until today, that is.

'*Une baguette, s'il vous plaît.*'

'*Avec plaisir, Monsieur.*'

I wrap a baguette in a piece of paper, take the euro and let it land in the empty till.

As Laurent turns to leave, I see Geneviève at the door. '*Bonjour.*'

'*Bonjour,*' she replies.

'*Une baguette, s'il vous plaît.*'

Suddenly I'm bursting with pride. She's come to buy my bread.

'I'm sorry I haven't been before,' she says. 'It is a change in routine.'

'What made you come today?' I ask.

'I became an aunt. My brother and his wife have wanted children for a long time. Last night, they had a baby girl. A new life. A new beginning. Life changes and it moves on for all of us. We should embrace change,' she says. 'But, of course, change comes at a different pace for everyone, like grief, like celebrating life.' She looks out of the doorway onto the square.

I hand over the baguette and she gives me the euro. I put it into the till to join the other, smiling. She has no idea how much this means to me. Or maybe she does.

I stand at the door and watch her leave as the other women gather around the vending machine, waiting for Claude to arrive and fill it. Despite my best efforts to spread the word that my shop is open, and despite some of them having tasted the bread, I still can't get them to change their routine. Not yet. Maybe never. To them I am just a British woman trying to be a baker who won't be here for long. And if Claude takes away his machine, they will have nothing.

Even if I can get them through the front door, will that be enough to keep the place going? It's been three weeks since we opened with Madame B's bread on 14 July – a day of liberty, resistance and equality. 'A day to celebrate the French spirit,' Madame B told me as we opened the doors. But resistance and French spirit are running thin here at the *boulangerie*. I need a miracle.

At the end of lunchtime I close the door and turn over the *'Fermé'* sign, with a tinkle from the bell.

I gather up the leftover baguettes into a basket. I lock up the shop and join Laurent for a coffee. Then we share lunch, handing out to the three men the bread we haven't sold. It's that or throw it away. They seem grateful, taking the baguettes straight home, instead of buying them from the vending machine they've been sent to use.

But now, as days pass, it has been four whole weeks, and I'm clearing away the plates and cups from our early-morning breakfast, wondering how to tell Madame B that we can't go on. We can't keep opening the door when no one other than Laurent and Geneviève are coming in. We've given it a really good shot, but I have just over two weeks left to prove why I should be allowed to stay. The *boulangerie* is alive, but I know that, really, we have come to the end of the road. We tried. But we can't keep baking bread that no one buys, that I'm giving away come lunchtime. Every morning they line up at the vending machine to buy their bread, none of them, other than Geneviève, prepared to break rank and give the new *boulangerie* a chance.

But this morning something different happens. The bell above the door rings, surprising us. It's too early for Laurent. Even for Geneviève.

'I'll go,' I say, propping up my broom by the big dough-mixer I've already cleaned.

There, standing in the doorway, small and neat and in low court shoes, is the wife of Gilles from the *tabac*.

I take a deep breath, wondering whether I'm about to

get the sharp end of her tongue again. I'm ready for her accusations, and as she looks around the inside of the bakery, her eyes narrow. 'Is it true?' she asks.

'Look, I'm not sure what you think is going on here but . . .'

'Is it true that the bread my husband has been bringing home every day at lunchtimes isn't from the machine? It's from here?'

Part of me wants to breathe a sigh of relief, but I'm unsure of how she feels about it. I lift my chin, as she does. I know Madame B, in the back room, is watching from the shadows.

'Why do you ask?' I say. Is she about to tell me to stop serving him? That I'm not wanted around here?

She looks back at me, then says, 'It's different. Better, much better.'

My heart slows and I gain confidence, like an oven beginning to warm in the early morning. 'If it has a shine and a crunch, and makes you want more,' I assert, 'then, yes, I'd say it's from here.'

Her shoulders drop and the tension visibly disappears from them. '*Merci*. And I'm sorry. I shouldn't have been so outspoken the other day. Or offended you. He brought the bread back to the house. Insisted I try it. Most insistent, in fact. And, well, I haven't enjoyed a meal with my husband like that in years,' she says. 'It was like old times. And the bread tasted just like it used to taste.'

'I'm using local flour, direct from the mill,' I say. 'The same ingredients. The same family farms supplying the wheat. The same family recipe.'

'But the knowledge, the *savoir faire*,' she adds, with suspicion, 'how did you know? You are a cake-maker from the UK.'

'You're right,' I reply, 'and I have a lot to learn. I'm still learning. Maybe that's the thing about when you get to this stage in life – it's not about what you already know but what you're prepared to learn. And I have an excellent *professeur*.'

I step aside from the doorway into the bakery where Madame B is standing, her white hair up in its usual soft quiff, her nails their trademark red, but her cheeks and apron are covered with flour.

'Charlotte!' exclaims the woman in the shop doorway.

Madame B gives a nod. '*Oui, c'est moi.*'

The other woman frowns, and points at the basket of baguettes on the counter. 'It's you who made the baguettes?'

She nods. '*Oui, c'est moi.* And now I am passing on the *savoir faire*.'

The woman looks shocked. 'All these years, the shop has been shut and we have lived with the vending machine. You said you would do whatever it took for it never to open again.'

Madame B nods once more. 'I lost sight of what was important. I forgot what it felt like to love. But now, I remember and it's there in my bread again.'

The woman is pale, as if she's seen a ghost.

'Would you like a drink of water, a coffee perhaps?' I ask.

She's grasping the back of the chair. '*Un café, merci*,' she says, sitting, and I go to the scullery and fetch a coffee, placing it on the table in front of her along with sugar and some water.

'What changed? This bread, it has changed everything for me. I wait for my husband Gilles to get home at lunchtime, keen to see him now. He even kisses me as he hands me the baguette. We smile at each other. The joy has come back into our lunches together. It's like we are seeing each other again for the first time in years. We look forward to *le déjeuner*.'

'Things have changed for me too,' says Madame B. 'I realised I shouldn't waste the love I once had and should remember the joy it brought me. So I have. Thanks to Juliet.'

'I must go,' says Gilles' wife, glancing nervously out of the window.

'Drink your coffee.' I smile. 'No one will see you this early, especially as the light is on the church, not here.'

She nods gratefully and I see her smiling, relaxed. 'And now I must take a baguette for breakfast,' she says.

'Of course,' I say.

She stands and hands over a euro from her pocket. 'But, please, don't tell anyone I was here. I can't be to blame if people stop buying from the machine and it disappears.'

'Of course,' I say again politely, but I'm dancing inside. 'I can save you a baguette for tomorrow, if you like?' I say, as I hold the door open for her, and Madame B picks up the broom.

She nods, taking the baguette for breakfast with her husband. '*Merci, Madame*,' she says, and heads for home in the early dewy morning.

Madame B is smiling, her arms crossed. 'That was a good sale,' she says.

'It was,' I agree, then remember the conversation that needs to be had. 'It's great, but three customers a day isn't going to keep us afloat. Unless I can make a profit, I can't get my visa.'

'Just wait,' she says to me. 'Just wait.'

I sigh. 'I can wait one more week,' I say, and then, voicing what needs to be said, like ripping off a plaster and knowing that it's going to hurt, 'then we'll have to close.'

Chapter 34

The following morning, the bell rings.

'I have your baguette, Madame,' I say, coming out of the kitchen holding a freshly baked, warm loaf. But I stop. It's not the woman I was expecting. It's another I recognise from the vending-machine queue.

'Madame?' I say tentatively.

'I could smell the ovens from outside when I was waiting,' she says, referring to the vending machine. 'It's like when I was a child and my mother would send me for bread. I would wait in the queue here. Talk to friends. It was a treat to be sent out to see people and to walk home eating the end of the bread before I got there.'

'Come in,' I say. 'Take a seat. It's warm out there this morning. A hot night. Would you like some water, a coffee maybe?'

'That would be lovely. And maybe . . . a baguette?'

'Of course.' I bring her a coffee and put down a baguette with the butter and jam from earlier.

She breaks some off the end of the baguette, and as I hear it crack, I smile with satisfaction. That crack tells me everything I need to know and have come to learn since I've been here. Her eyes close as she bites into the bread, then lets it sit in her mouth just for a moment before chewing and swallowing. 'It is perfect,' she says, then whispers, 'I saw Charlotte out of her apartment the other day. Is she quite well?'

'I'm more than well,' says Madame B, appearing from the back room and standing with a smile on her face, in the doorway behind the counter. 'I am happy. Back where I belong.'

The woman stares open-mouthed when the bell over the door sounds and we turn to see Gilles' wife.

'Gabrielle!'

'Thérése!'

They gawp at each other.

'I just thought . . .'

'I didn't know . . .'

'Can I get you some coffee?' I say to Thérése.

'Join me,' says Gabrielle, already sitting at the table.

'Well, why not? Gilles will still be snoring and won't notice if I'm not home for a bit.'

'Nor Hubert. But he'll wake when he smells the coffee and this bread.'

I make more coffee when the bell over the door rings again.

'Béatrice!'

The three women look at each other, startled, then laugh.

I bring out a third cup, and they share the baguette on the table with coffee and stories of the *boulangerie* and the mill in their younger days. They talk of picnics on the lakeside, first dates and kisses, broken hearts and tears, illicit bottles of wine and new flirtations. They laugh and laugh, and the *boulangerie* is not only filled with the smell of freshly baking bread, but the sound of nostalgia and joy too.

'You must keep going. Don't let anyone stop you!' says Thérése, peering out onto the square as if searching for signs of trouble.

'*Non*, be strong. Now, I should be getting back before anyone sees me. Keep a baguette for me tomorrow,' says Gabrielle. 'This is for the baguette and the *café*.' She gives me some money.

'And me, see you tomorrow,' says the third of the ladies. '*Merci*. You have brought joy back to the village,' she says, and tears spring to my eyes. 'Please keep going. Everyone should taste this bread. It is the work of a master baker. *Merci*, Charlotte,' she calls, over my shoulder.

Madame B smiles, having reapplied her lipstick.

The three women open the door, and slide silently out into the warm morning, pulling light headscarves over their neatly kept hair as they set off in different directions. Their baguettes are hidden under a shawl, in a large shopping bag and up the sleeve of a raincoat – which in itself is fairly conspicuous, given the warm morning, heralding a hot day.

Madame B is smiling at me.

I know what she's thinking. 'But this still isn't enough to cover the rent on this place. We need to sell more to stay open.'

'Well,' she says slowly, 'if the customers aren't coming

to us, you need to take the bread to the customers.' I wasn't expecting that.

I stare out onto the square as Claude's van arrives to fill the vending machine with baguettes. He closes it, looks at the *boulangerie* and smirks, as if seeing me hiding behind the net curtain. 'Madame B?'

'Juliet,' she says.

I'm thinking, possibly out loud. 'Where is the nearest market today?'

'It's in the next village. In the opposite direction to Claude's bakery. He has a machine there too. The weather is good. There will be lots of holidaymakers.'

Without any real thought other than to wipe the smirk off Claude's face, I pick up the basket of baguettes and swing out of the shop.

'Wait!' she says.

I turn back.

'Where are you going?'

'To take the bread to the people, like you said. I'm going to market. I'm not going to let him win.'

She grins. '*Bon courage! Bon profitez!* Oh, and, Juliet?'

'Oui, Madame? Sorry, I should have said *au revoir* . . .' I remember my etiquette.

She smiles again. 'I think you must call me Charlotte now. After all, we are friends.'

'*Au revoir, Charlotte,*' I say, feeling more than a little touched.

I walk towards my dusty little car, waving to Laurent as I pass the *tabac*, my basket full of baguettes and hope.

Chapter 35

'How was it?'

Madame B is in the bakery, leaning on the broom, brushing her white hair off her face with her forearm. It is covered with flour, which is now spread across her forehead. She is beaming.

'Lots of tourists browsing. Not buying much. And all the locals were already walking around with their baguettes from the machine,' I say, sitting down heavily on the chair at the table in the window. I help myself to water from the jug and the little stack of glasses I placed there this morning for the women buying their early-morning baguettes and staying for coffee. 'I mean, who is going to buy bread from the British woman in the Fiat Panda?'

I'd tried offering samples but got the same answer from everyone: '*Non*.' And sometimes a '*Non, merci*' as they hurried past me to the vending machine.

'If we can get the locals on board, we will have to start baking a second batch in the afternoon for *le dîner*, when word gets around,' says Madame B, clearly ignoring the fact that I haven't sold anything this morning.

Through the clean white net curtains hanging halfway across the front window, I see Claude's van pull up at the vending machine, ready to fill it with baguettes for lunchtime. I slide lower in my seat, hoping he won't see me, and praying he won't come in. I don't want to face him until I'm making a go of this place.

'Laurent was asking where you were when he came in for his baguette. He says he'll be at the mill to make more flour this weekend.'

I feel a flutter of excitement. A weekend with Laurent at the mill . . . My thoughts turn to the picnics we'll share on the lawn, reminding me to cut the grass. I stand and take my glass to the kitchen. Madame B is finishing the tidying.

The bell tinkles. I finish washing my glass and wipe down the draining board, then hurry out as I'm drying my hands on a tea-towel.

'Sorry, *je m'excuse*, how can I help?' I stop in my tracks. There, standing in the doorway, is Claude's wife. The woman I met at his bakery, the one who sold me the stale croissant. A way of warning me off. I feel myself go cold.

She stares at me with her hooded eyes. 'I am Vivianne, Claude's wife.'

I forget all etiquette, totally at a loss in situations like this. 'I know.' My cheeks are burning, as if I've been slapped. I don't know what to say. If I didn't know better, I'd say even my eyeballs were sweating.

'Look I'm sorry,' I attempt to say. 'I didn't kno—'

She cuts across me crisply. 'I know that you and my husband kissed. He says you were chasing him.'

I feel sick. Like a silly girl, rather than the mature woman I am. What was I doing, thinking I was having some sort of Shirley Valentine moment? I left the UK to just be me, to be Juliet. To be seen. Now, I was anything but that . . .

'Please, I can only apologise, but it wasn't like that. For a start, I didn't know he was married. I was flattered by the attention at first . . . And he kissed me. It certainly wasn't the other way round. And then he told me he was married and I told him to leave. I actually can't stand him. I'm sure you find him . . .' I swallow.

I'm making a pig's ear of this. I've never been in this situation. Not even when I was younger. I met Pete and we were never apart from then.

Suddenly I feel very foolish for thinking I could do this on my own. I've made an idiot of myself and now a woman is standing in front of me, as if we're in a spaghetti western, guns drawn, but I have no desire to fight over her man. Neither do I know what she's likely to do now. What I do know is that I don't want anyone else to find out about this.

'Please, I really didn't . . . It's so out of character for me.'

She holds up a hand. 'No, it's me who's here to apologise. The croissant I gave you was stale. I knew it was. I didn't want you to have a fresh one. I didn't want you to stay. I knew he would find you attractive. You're his type. I wanted you not to feel welcome. I wanted to believe it was you making a move on him and not the other way round. But I knew that really it wasn't the case. I'm sorry.'

'What? You can't apologise for your husband's behaviour! And the croissant – honestly, forget it.'

'No, I'm apologising for me. I should have left him a long time ago. I've come to thank you. I knew when he said you were . . . chasing him, it was all him. It always is. He was doing it again. But you being here, staying and confronting him, has made me realize, I need to stand up to him. I shouldn't stay a moment longer. I'm leaving him. Finally. I have run the shop for him, filled the vending machines when he is too lazy or busy elsewhere to do it. And, above all, I have believed his lies and ignored his affairs.'

'Really, it wasn't an affair!'

'But others were.'

I shake my head. 'So he does this a lot?'

She nods. 'And I always ignore. The most I can do is give out stale croissants! And even then, the majority of people would have complained and I'd've exchanged them. I knew when you didn't say anything that you would be an easy target for him.'

I cough, my mouth dry with embarrassment.

'He says other women want him and I am lucky. He relishes telling me how attractive other women find him.' She looks around the shop. 'I expect he thought you wouldn't still be here by now.'

'Well, I . . .' I take a deep breath, enraged. 'I may have been foolish then, but I have since discovered what matters, and I mean to make sure he knows I'm not going anywhere.'

'I am pleased,' says Vivianne. 'He needs some good competition.'

'But where will you go?' I ask.

'To my sister. She will be happy to see me. She has been telling me to leave him for a long time.' She gives the tiniest hint of a smile, and seems to straighten a little. There is a glint of light in her eyes. 'It is a new beginning.'

'Stay strong,' I tell her.

'*Bonne chance*,' she says, as she turns to leave. 'By the way, I reset his alarm clock before I left. He will struggle to do everything and get to market tomorrow morning.'

She gives a small, satisfied smile.

And I have just been given the information I need to beat Claude at his own game.

'Oh, I nearly forgot.' She turns back to me, looking lighter than when she arrived, and passes me a paper bag. 'Fresh croissants. I'm sorry again about the other one.'

'*Merci*. And good luck,' I say.

Chapter 36

'You sold out!' says Madame B, as I present her with the empty basket when I return to the *boulangerie* the next day at lunchtime. She proffers a glass of water.

I'm hot and exhausted, but on top of the world. I hand over my bag, weighed down with euro coins. 'Vivianne was right. There were no baguettes in the vending machine this morning. The locals weren't happy, but I gave samples to everyone waiting. The women were hesitant at first, but when I explained that the mill and *boulangerie* are working again and using traditional ingredients, one lady at the front tried a piece and the rest followed. I'd sold out by the time Claude was pulling up in his van.'

Madame B giggles. 'I bet he wasn't happy when he turned up and you'd managed to tempt his customers away.'

'I didn't stick around to find out!' I say, although I can only imagine the expression on Claude's face when he went to restock the vending machine and didn't find the queue that would usually be waiting there . . .

The following morning, I take the same route, having worked out which way Claude does his round. I drive to the next town from yesterday's, managing to beat him there. Again, a small queue is waiting for the vending machine to be filled. I offer the samples and, with no sign of Claude, they buy their bread from me.

On the third morning, I'm smiling as I pull up in another village with a vending machine, skipping the two I've visited over the past couple of days, and offer samples. I sell out in no time, handing round the cards I've written to let people know where we are, but promising I'll be back next week at their local market. I wish I could find a way of making more regular visits. My last customer takes the final two baguettes, and as she hands me her money, I hear beeping behind me. It's Claude, trying to move his van into the market square.

I give the woman some change and a business card, then quickly bid her good day. The coins land in her hand safely, and I disappear into the market throng. But as I do, the card flutters from my customer's full hands and catches on the wind, which whips it up, then lets it fall. I put my head down and carry on into the growing crowds of the market. I snatch a glance back and see Claude pick up the card and read it. I hurry to my car and get on the road home, my heart thumping.

At lunchtime, I'm with Laurent, at the *tabac*. Madame B has made extra loaves for me to fill for people wanting sandwiches, walkers mostly. Clearly word has got around and there's an appetite for them, along with the mini Victoria sponges and chocolate and beetroot brownies I've made. The soft, gooey chocolate squares, with extra richness from the beetroot, are sprinkled with icing sugar and seem to be going down a treat with my three taste-testers at the bar, already armed with their baguettes to take home for lunch.

'You'll need extra help at the *boulangerie* at this rate,' says Laurent.

'Maybe I will,' I reply.

'And you'll be able to prove your income to get your visa!'

With the deadline looming, in under two weeks, I may be able to do it.

The next morning, I'm up and ready to drive to one of the small villages. I know, if I leave early enough, I should get there ahead of Claude. Once the loaves are out of the oven, I load them into my basket and I'm off, out of the village and down to the main road. It's warm already, and there are plenty of bees in the hedgerows bordering the narrow country lane.

I'm concentrating hard, counting up the number of baguettes I need to sell over the next fortnight, to prove my profits to the mayor, when I hear a car travelling up quickly behind me. Too quickly, I think. There's a blind corner coming up. I move out into the road, just enough to ensure the idiot driver doesn't try to overtake me on the bend.

I hear the engine revving, then the familiar beeping,

and know exactly who it is. My jaw tightens and my foot pushes a little harder to the floor. I see him edging closer to me in my rear-view mirror, as is the bend in the road. Claude's edging out as if to overtake, and I move over to stop him. The village is just around the corner. There is a chance I could still make it there first, if I can get the baguettes out quicker than he can empty and reload the vending machine.

Suddenly he swings out ahead of an oncoming car, then back onto my side of the road, cutting right in front of me. I have to swerve violently, straight into the ditch, with a bump, bump, bump and a thump as the front end of my car slams into the ground. I catapult forward, then back – shocked, but saved by my seatbelt – followed by a shower of baguettes from the back seat.

My heart hammers. I sit there for a moment, working out if I'm injured, as the van speeds off in a cloud of exhaust fumes. I take a deep breath. I'm not hurt – my pride is wounded more than anything else. I push open the car door and climb out, staring at the white van disappearing into the distance. Frustration and fury bubble inside me. I reach back into the car and gather up the baguettes, straightening some and placing them back in the basket. Only a couple are bent and broken. I still have plenty to sell, except it's too late – Claude will have beaten me to the market and probably told the waiting queue that I won't be coming today. I look at my dented bumper and wonder how to reverse out of the ditch, with thorns and prickles scratching and stinging my ankles.

My phone pings with a message. There are two.

One is from Pete, asking how things are.

The other is from Annie's husband, telling me she's received all my messages, and he's been reading them to her. She's too weak to reply just now, but is loving hearing all about my adventure. He thanks me for providing them with a little escape from what's going on.

Angry tears fill my eyes. I get back in the car, grab the ignition key and try starting the engine, hitting the accelerator with force. It roars into life. I shove the gearstick into reverse, but the wheels spin, showering dust from the ditch. I try again, harder, but they spin until the engine splutters and cuts out.

'Damn!' I say angrily, getting out of the car and slamming the door, fuelled by frustration and fury as I process Annie's news. I hear a tractor coming down the lane and it stops beside me. It's Hubert, one of the *tabac*'s regular customers.

'*Bonjour, Madame.*'

'*Bonjour, Monsieur.*' I manage to hang on to my manners even in times of trouble, I think, and smile to myself. 'What are you doing here?'

'Helping my brother-in-law with some farm work,' You have a problem?' he asks, in stilted English.

'You could say that. Claude ran me off the road. He doesn't want me to sell at the market today . . . or any other day,' I explain, my voice more high-pitched, almost hysterical, because this is all madness. 'I had to get there before him, to sell my bread, but he'll beat me now, so I may as well go home.'

Hubert looks at me. 'Maybe he has beaten you to the next town,' he nods straight ahead, 'but not to the one after that. They have a market today too. Claude will be going there afterwards.' He grins. 'We can beat him!'

I laugh, and shake my head. 'No, my car is stuck.'

'We will come back for the car and tow it. First, we will take the tractor,' he says, tapping the steering wheel. 'How do you say? Across the country! He won't beat us then. You have bread to sell. We need you in our village. I need your bread . . . and your Sandwich of Victoria!'

I laugh, but little tears well in my eyes and I'm not sure if they're for me, Annie or his kindness. A feeling of belonging has come over me like I've never experienced before.

'Come,' he says, offering a hand to me.

I can't quite believe I'm doing this, but I hold up the basket of bread, which he takes from me. Then he puts out his hand again and hauls me into the cab to sit beside him. Cross-country it is!

'*Prêt?*' he asks.

I'm not ready for any of this, but I'll be messaging Annie all about it when I get back.

'Why not?' I say, laughing. '*Pourquoi pas?* I'm ready.'

And with that, we're bumping across the fields to the next town but one, where there is a queue by the vending machine. Hubert gets down from his tractor cab and explains to those waiting that this is the bread being sold today and he can personally recommend it, along with all his neighbours in the village where it comes from. It's made with the flour from the old mill there, he tells them, by a baker who has come out of retirement to give the village its soul back.

The baguettes are sold in minutes and the queue disappears.

We're laughing as we set off for home, passing a bemused Claude, who had just arrived in the square to find his regular customers leaving with their baguettes in hand. But these baguettes bear the signature of a different baker from him. These baguettes are made with love by Madame B.

Back at the village, I gather along with Laurent, Hubert, Gilles and Eric, Béatrice's husband, at the *tabac*. Madame B and Bibi come to join us, too. She has made more bread and I explain how Hubert came to my rescue as we hand round freshly baked, filled baguettes, *jambon-beurre* and *tomate et Camembert*.

Laurent fills a carafe with wine and puts it on the bar. Everyone takes a glass and raises it to '*le baguette*'. And when we've explained our escapade and laughed all over again, everyone leaves for home. Madame B tells me she has an old bicycle that she will get out for me to use while my car is being fixed.

'*Merci, Hubert*,' I say.

'*De rien*,' he says. 'And now you will stay open, yes?'

'Well,' I wince, 'I don't have a car right now . . .' *Or the money to fix it.* 'Or a tractor to borrow every day.' I try to laugh. 'And I'm not sure Madame B's bicycle is enough.' I'm making light of the situation, but inside I'm devastated. If I could just have kept going until the end of the month . . .

He nods slowly. 'I understand,' he says, and glances at Gilles, who does the same.

We clear away the remnants of lunch and I head back to the mill with the last of the day's bread. With a wave to the fisherwomen, I stand outside. It's raining, a summer shower.

I throw large pieces of bread into the lake, ripping up the baguettes. Tears trickle down my cheeks, mixing with the rain.

The ducks land and paddle happily, scooping up the bread. I have no idea if they should be eating it or not. I break off another piece and then, in frustration, just throw half of the baguette into the water, narrowly missing a duck that squawks and flaps its wings in indignation.

'I don't know what you do in your country, but around here we tend not to throw missiles at the wildlife.'

I whirl around and see Laurent.

I attempt to brush away the tears and can't help but laugh at little. 'Sorry, I wasn't, I mean . . .'

'I came to see if you were okay.'

I take a deep breath. 'I've realised this has all been a mistake. The mill, I mean. I'm never going to be able to make this business work, and I should sell it to you. It's yours if you want it.'

He sighs. 'I'm afraid that may not be possible.'

'Why not?'

'I'm not in a position to buy right now.'

'Really?'

He nods. 'I had other ways I needed to spend my savings. Sorry.' And with that he walks away, clearly as upset as I am.

I'm done.

Chapter 37

There is knocking on the front door, rousing me from my deep sleep.

'*Oui, j'arrive,*' I say, realising I'm automatically speaking French now and will have to change to English when I'm back home. Home . . . Where is home? Where will I stay?

I messaged Pete when I got back to the mill, letting him know that I was unlikely to get my visa to stay on, so would be making plans to come back. Pete replied, *Are you sure? Isn't there any way for you to stay?* Which took me by surprise.

I wish there was, I typed, making it clear my heart is still very much here.

Let me know if I can do anything to help, he said, and I realised he's not waiting for me to come home. We've both had a taste of a different way of life, one without the other in it, and we're happy.

Bang, bang, bang comes the knocking, and I stumble from bed, where I've been napping, down the wooden steps and through the main room to pull open the door.

It's Madame B.

'*Bon après-midi*,' she says. 'Come, we have somewhere we need to be.' She puts out her cigarette on the ground with a flourish of her foot, then picks up the stub.

I get my bag and close the door behind me. 'Where are we going? What's going on? Is it the *boulangerie*?'

'You'll see,' she says, walking beside me in smart red shoes with gold buckles, matching her trademark red nails. The ends of her short silk scarf catch in the wind. Bibi trots along beside her, taking in the smells, clearly enjoying the change from being in the apartment all day.

We arrive in the square after our short walk, and there, outside the *boulangerie*, is an old bicycle, propped against the window. My spirits dip. As kind as it is of her, the bicycle won't help me do bread rounds big enough for whole towns. Then I hear jovial voices and laughter. Beside the *tabac* there is a building with two garage doors, a fading sign over one, indicating it was once a car mechanic's workshop. There, in front of the dark blue, worn wooden doors, stand Gilles, Hubert and Eric, beaming.

'What's going on?' I ask.

'You'll see,' says Madame B, reverting to her usual clipped tones and lighting another cigarette. I look back at the *boulangerie* to where my car is parked in front of it, dented at the front. They must have towed it back for me while I was napping. It's so good of them. I should have gone with them.

'That is really kind, *merci*,' I say.

'No, that is not it.' Madame B turns back towards the big wooden doors of the garage.

'*Allez!*' Madame B commands, waving a red talon.

The three men step forward and start to pull back the dusty wooden doors, their paint peeling, under the faded sign. As they do, I sense Laurent has come to stand behind me. I can feel him without having to turn. I wish I didn't, but I do. I can smell him, coffee and sunshine – a scent I am coming to find familiar and comforting mixed with that of the mill when the grain has been freshly ground.

'Come on, put your backs into it,' he jokes in French, and rests a hand on my shoulder. My nerve ends stand to attention and my stomach feels as if the kingfishers are darting from one side of it to the other. But the doors are stiff and Laurent skirts around me to help. They eventually pull back, and the men stand and smile. I have no idea what we're looking at. It's a deep building, with tools on a bench down one side, beams overhead.

Gilles walks in and my eyes adjust to the darkness within as he starts pulling at a tarpaulin. The other men go to help. I step forward, curious as to what they're doing and baffled as to why I'm here to witness it.

Finally, the tarpaulin is released and comes away, landing in a pile on the concrete floor, and there, staring back at me, are two big round eyes. Well, they look like eyes, but they're actually headlights – round headlights on the front of an old van. It almost looks as if it has a personality of its own.

There are suddenly raised voices as Gilles shouts enthusiastically that he has found the key. He climbs into the driver's seat and takes hold of the wheel, puts the key into the ignition and turns it. There is a murmur of life and the men cheer. I have no idea why I'm here, but their excitement is infectious. Gilles tries the engine again. It murmurs and dies.

Then, with lots of shouting to each other and help from Laurent, they push the van out of the garage, into the sunlight and onto the forecourt.

'*Allez, allez,*' calls Gilles, and instinctively we get behind the cream van and help to push it down the little hill.

'*Allez, allez,*' we call, as the van rumbles down the gentle incline in the road. We stand back and watch her go. As she nears the end and turns left towards the old mill, she belches into life, and everyone cheers.

We wait under the plane trees in the square, wondering if Gilles is going to return.

'Well, I'd better be getting back,' I say to Madame B.

'What? No, you cannot go yet.'

'I'm not sure they need me to help.'

'Gilles was a mechanic. He'll get it going, you'll see.' She's smiling.

'That's great. But I need to start making plans. Next week, I'm meeting the mayor and I won't have been able to do what I said I could. I'll have to leave France.'

'But Gilles is doing this for you – so you can stay.'

'For me?'

'Yes. Instead of your little car. When I asked Gilles to open the old garage to get my bicycle out where I had stored it, he remembered the van. It's been mouldering in there for years, ever since he closed the business. He'll get it going again and you can take the bread to the markets.'

'What?' My jaw drops. 'A bakery van?'

'Yes, exactly. A bakery van. I will bake and you will take the bread out to the markets. The people will much prefer to buy from a bakery van than a vending machine! It's what they were used to.' She beams.

'But . . . why would he?'

'He says the bread has changed his home life. Life in the village. It is a thank-you. Everyone wants to help. And . . .' She raises an eyebrow, and a small smile tugs at the corner of her painted lips '. . . let's just say he always had a soft spot for me. He is happy to see me out of the apartment.' And then, more seriously, 'Not that I would ever feel the same way. Just don't tell his wife.' Her face softens and glows. 'He asked her to marry him after I turned him down. There was never anyone for me except Raoul, even if it was all in my head.'

'And in your heart,' I tell her. 'You loved him. He just wasn't in a position to love you back.'

There is a rumble and a crunch of gears, and Gilles appears from the corner at the top of the village, clearly having done a loop around it. The cheers gather as he pulls up in front of the garage next to the *tabac*. He climbs out and walks over to me, grinning. 'We'll get her ready for the road, don't worry. You'll have wheels. It may take a day or so, but she'll be fixed.'

'Really?' I stare at him, then at the vintage Citroën van, and feel as if I've fallen in love. 'She's beautiful,' I say.

I walk slowly around the van and can't help but put out my hand and run it over her cream, corrugated sides. She needs a good clean, and she has some marks on the bodywork, but nothing major. 'She's beautiful,' I repeat.

'She?' Laurent laughs.

'She's definitely a she!' I look at her dents and scuffs.

'She's a little battle-scarred,' he says.

'Aren't we all?' I say quietly.

'But still beautiful,' he adds. I turn back to face him and feel a rush of affection for this man.

'She will help us get the bread out there,' says Madame B.

'But how can I pay for her? I need every euro right now.'

'It was owned by a local man, delivering groceries around the villages. But he died. His wife left the van here in return for his garage bills. It is good to see it being used!' says Laurent quickly.

There's a bit of dust and mould inside, but nothing that stops me seeing what a beautiful little van this is, with its drop-down hatch on the side. And I can see it now, covered with bunting and baskets of baguettes on the counter. 'She's perfect!' I say. 'Thank you! I'd better get cleaning!' I beam. 'And *merci*, Gilles,' I say, as I step forward and hug him – not what he was expecting, but he chuckles and pats my back.

We all spring into action. The three men lift the bonnet and start checking the oil. I go to the *boulangerie* and fill a washing-up bowl with soapy water. We spend the rest of the afternoon, the evening and the following day getting the van spruced up. While the three men and Laurent work under the bonnet, Madame B, the three wives and I scrub with long-handled brooms and mops until she is gleaming and ready for her big day out.

Chapter 38

The next day, I'm as excited as a child on Christmas morning. I hurriedly get dressed in a light cotton jumpsuit, and instead of putting my scarf around my neck, like Madame B does, I tie it around my head to keep my hair off my face. I may not look French, but I feel more like me than I ever have. I walk quickly through the darkness before dawn, the moon lighting my way to the bakery where the orange glow spills out, letting me know that Madame B is up and the ovens are on.

Outside the *tabac*, on the old garage forecourt, I can see the bakery van. I've named her Dolly after Dolly Parton, who always wears her heart on her sleeve, a bit like my van with her touched-up scuffs and bumps. She's loud, fun and is going to bring lots of joy. It suits her. I stop to run my hand over her bonnet and pat her, then head to the *boulangerie*.

But at the door, I see another baguette on the front step, laid upside down. I know it's not a good sign.

I pick it up and go into the shop. This time I know exactly what to do to ward off any evil threats. I score a cross in the back of the bread, then open the door and toss it to the crows waiting on the square.

I'm not being scared off, no way. I have a bakery van to get ready.

Once the baguettes have been loaded into the van, I start the engine just as dawn begins to break, to a cheer from Madame B. Then, with a toot of the horn, I drive to the neighbouring town.

The women look at me warily as they arrive at the vending machine. I pull the side hatch down quickly and smile to encourage them, but the more I do, the more they seem to back off or walk away.

I take a piece from the plate of cut-up bread I've put out, and walk towards a small dog lying in the morning sunshine. I sit on a bench in the square, looking up at the church. I have no idea how to connect with these women. How can I be myself if they won't even engage with me?

I start to eat the bit of baguette, tossing a little to the pigeons. The little dog approaches and I give him a small piece too.

'Madame!' I hear a sharp voice behind me.

'*Désolée*,' I say automatically, assuming I'm in trouble for feeding the dog, or the pigeons, or both. 'I'll go!'

'*Une baguette, s'il vous plait*,' says a woman, holding a half-eaten sample. Another woman has the plate and is passing it around.

'It's like we used to get from the mill,' another is saying.

'Its own unique taste.'

'I remember it well.'

'I will take two,' says another woman.

I don't need asking twice. I hurry back into the van and take their money, thanking them, and handing over baguettes. The line of curious women grows and in no time I'm out of bread, shutting down the hatch and heading for home. It seems curiosity got the better of them. I just needed to let them find their way to our bread in their own time.

The next morning, Madame B and I bake twice as much in the hope I can make it to two towns, and again, in no time at all, the bread is sold out. The vending machines are ignored. That afternoon, I plan which markets I can get to the following day to sell baguettes to those who would rather buy from the bakery van than a vending machine.

When I return to the *boulangerie* with an empty basket, I know what I have to do. I must make my appointment with the mayor. I add up the takings, deducting costs, rent and very minimal wages. And we've done it, by the skin of our teeth. The bakery van has brought us in all the business we needed this week, and I can proudly say I'm making a profit. Okay, we need to start paying ourselves properly soon, but this month we have made money. And I cannot wait to show the mayor.

'I'm taking Bibi out the back for a *pi-pi*,' says Madame B.

'No problem,' I say. 'I'll go to the bank when you're back. And then I'll make an appointment at the mayor's office for next week to show our profits and agree my visa.' I beam, and skip into the kitchen to finish clearing up.

The bell over the door rings.

'*J'arrive!*' I call happily and hurry into the shop, where I stop, suddenly feeling cold.

Chapter 39

'So,' Claude says, walking around the shop, as if inspecting it for signs of dust or things out of place, 'you have decided to take on one of the biggest baking families around here,' he says scornfully, 'with your pathetic little bakery van.'

'I know it was you who left the baguette, Claude.' My heart is thundering. 'You might have scared others off, but it won't work with me. The villagers like having a *boulangerie* back.'

'They might tell you that, but they won't change from my bread. They might like to try what's on offer, but it won't be better than they're used to.' He raises an eyebrow. 'In fact, it's probably quite a let-down,' he says, in a loaded way.

I pull myself up tall. 'Our bread is far superior to yours. People are letting you know that. They are buying our bread. It is made with quality ingredients, not cheap ones to give the biggest profit. This is proper artisan bread. There is a place for the *boulangerie* in the village and for the van in villages where the *boulangeries* have gone. They like having the van arriving rather than queuing at a soulless vending machine.'

'For now. But,' he shrugs, 'who will take it on when you have to leave? No one wants to.'

For a moment I'm not so sure-footed.

He walks through the shop and I feel as if he's infecting its gloriously warm welcoming ambience with his insidious, poisonous air.

He is by the end of the old wooden counter now, by the old-fashioned till. He leans on the return of the counter. 'I'm here to tell you there isn't room for both of us and you will be leaving. I'm not sure if you play by different rules back home, but here in France, if you steal something from someone, you have to pay them back. You are stealing my customers. And so you will have to pay.'

'Don't be ridiculous!'

He presses down on the till button and the drawer pings open. 'Why don't we start with today's takings? Looks like it's been a good day!'

'No, you can't. I need that money!'

He holds his leather satchel open, looks at me and starts to fill it with coins and notes. 'It's money you took from me.'

'I didn't take your money!'

'You took custom that belonged to me. If I took all your baguettes, that would be stealing, wouldn't it? I would owe you money. It is only right.'

I look for some way out of this, wishing Madame B will reappear.

I try to slam the till drawer shut, hoping to catch his fingers. But he grabs it and empties it.

'*Merci.*'

'It is a shame. We could have done good business together. I could have taught you a lot,' he says, leaning in. I can smell yesterday's garlic and wine on today's cigarette breath, making me want to gag. I can't move.

'I will go to the *gendarmes*,' I tell him.

'Yes. You could, but I wouldn't bother. I am a local businessman, and we go back a long way – they'll never believe your word over mine. And if you were to take your chances and find out, I could always tell your new love interest that you and I shared a passionate kiss. That you wanted me, were begging me to become your lover.'

'That's not true.'

'We kissed, did we not?'

I feel frozen to the spot. He's blackmailing me. He'd tell Laurent the one thing that will hurt him most: that another member of his family has taken what they want without a care for others. I'm furious with myself.

Suddenly the door opens and the bell rings. Claude turns to see Laurent standing there.

'Claude,' he states, rather than asks.

'Laurent! *Bonjour*,' he says, turning away from the counter and me. I let myself breathe.

'Were you just leaving?'

'Yes. Thank you. *Merci* . . . Julie?'

'Juliet,' I say, through gritted teeth.

He looks at me, then at Laurent. 'Lovely to see two people so happy in each other's company,' he says with a sickly smile. 'I hope nothing comes in the path of such a blossoming friendship.' He smirks and Laurent narrows his eyes as my mouth goes dry.

'Well, thanks for popping in, Claude,' I say, my fight reignited. 'I'm sure we'll work things out.' I'm not sure if I'm referring to him and me, or Laurent and me. 'Plenty of room for us all here, I'm sure. See you at the market.' I skirt around him and hold the door open, the bell tinkling.

He leaves, slowly, still smirking. His snake eyes mirror how they looked on that regrettable day. I was desperate to find myself but, instead, I found someone I didn't like – in him, and in me. I want him out of the bakery, because it's here I've finally found my happy place. Being here, with Madame B, in the early-morning glow of the lights and the hum of the ovens. In the smell of the bread as it starts to bake. The arrival of our first customers. The coffee and the greeting ritual, the chatter from the women, meeting and buying their bread, gathering around the table.

I've found my purpose. I look at Laurent. But I know Claude is right. I can't get close to this man. I can't – not after what I've done, with the one man he hates, whose grandfather nearly destroyed his family for good. I can't ever let him know that I nearly made the same dreadful mistake, almost choosing the wrong man. But I can still enjoy his company, share his love of producing flour at the mill, and the bread we make with it. A mutual pride and passion, which includes the friendship I've made with Madame B. Like leaving the dough to prove over-night, good things take time and judgement. They take *savoir faire*.

And Claude may have taken today's money – which I needed in my bank account to show the mayor I was in profit – but I'm not done yet. I'll do everything to stop that man running me out of town.

Madame B comes back into the shop with Bibi on a lead.

'I'll take all the baguettes we've got left, and then as many as you can bake while I'm out. I'm going to get to as many villages as I can, visit farms and hamlets, see if they'd like bread brought to them. It could be a regular thing.'

She nods and gets to work.

'Do you need a hand?' asks Laurent. 'You look like you're on a mission.'

I smile. 'That would be very kind. And, yes, I am.'

With twice as many pairs of hands, we sell twice as much bread. We arrive in small hamlets with a toot of the horn, dropping down Dolly's hatch and selling to the queue that quickly forms when they hear we've arrived. Then we move on to the next village, where people are getting to know us and ignoring the vending machine.

We even return to the bakery and load up again, making afternoon visits to other villages, pulling up in the squares, selling to people who are keen to know the story of the mill coming back to life and quick to grab their purses to buy from us. We hear people say they hope we'll be back soon as we drive away.

Laurent and I work around each other in the small, intimate space of Dolly, with jokes and laughter, smiling at the customers who are sharing their appreciation for the bread, talking with each other and catching up on news. Getting daily bread is so much more than coming home with a baguette from the vending machine.

'Are you sure the *tabac* isn't missing you?' I ask Laurent, on his third day out with me.

He laughs. 'Have you seen how many customers I don't have?'

The following morning, the village women are in to buy baguettes as we load the bakery van. By the time we return to the *boulangerie*, the netting in the front window has been pulled to the side – there are no more secrets. Those three women are enjoying their coffee and a catch-up as their husbands do the same on the other side of the glass outside.

Laurent and I soon get in a routine with Dolly. As we pull up in the next hamlet, Laurent engages the hand-brake and I open the side hatch, straightening the bunting that catches and flutters on the breeze. By the time I've done that, he's in the van, ready to serve customers, and we work comfortably, side by side, feeling the excitement of the sales, and each other's presence. Our bodies are close enough that can smell his cologne, and I smile at the frequency with which we catch each other's eye. We share satisfaction at the sight of the sidelined vending machines, full of unsold bread. The only cloud on the horizon is Claude, who sometimes pulls up at the vending machines, next to the bakery van. He's not happy, not happy at all.

I have just days left to show the mayor I'm making a profit before I can start to believe that I may be here for good.

Chapter 40

I'm preparing to close the *boulangerie* at the end of the day and it's really hot. The air feels thick and heavy, and I have the day's takings in my bag, slung across my shoulder.

'Now, go home and change. It's the village dinner this evening and I'm taking you as my guest,' Laurent says firmly. 'You could do with a night to enjoy yourself. Everyone will be there and you're part of this village now. They're expecting you. We can celebrate your profits!'

'But what about Aimée, from the *mairie*? Won't she be hoping you'll take her?'

He shakes his head. 'Despite what you might have heard, I am not someone who wants a fling, a relationship because it is convenient. Aimée knows that. Besides, she and Claude were in a relationship for a long time. She is a very bad judge of character.'

'While he was married?'

He nods. 'When I find someone I want to be with, I

will give my whole heart. I firmly believe that if you find the right person, you feel seen every day.'

He looks at me and our fingertips touch. I shiver with the passion of his words and the ridiculous hope that maybe that person could be me. To feel like this, to feel really seen by one person, the right person . . . like no one else can see us at all.

'*Alors* . . .' says Madame B, coming out of the kitchen, pulling off her apron and pushing her fingers through her soft quiff. 'Time to change. Then time to raise a glass to the *boulangerie*'s success. I have the bread ready for the meal. Oh, and I've been trying out some other loaves. Next week we can start offering different types of bread as well as the baguette.'

Laurent and I turn to her. She is oblivious to the moment that has just passed between us. We give each other a shy smile and I wish we could talk more.

'Come on, let's celebrate,' he says, opening the *boulangerie* door and ushering us out with Bibi.

I'm on cloud nine. Happier than I've felt in a very long time. Laurent's right; it's time to celebrate. It's been a really good week in the bread van. The money has been banked and I'm ready to meet the mayor.

'Okay. I'll go back and change. Meet you back here,' I tell him. 'Give me twenty minutes.' It's all I can do not to lean in and kiss him. But I don't, despite the slow burn building inside me.

The dough is ready for the morning and I've even made more mini Victoria Sandwich cakes to take on the van tomorrow. I have plans for the front window of the *boulangerie* now that the netting is down, and dressing the table with some flowers. Everything is ready. *Mise en place*. Madame B has worked so hard to keep up with my plans. And I am a little worried that she must be exhausted.

As I leave the bakery, I take in the tables under the plane trees that have been laid with plates, glasses, water jugs and cutlery. The corners of their cloths flick up and flap in the warm wind. Smartly dressed villagers are already arriving in the square. I spot Gilles with his wife. He's carrying a covered dish and a bottle of wine, and she smiles as they greet Hubert and Gabrielle, then Eric and Béatrice. Madame B's bike is parked in front of the *boulangerie*, and someone has put a red geranium in its basket. I think it looks very in keeping and should stay there. I turn towards the bakery van and see a figure standing beside it in the shadows. It takes me a moment to recognise who it is. But then I see it's Claude's wife, Vivianne. She looks anxious.

'*Bonjour, Madame*. Is everything okay with you?'

She is holding her hands together, wringing them. 'It's Claude,' she says, worry etched on her face. 'He's gone to the mill. He . . .' she swallows hard '. . . he means to do damage.'

'To the mill?'

She nods. Tears are pricking her eyes.

'I went back to the house to pick up my belongings. He is consumed with fury. He never believed I would leave and thinks I am ruining his reputation at the bakery. People have stopped coming. The bread is not like it was when I was there helping him – customers have told me. And he blames you, too – says you are

· 283 ·

taking what is his, the customers. We had a row. I told him he had done this to himself. He hates to be wrong or challenged in any way. He knows that everyone will be at the village dinner this evening.'

I grapple for the keys to the van and climb into Dolly as I hear thunder rumbling in the distance. Raindrops begin to fall.

'Laurent, I'm going to the mill!' I call over the ominous sound of the sky and people hurrying to shelter beneath the trees.

'It's raining!' someone calls.

'*C'est dommage!*' says someone else.

'Where shall we go?' I hear.

'Bring the plates and food,' says one of the women.

'They're going to the old mill!' I hear someone call.

'To the mill, out of the rain, everyone!' another shouts.

The van roars into life and I push it into gear. Dolly jolts, then gathers, and I set off.

The first thing I see when I arrive is Claude's white van. I jump out and run up the grassy drive, up the slope, slipping in my eagerness to get there, falling forwards on my hands. I stand and hurry up the rest of the slope and onto the lawn, where I see Claude standing by the water wheel. He's holding the handle to the sluice gate and it's clear he intends to close it. He's going to flood the mill.

'Stop! *Arrêt!*' I shout.

'Ah, so you've come to save the mill. Or maybe it is Laurent you want to protect, and save his family's reputation. The family who are known for their women leaving them for something far better on offer.'

'That's not true. He is a good man. Better than you will ever be.'

'You still owe me. You have stolen my customers and the debt is going up.' He holds the sluice gate poised to drop it into position as the rain continues to fall in fat, heavy drops, rolling down my face and back. There's a flash of lightning and a crack of thunder.

'I'm not paying you, Claude. You're not getting a single euro out of me.'

'From what I understand, you're making quite a profit from the bakery van.'

'I need that money. I'm not paying you!' I say, as another clap of thunder crashes out, making me jump.

'There is only room for one baker around here. And it won't be you.'

He goes to close the sluice gate. My heart lurches.

'Stop! Okay,' I raise my hands. 'I'll leave. If that's what it takes. Close the *boulangerie*. I'll do whatever it takes. Just leave the mill alone.'

I take in what I've just said in desperation. *I'll leave.* But I don't want Laurent to lose the mill again.

Claude sneers at me. 'You think I can leave the mill like this, so your boyfriend can carry on here, and your baker can keep on baking? You've taken everything that matters to me, Julie.'

'It's *Juliet*,' I say, knowing he misnames me on purpose.

'Well, *Juliet*, as I said, there is only room for one baker around here. And it will continue to be me.'

He lifts his hand to turn the sluice-gate wheel as an arm reaches out across my shoulder. Again, I don't need to turn to know it's Laurent. My heart is thundering and rain is starting to hit and run down my face.

'I wouldn't touch me, if I were you. This mill needs to stay decommissioned,' shouts Claude.

'Not on my watch!' Laurent growls. His hair is wet, his face angry and set. 'Go and crawl back under whatever rock you came out from, Claude. You and your family won't just help yourselves to whatever you want around here any more.'

'Really?' He raises an eyebrow. 'From where I'm standing, everything is being offered on a plate! Just like your grandmother, the women in your life always did prefer the Guiomar men.'

Behind me I can hear a crowd of people arriving at the mill, bottles chinking, cutlery and crockery being carried too.

'Shall we go inside?' someone asks.

'Laurent? Shall we go in?' calls Gilles, as the locals gather around the front door. But Laurent is too focused on Claude to hear him.

'Just leave, Claude,' Laurent growls.

'Not until you know the truth about your new lady friend.'

I turn to Laurent in panic. Claude is determined to hurt him. I have to say something before Claude does and Laurent discovers I've been keeping a secret. And I know this is really the end now. I'll be leaving. Laurent won't want to be around me after this.

'Claude and me, we kissed!' I suddenly blurt out. '*He* kissed *me* – it was a moment of stupidity.'

There is a clap of thunder, a flash of lightning and a group intake of breath. No one says anything.

'I didn't know he . . .' but I stop. It's useless trying to explain or excuse my behaviour. It was a moment of stupidity, but it's also the truth. And now I know that I have broken Laurent's trust. I kissed the man he hates for ruining the thing he loved most: his family. And now I've done the same. I've let myself fall in love with Laurent, and from what I see, I think the feeling is reciprocated . . . but I realise I've crushed whatever we had by letting history repeat itself. And I know there will be no way to put it back to how it was.

Laurent stares at Claude as if he'd like to kill him. Then, in a low, hard, cold voice, he says, 'You're not worth it.' He drops his hand, turns and walks away in the pouring rain, the wheel turning and turning.

I glare at Claude and narrow my eyes. 'Happy now? Got what you wanted?'

'I will do when I have your takings from today. You took my customers, remember? I'm owed.'

I pull the bag of coins out of my bag and throw it at his feet.

'Here, have the lot!'

He bends and picks up the money bag. '*Merci.*' He lets go of the sluice-gate handle and the water continues to flow, its path uninterrupted. The mill is safe, for now.

Claude steps forward and brushes past me. 'Enjoy your dinner. *Bon appétit.* Looks like it could be your leaving party!' As he leaves, I see Madame B looking at me, as is everyone else, clearly happy to see the back of Claude. She ushers them quickly into the mill and out of the rain.

I follow, trying to hide my embarrassment and my pain by slipping on a smile and making sure everyone is okay. 'Come in, come in. Let's find you all somewhere to sit,' I say as they enter. I see them all admiring the clean, whitewashed walls and polished workings of the millstones – Laurent's passion, his pride and joy.

The villagers happily throng out of the rain, seemingly having forgotten the scene outside, but I know I've ruined everything with Laurent and now, even if there was a way to get my visa, I can't bear to stay. Even if I was to explain to him that Claude kissed me and I was flattered by the attention, before I realised what kind of man he was, I'm not sure things would ever go back to how they were. I don't think I could bear to see him every day, thinking about what might have been.

I hear more cars pulling up outside, and it's the fisher-women, arriving with the tables and chairs from the square. 'I can bring the rest in the van,' I say, and grab the keys. I drive up to the square, looking for Laurent through the rain, but he's nowhere to be seen.

When I get back, everyone helps unload the tables and chairs, and lays out the food in the dishes they've all brought. We're in the big room of the mill and, all of a sudden, I can see exactly how this place would have looked if it had become the *salon de thé*. There is excited chatter as the food is served, and the bread that Madame B has brought from the boulangerie is put out along the tables.

Plates are laid out, with platters of cheese, cold meats and big green salads. There are desserts too: the chocolate and beetroot brownies I've made, and mini Victoria

Sandwich cakes, as well as a *tarte aux pommes* with bowls of crème fraîche on a table in front of the window overlooking the lake.

Bertrand, the mayor, has arrived, beaming and soaking up the atmosphere in the big room, as are the fisherwomen with their partners, parents and children. Madame B is smiling, and I think it may be because she's in her happy place, with her memories of the man she loved, even if he couldn't love her back.

I think of what Laurent said, back when we were first getting to know each other: *They say that if you throw yourself into what you love doing, you'll end up finding yourself there.*

Laurent loves this place. The mill, the lake, the swimming hole – where he always went when he needed to think. And at that moment, I realise that's where he'll be. I need to explain to him that I didn't kiss Claude and then hide it from him on purpose. Well, I did hide it from him, but only because when I realised I had feelings for him, I knew it was the one thing I couldn't bear to have him know. It was just part of my journey . . . albeit a very bumpy part.

'I'll be back in a minute,' I tell Madame B. 'Keep things going here. It's wonderful.' I look around at the lit fire and the smiling faces.

I head out to the lakeside and the canoe, grabbing hold of it and tipping it on its side to let out any water. Laurent said the only way to get to the swimming hole was by boat. But the last time I tried to face my fear of being on the water, we nearly capsized.

I stare at the now-empty canoe. I have to do this! I

need to find him and explain that what happened with Claude was when I wanted to feel seen. And now I realise what I really needed was to feel like me . . . and let other people see the real me. I stretch out a leg and move my weight from my back foot to the front and step in the canoe – well, more stumble forwards.

'Oh, my word, oh, my word,' I say, as the boat wobbles this way and that on the swollen lake. I grab the sides and sit down quickly, remembering Laurent's words: *Keep paddling*. I lean forward, unhook the canoe from its mooring, then sit down again in the middle, the whole thing jiggling under me. I pull out the paddle, dip it into the water and pull back, then change sides. Soon, I'm starting to make headway. *Keep paddling*, I tell myself, *or you'll go under. Keep doing it.*

By the time I reach the swimming hole, my arms are aching. I have to tell him I'm sorry. I didn't mean to cause him any hurt or embarrassment. I look around, but he's nowhere to be seen. I drop the paddle into the boat and put my head into my hands. The boat rocks from side to side and, right now, I don't care if I capsize. I'm exhausted. I've tried everything to make things work here. Then I hear a voice.

'The last time you took to the water, you nearly drowned me! Left me in the middle of the lake. Have you come to finish the job?'

I look up. He's wet and pulling on his shirt, which clings to him. He's clearly getting dressed after a swim. I swallow, wishing I wasn't so attracted to him – not just because of his good looks, but his kindness, trustworthiness and loyalty to the village, the mill, the people . . .

and, more recently, to me. I hurt him. I fell for the fake charms of the one man he has always mistrusted and disliked. I did the one thing that would hurt him most.

'I thought you might have gone. Left . . .' I say. 'I've ruined everything. I gave Claude my money bag.'

He shakes his head. 'That man has a way of getting what he wants.'

'Yes, without my earnings, I'll have to leave anyway. But, regardless of the visa situation, I couldn't bear to hurt you any more than I have by staying around. The mill will be sold.'

He nods in understanding, his dark hair clinging to the back of his shirt, rivulets of water sticking the cotton to his skin.

Then I say gently, 'I'll sell the mill to you, if that's what you want. You can have first refusal, just as the mayor originally promised. Could you raise the funds now, do you think?'

Laurent laughs. 'What money I had went on buying the bakery van.'

'What? That was you? There wasn't really an old man with outstanding debts?'

He shakes his head.

'But why?'

'Because I wanted you to have it. I wanted this to work. You at the bakery, me at the mill.'

'Getting one over on Claude?'

He nods.

'Maybe we'd both become obsessed on that front. I wanted to hurt him,' I say. 'I felt foolish after he kissed me, and then I found out he was married.'

'Ah, for me it was about the past, his family trying to destroy mine.'

'What will you do? Leave too? Now that the mill will be sold.'

'I thought about it.' He's gazing straight ahead into the woods. 'But then I came here.' He waves at the canoe. 'Throw me the rope,' he says, holding out a hand.

I toss it to him and he catches it effortlessly, then pulls the canoe towards the bank with me clinging to the sides. Once he's secured it to a nearby tree trunk, I crawl across the seats to the side. He pulls me out and onto the bank, and I fall forwards, wishing my treacherous heart would stop thumping. Then he manages a smile. 'You actually did that, got all the way up here on your own! Kept paddling.'

'I know what you must think of me,' I say.

And then I see it. The rain has stopped and the flash of blue from the kingfishers darts across the lake.

'I'll miss them,' I whisper. 'And I can only imagine how hard this will be for you.'

'It's like history repeating itself,' he says, sitting on a large rock, watching the kingfishers.

'Yes,' I say.

'Claude has all the power. He always has. You shouldn't have paid him.'

'I thought he would leave the mill alone. I hoped you could still run it if he went away.'

'And now you've paid him off, you can't stay?' he adds.

I shake my head. The rain has stopped and drops of water on the leaves above us occasionally fall. 'I can't show the profit I made without that money. It's not enough. The business had to make a profit. I need to deposit it in the bank and for it to show there. I thought he would go and you could take over the mill. That you'd still be able to keep doing this. But . . .'

Now it's his turn to shake his head.

'I can't. I don't have the finances any more.'

We both look out over the water, watching the flashes of blue.

'So now what?'

'Go back, I suppose. To where I came from. Disappear into the life I had as if none of this had ever happened. Chalk it up as some mad Shirley Valentine adventure that didn't have its happy-ever-after.'

We fall silent.

'I'm sorry,' he says, finally.

'I'm sorry too. I wish this could have worked out for you, for us. Madame B was right. Other people have tried to make that bakery work. Why should I be any different? Claude clearly means to intimidate anyone who takes it over and get them to leave, one way or another.'

We can hear music in the distance. The mayor must have put his record player on. I can just imagine people dancing. The mill sounds as I hoped it would on Sunday afternoons – full of people enjoying a tea dance.

'You deserved a fair shot at this,' Laurent says.

'I made my own mistakes. I guess I'm paying for them.'

'No. You're paying for the mistakes of the past. It has to stop somewhere. We can't let that family keep ruling our village – who we buy bread from, who we fall in love with . . .'

He stares at me and I stare at him, wondering if I've heard him correctly.

'I . . .'

'Ssh, say nothing,' he says, putting his fingers to my lips. Then he leans in: 'Is this okay?'

I nod. *More than okay!*

He kisses me, softly at first, then more intensely, and my senses go through the roof.

I pull back. 'I don't want you to think I make a habit of doing this,' I say with a smile.

'Like I say, we all make mistakes. I should know. My mistakes have never left me or let me move on. I was so cross when you bought the mill. I thought you were going to rip the heart out of it, paint over the memories, *my* memories. I couldn't move on from the past . . . It was me who left the first baguette on your doorstep.'

I recoil. 'You?' I say, standing up from the rock.

'I thought you might leave. That I'd still be able to get the mill. But this place is nothing without you . . . without you pulling us all together.'

'You wanted me to go that badly?'

'Then I did, but not now.'

I sit down again. I can't believe it. This isn't the Laurent I've come to know. Leaving an upside-down baguette is a sinister act that I might have expected from Claude, but not Laurent. I had come to trust him, but now he's crushed all of that, all of the feelings I had for him. The tears well in my eyes. My voice wobbles and I try to steady it and speak slowly, but a slight quiver betrays me as I say, 'Well, you've got what you wanted all along. I'll be leaving.'

I turn to go. He doesn't move.

'You know,' he says then, stopping me in my tracks, 'they say that seeing kingfishers is good luck. It's a sign of a new beginning.'

'I hope so.' I turn away again, tears rolling down my face, feeling foolish and betrayed. 'Good luck, Laurent.'

Chapter 41

By the time I'm back at the mill, the tea dance is ending. People are taking their chairs, plates and cutlery and weaving their way back to town. As they leave, they wish each other and me a '*bonne soirée*'.

The place is spotless. You would never think there had been such a party here. I brush away any stray tears and take a deep breath, hoping the quiver has gone from my voice.

'Day off tomorrow, Madame B. It's needed,' I tell her firmly, and she agrees. I know she wants to say something, but we're interrupted.

'So, I'll see you tomorrow and we'll talk business,' says the mayor, carrying his record player. 'I'm looking forward to hearing the plans for this place.'

My heart plummets. The only plan I have is to put it back on the market.

As the villagers leave, my phone pings.

It's Annie's husband, texting news I wanted never to hear but knew would come some day soon: *It is with deep*

*sadness I have to tell you that my darling Annie passed
away peacefully this afternoon.*

The following morning, I'm red-eyed from crying
and lack of sleep. I take my coffee and sit outside. In
no time at all, the kingfishers reappear. The message
from Annie's husband seems to have put everything
in perspective. Laurent's prank with the baguette,
our argument – it all seems irrelevant and stupid now.
What's the point in holding a grudge about something,
when none of us knows what's around the corner? All
I can think about is Annie, her husband and children,
robbed of their future together.

'Thank you for being here,' I say quietly to the kingfishers. 'You have been my constant company when I
needed you.' I'm choked thinking about Annie. It's too
soon, too unfair. I wish I could have done this for her,
like she told me – to go and live life. But I couldn't make
it work and I feel wretched.

I message the family WhatsApp group and tell them
the sad news about Annie, and that I'll be leaving France
soon. I can't wait to see them all.

I have the key in my bag to the *boulangerie*, ready to
return it to the mayor. Then I will have to explain to
Madame B that I'm shutting up shop and leaving.

I drive up to the square, ready to hand the keys to the
bakery van back to Laurent. As I turn towards the *boulangerie* to park, I wonder if I'm seeing things: there are
tables and chairs outside, clearly from yesterday's lunch,
with people sitting at them. They seem to be chatting,

drinking coffee, eating bread – and it's more than just the locals, I notice.

Just then, Laurent comes out of the *boulangerie* with a tray of coffee and a couple of the brownies from yesterday and puts them on the table. He's wearing a black baker's hat, white T-shirt and black jeans. He looks more than handsome. He stops and stares at me, making my insides leap.

I slide down from the driver's seat and shut the door.

Everyone, it seems, is at the *boulangerie*, either helping or sitting and enjoying the early September weather, when the sun shines lazily, without June and July's ferocity.

I walk across the square to where Gilles, his wife and friends are sitting together, drinking coffee and eating bread and butter with homemade jam. The fisherwomen, with their husbands and children, are there. The square is full of life as the children play and families gather with coffee and chat to one another. Even Bibi and the mayor's cat have made friends and are snuggled up together in the sun under one of the plane trees.

'I thought I'd told Madame B we wouldn't be opening today,' I say to Laurent, as I look at the busy space in front of the *boulangerie*.

'It seems the baker and the people wanting your bread had other ideas. When the van didn't turn up, they came here to buy it. I brought the coffee machine over. I thought it might be useful. For your customers and the till.'

'But what about the *tabac*?'

'This village can't survive on coffee alone. It needs

both: bread and coffee. The perfect partnership. Maybe even some British cakes.' He smiles.

I shake my head. 'But . . . I'm leaving.'

'Not if we've made enough money,' he says. 'And not if you don't want to.'

'And,' I say tentatively, 'would that be okay with you?'

'More than okay. Like I say, it's time the past stayed exactly where it is. And I take the kingfishers as a sign that it's time for a new, hopeful beginning. What about you? Can you forgive me for leaving that baguette?'

I can barely breathe I want this so much. I know what Annie would say: *Forgive him, forget what doesn't matter, and seize the day. Life is for living.*

I nod and smile. 'A line in the sand. Today is a new beginning.'

Then he takes my hand and leads me to the till, which he opens with a ping. Madame B is standing in the kitchen doorway, grinning expectantly.

'Shall we?' he says, and thrusts a handful of coins into my palm.

We start to count out the money, but as we're nearing the end of the takings, I know it won't be enough. 'If I hadn't had to give that money to Claude, we'd've made it.'

Madame B comes to stand beside me. 'When someone loves you as much as you love them, don't let them get away,' she says quietly to me, and carries on outside into the sunshine, leaving me with Laurent.

'It isn't Claude or his bread or his vending machines that we all love around here. It's you. We want you to stay. Whatever it takes.' Laurent slides his hat from his head. 'Tout le monde,' he says, as he steps out into the sunlight, addressing the customers.

'No, Laurent, really, please don't,' I call after him.

But he takes no notice and begins in French: 'I may not have been the most welcoming of neighbours when Juliet first arrived in our village. In fact, I was pretty confident she wasn't going to be sticking around and even left her an unwelcome gift on the doorstep to let her know so. I was furious when the mill was sold, but I've come to realise it couldn't be in better hands. Between the mill and the bakery, this village finally has its heart back.'

I look at Madame B blushing, standing next to the mayor. And I wonder if the confirmed bachelorette may be changing her mind about life outside her apartment.

'This bakery will only carry on if we all pull together, and we need to help Juliet here to make sure that happens, for the bakery van to keep doing its rounds . . . unless you'd rather go back to a vending machine for your daily bread.'

'Non, non!' I hear.

'There is a story about an old man who had nothing. He put on a pan of water to cook over an open fire and put a stone into it. A neighbour passed and asked what he was cooking, and he said it was stone soup. The neighbour was intrigued, and offered to bring some vegetables to add to it. Another neighbour passed and also offered a contribution. And so it went on, until there was a delicious pot of soup for everyone to share, at which point the old man took out the stone. Stone soup is about the community.'

He reaches into his top pocket, pulls out a euro and drops it into the hat. And then the hat is being passed around, and as well as can the coins being dropped in, I see notes too.

Laurent smiles at me. 'One euro can get you out of a lot of trouble.'

'Or into it,' I say, and giggle.

The hat comes round again and is handed back to Laurent. 'I'm pretty sure that will cover what went to Claude.'

'Wait. I haven't put mine in. How much do you need?' says the mayor, raising a hand.

Laurent proffers the hat.

Mayor Bertrand puts in a euro. 'And if you need any more, I have a jar of lucky euros for just this kind of moment.' He beams. 'We all want you to stay, Juliet, if you will,' he says.

I look at Laurent. 'Say yes,' he says. 'Say *oui!*'

'And if you want to turn the mill into a *salon de thé*, you have my permission,' calls the mayor.

'I think,' I say, 'I'm happy being a baker's assistant and driving my van.'

'If you're looking for another baker's assistant,' Vivianne, Claude's wife, steps forward, 'I know my way around a *boulangerie*.'

'That would be marvellous,' I tell her.

'And, erm . . . I was wondering how you'd feel about expanding into coffee and hot chocolate?' asks Laurent.

'But the *tabac*?'

'Better that we work as a team. I could make sandwiches for customers here too.'

'Excellent idea,' I say.

He leans in. 'May I?'

'Forget the etiquette, just kiss me.' And he does.

Suddenly there is a loud bang. It's Monsieur Martin, in his electric car, reversing and hitting the vending machine.

'Looks like we'll all need to get our bread from somewhere else,' says Laurent.

A cheer breaks out among the crowd gathered there, and we hear the slam of a car door as Claude parks his white van and gets out, furious with Monsieur Martin.

'I know a good miller,' I say.

'The miller and the baker should always be good friends, very good friends.'

'What about more than friends?'

'In this case, definitely more than friends,' he says, and kisses me again. And I know I'm exactly where I want to be: at the heart of this little French village.

'Ouch,' I say, as I lean into him.

'What's up?'

I reach in and pull the euro from my top pocket. It was pressing sideways into me. 'Someone once told me I should never be without one. It's my lucky euro.'

'You never know when you might need it,' he reminds me. 'Or where it might take you!'

He kisses me again, and it's as if I'm waking after a long winter hibernation, emerging where bright, brilliant sunshine bounces off the lake and there is always a flash of the kingfishers' blue to remind me of good things to come.

Epilogue

I pull up in the bakery van outside the *boulangerie* from a last round of visits to the four villages that used to depend on vending machines for their bread and now wait for Dolly and me to arrive each day. The machines have been covered with black sacking, no doubt waiting to be moved on to other small villages that don't have a local *boulangerie* any more. Claude's is closed and standing empty, after he tried to upscale his side hustle and sell drugs from under the counter at the shop. It wasn't long before the *gendarmes* got wind of it – it seems that Claude wasn't so close and friendly with the local police force as he claimed he was. A cheer went up when he was charged, while angry parents and shopkeepers alike celebrated getting rid of him and his clients, and vowed to boycott the shop.

I've visited some of the nearby farms and hamlets that I regularly deliver to and received gifts of wine, homemade pâté and local cheeses to wish me a happy

Christmas. I can't wait to share them with Laurent and Madame B. Everyone in France is getting ready for the big Christmas Eve dinner. They've been preparing it for weeks, and I'm no exception. I have everything planned and ready at the mill. There is a table in the middle of the room, covered in a white cloth with red candles and dark green ivy trailing down it. A huge tree stands beside the millstones, decorated with red and gold baubles, lights and holly decorating the mantelpiece over the fire that is laid and ready to light. Festive cards are strung up either side of it with Christmas wishes from back home, including one from Pete and Mandy with a snowy golf buggy and a little Jack Russell in a Santa hat driving it on the front. It's a big tree for just Laurent, me and Madame B. *But why not?* I thought. We have the space.

I switch off the Christmas music I'm playing from my phone on the van's dashboard, then duck out beneath festooned paper chains and bunting. I pick up the empty baskets and make sure the side hatch is secure, then step out into the cold, dark, crisp Christmas Eve. The church bells are pealing and people are on the steps, greeting each other with kisses and wishing each other '*Joyeux Noël.*' The lights are twinkling in the square, multicoloured bulbs strung between the plane trees – it was a spectacle in itself watching Gilles and the others with the tractor putting them up. It couldn't feel more festive.

I look to where the *tabac* once was and wave at the new owners of the wine shop and deli, selling meats and cheeses from the local area. They wish me a *joyeux Noël* and I tell them I look forward to seeing them at the mill for drinks tomorrow – Christmas morning – with Gilles and his wife and the others from the village. And Bertrand the mayor, of course.

I look back at the *boulangerie* with its newly painted sign, *Annie's* in gold, shining brightly, making my eyes sparkle with a few tears for a friend who should still be here. 'Because she couldn't be,' I told Laurent, when I finally settled on a name.

'It's perfect,' he said. 'It's your second chance, and she would be cheering you on all the way. Just as she did from the start.'

I can't wait for Annie's husband and the children to visit in the spring, as we've agreed, when the weather is warmer and they can enjoy exploring the woods and playing in the swimming hole.

The lights are on in the *boulangerie* and the orange glow I love to see is as bright as ever. I head to the shop and push open the door, hearing the tinkle of the bell. I stand for a moment, taking in the rush of warmth from the ovens, the voices and laughter. Suddenly, the room falls quiet and I hear, 'Mum!'

'Surprise!'

Maddie, Jake, and Becky! I rush forward and hug them tightly. 'You're here!' I say, with a crack in my voice.

'Well, we knew you wouldn't be able to get away now you have the bakery van.'

'Dolly,' Madame B corrects.

'Dolly.' Maddie laughs. 'So we came to see you!'

'Oh, this is wonderful.' I look at Laurent. 'Did you know?'

He shrugs. 'I may have had an idea. Maddie wanted to surprise you and asked if I thought it would be okay.'

'I thought we agreed no more secrets!' I say, then laugh. 'Unless they're glorious ones like this!'

I hear a pop. Madame B has bottles of *crémant* in an ice bucket on the table, and glasses. Tea lights flicker against the dark night outside. There are little rounds of toasted French bread topped with grilled goat's cheese and pâté.

'A little aperitif before dinner,' she suggests, and I think about the turkey that's cooking in the oven at the mill, far too big for the three of us. And there's a Bûche de Noël, a chocolate log, and, of course, a cheese board that will feed us for days to come.

Laurent is filling the glasses and handing them round. I take one and turn back to Maddie and Jake. 'But what about your dad? Did he mind you leaving him at Christmas?'

'No,' says Jake. 'He's spending it with Mandy. Lunch at the golf club.'

'Oh, that's great.' I smile.

'He's good, Mum. Really good. They're enjoying each other's company,' says Maddie.

'I'm happy for him, for them.'

'And they're thinking of mixing things up and creating a new tradition: presents after lunch instead of before!'

We laugh fondly.

'And what about Heidi?' I ask Maddie.

She takes a sip of the sparkling wine. 'Actually, Mum, I'm taking a leaf out of your book, having some time on my own to find out who the real me is.'

'Well, you know how that turned out for me!' I look at Laurent and we chuckle. 'And what about you two? How are plans for a full-time life in Spain going?'

'Ah, well, that's been put on the back-burner,'

'It's not for us,' says Becky. 'We're slowing down a bit.'

'Becky is pregnant,' says Jake, suddenly.

'Oh, what lovely news,' I say, and hug them both.

'Not what we'd planned, but we're thrilled – even if we are still getting our heads around it! We're considering how to make it all work between us. Djing in Spain doesn't seem quite right now . . . so we're looking for new opportunities. A bit more of a settled life. I just want to be the best dad I can be. In fact, this is just the sort of place I'd love to bring up our child. Especially being close to family. I'm beginning to realise that matters. Being part of a community.'

And I hug my two children all over again.

Madame B coughs. 'Well, I won't be baking for ever, and with your mother driving the bakery van and Vivienne running the shop, it won't be long before we'll be looking for an assistant to learn the *savoir faire* and help with the baking . . .'

Jake looks at me. 'Really?'

'If it's okay with Madame B, it's fine by me!'

'I'd love that!'

'You'd be brilliant, Jake,' says Becky.

'Yes, please,' he says. 'I mean, *oui, merci*!'

'Well, this might just be the best Christmas present ever,' I say. I lift my glass. 'To health and happiness.'

And the church bells continue to ring as the families head home for their Christmas Eve feast.

'To a wonderful day with you all tomorrow. Madame B, is the mayor bringing you to the mill for drinks?'

'He is,' she answers, and I swear I see sudden pink in her cheeks.

'What about you, Mum?' Maddie asks. 'You seem happy!'

'I couldn't be happier,' I say. 'I won't ever be French, but I'm not defined by being British any more. I'm just Juliet, and I'm loving being on this journey with her.'

Laurent pulls me close and drops a kiss on my lips.

'*Merci*,' I whisper. 'For everything.'

'And you,' he says quietly, and I feel the heat from his body close to mine and know I'm exactly where I want to be, in the bakery, with the ones I love. And as I look through the window, with Annie's name in gold across the glass, I smile at the Christmassy square. I look above the church, and a shooting star arcs across the dark, diamond-studded sky. I make a promise to keep seizing the day, not to let anything stop me living it to the full. I'll make the most of what I have, loving deeply, every single day, for as long as I live.

Acknowledgements

This is my twenty-first book, and I'm so delighted to be working with my new publishers at Pan Macmillan to bring it to life. Thank you to my fabulous editor, Katie Loughnane, and her assistant, Maddie Thornham, for making this book the best it could be. Thank you also to the rest of the Pan Macmillan team who have helped share the *French Bakery* love. Rosie Friis in publicity, Natasha Tulett in marketing, and Stuart Dwyer for getting the books into the bookshops and on the shelves.

And of course, as always, a huge thank you to my lovely agent, David Headley, for steering the ship onwards and upwards.

This book wouldn't have been possible if it had not been for family friends of my parents, Jill and John Mather. John bought Le Moulin, the old mill in Saint-Just, and was slowly renovating it. It became a place of healing and laughter for my mother after my father died – particularly because of the kingfishers, which she loved to watch over the lake. Their generosity allowed my husband and me to stay and spend time there, and we loved the place. There are so many memories from this time: from canoeing to get wood, to the big bat that flew in through one window, through the bedroom and out the window on the other side. Then, of course, there were our daily walks up to the village to get coffee and croissants in the mornings, and Sunday lunch in the one local café. There were big huge platters of seafood: piles of langoustines, slowly peeled and dipped in garlic mayonnaise; fish cooked in butter sauce with capers; steak with chips and carafes of rosé wine. I have never forgotten these meals. It's memories that make up so much of this book – the place, the feeling of being there, the stillness. Thank you for the memories, Le Moulin du Haut, and Jill and John.

Curl up with Jo Thomas's
festive new book

LOVE FROM CHRISTMAS
TREE FARM

Available to order now!

Read on for an extract . . .

Chapter 1

'It's like Caractacus Potts's inventing room!' I say with a smile to Tegan, my small Pembrokeshire Corgi, who sneezes loudly at the dust, surprising herself and then turning in disgust and waddling out of the big barn into the windy, chilly autumnal morning.

I watch her go, still smiling. I know exactly where she's off to. She's heading back into the farmhouse to settle down on the patchwork-covered sofa in the kitchen; in front of the Aga that will be giving out its gentle heat like a hug, keeping the one room warm, whilst I shut the doors on all the others and try and forget they're there. I'm happy in the kitchen, just me and Tegan. There's the sofa, a little saggy, and a small television that I rarely watch; I find I'm happier with the radio in the evenings these days. Sometimes I go out to the local cinema, theatre or even have lunch on a Sunday at the local pub. I mean, I've seen some great stuff and some awful stuff, but you have to support them, don't you? Otherwise, we'd lose them. And I need to keep doing things, like I promised Paddy, my late husband, I would. Keep moving forwards.

I shiver and my breath comes out like a plume of smoke in the cold, fresh air which comes in through the barn's open doors. I bang my hands together in their almost-matching fingerless gloves. I think I'd rather be in the kitchen with Tegan, but this job has to be done. With the farm officially on the market and viewers keen to see it, I need to start getting rid of everything I'm not going to take with me to the new place. There's no room for clutter in a brand-new one-bedroomed flat with sea views over the Cardiganshire coastline. It's time to clear things out. It's time to leave this place behind. I look around: so quiet and still. So different from when Paddy was here and this place was his world. It was always a hive of activity, with Radio 2 playing on his old vintage Roberts radio and a cup of coffee – inevitably left to go cold on the workbench because he'd got so involved in whatever he was doing. He always had little projects on the go all over the place: signs for the Christmas tree farm, repairing the henhouse, bagging up mulch to sell at the farm gates. My nose tickles and I give a little sniff and then take a deep breath. I roll my shoulders and set them firmly, then look up at the wooden staircase in the barn and the door in the chipboard wall where Paddy made a big studio room for my crafting. A surprise for me that he'd been working on before he got ill. I've only been up there a couple of times, with him, to see the progress and the final build. When he passed, I shut the door on it and haven't ventured up there since. My nose tickles again and there's a dull ache in my chest; a sense of longing and loneliness that actually hurts. I take a deep breath and look around at the listing and leaning boxes stacked up in his workshop area and beyond the straw bales. Far too much straw for three ducks and a chicken. I'm hoping the new owners, whoever they may be, will take them on. But Paddy was always kind and didn't feel he could just order a couple of bales from the neighbouring farmer – he always took a small load instead.

I walk towards the workbench, where Paddy would stand and fix things. It's what Paddy did: fix things. And if something couldn't be fixed, he'd keep it in case whatever it was could be used to fix something else. I put my hands on the worn workbench where his hands would have been, feeling I'm in his space – feeling like he's right here. If only he could have fixed this. Fixed me, right here, without him. Our time at the farm is over, way before we wanted it to be. I rub the worn wood where my hands have rested. Then, I stand up on tiptoes and peer into one of the boxes. Its contents a mix of cables, wires, tubs and tubes. I put my heels to the floor and let out a long, slow sigh. I have no idea where to start.

Who knew one person's treasure in his large barn-cum-garage could be quite so overwhelming and baffling to another? I don't know what half of this – correction – *most* of this stuff is. I look around and peek into other boxes, full of nails, screws, bits of rope and extension cables. Almost as chaotic as my crafting room at the back of the house, I think with a fond smile. That's another room that is going to have to be cleared out soon. Decluttering, they call it these days – not just sorting out, or throwing out. It's got an actual name and people talk about it online! Make money from it! I wish I could make money from it. I've sunk every last penny I've got into the new flat, putting down a deposit to secure the place. I need to get the farm sold. So, I might not be decluttering, but – not for the first time lately – I have to pull up my big girl pants and be brave. I need to chuck out what hasn't been used in ages and won't be used again. It's like ripping off a plaster fast; I know it's going to hurt before it gets better.

The estate agent already has people wanting to view the house and farm, and who knows, maybe someone will make an offer soon. So, this barn needs to be sorted and emptied and most of it taken to the dump. I can just imagine Paddy's look of horror as I throw out his precious boxes of 'just in case it's ever needed'. On the other hand, he'd be finding this highly amusing. We used to joke that we should have a good sort-out, or one of us would be left with a heck of a job if the other went first. It was years of his family's clutter, left over from before we took the farm.

Well, here I am, with the heck of a job! And it needs to be done if I want to secure a sale, finish packing and move into the new flat – a brand-new block, everything pristine and in working order, overlooking the sea. No leaking loos, draughty hallways, broken light fittings or temperamental heating. All of which Paddy tackled – until he wasn't here to. It's time for a fresh start. My time to move on and leave this place and its memories behind. I blink hard, holding back the unshed tears. *It's a good thing*, I tell myself firmly. Paddy would say so, I'm sure. It's going to be good, living somewhere I don't have to worry about roof tiles shifting in high winds, trees coming down in the forests or air in the pipes that makes a ticking noise all night long. It will be a life free from quirks. I take a deep breath. It will be ordered, tidied and calm.

'It's been three years now Paddy,' I say out loud with a crack in my voice. 'It's time to move on.' And I pick up a box and carry it to the barn door.

I don't talk to Paddy as regularly any more. The first year, yes – I sat and cried for most of it. Getting out of bed was a struggle. But now, I get up and go about the farm, letting out the three ducks – Hughie, Louis and Dewi – as well as Gloria, the remaining chicken. Every day I take Tegan out for a stroll down the long drive. I even tried using a dating app to arrange a few dates to the cinema, or a meal out. But none of them went beyond the first couple of dates. And inviting anyone to dinner at the house was always a bit testing: a high-end micro-wavable ready meal, the lamp with the wonky shade, and me having to give instructions on how to use the down-stairs loo – two short, sharp tugs on the chain – because things in my world don't always work as they should. I think there was one who saw pound signs when I said I lived on the farm, and then realised the farm wasn't quite the meal ticket he was looking for. Another who found me a little 'too quirky' and another who thought I'd ghosted him because I've never been very good at keep-ing my mobile phone close to hand.

I'm not looking for another full-time relationship. That was Paddy. There will never be another Paddy: someone I loved and trusted with all my heart. I'm not looking to replace what I had with him – I know that was a one-off. He was the other half of me. However, I quite like the idea of company every now and again. And now I'm moving, I hope I'll become part of a community. I'll find people to talk to, shops and cafés to visit. There are some crafting groups I could join. It'll be different. Not so lonely.

I look out onto the yard. The cold morning wind has picked up and the sky has turned darker while I've been standing in here. Now, I can hear the first drops of rain on the corrugated iron roof. The downpour quickens, the volume increasing until it's thundering above me, blocking out all other noise. I turn and carry another box to the door. In the distance, I can just make out a volley of barks from Tegan; despite her age, her hearing hasn't faded. The ducks start up quacking too, and I think there must be a fox in the yard. I pull my coat around myself, tugging the hood over my head, and hurry out of the barn into the cold rain to shoo him away. But to my surprise, it isn't a fox. It's a car – a small Fiat Panda, its windscreen wipers working at full speed to swish away the fat, fast raindrops. Who would be visiting me out of the blue? *Let's hope it's someone from the lottery telling me I've had a big win*, I smile to myself. *I could pay for declutterers*, I think, looking skyward to share the joke with Paddy.

Turn the page for a delicious recipe
inspired by the story in

Summer at the French Bakery

and recommended by

Jo Thomas!

French onion soup

A classic bowl of French onion soup is the perfect winter warmer for you and the guests who join you at your table. Its comforting flavours are helped by sweet, caramelised, slow-cooked onions and soft, melting Gruyère cheese.

Ingredients – serves 4

- 1kg onions, peeled and thinly sliced

- 50g butter

- 1 tablespoon olive oil

- 1 teaspoon sugar

- 2 cloves garlic, crushed

- 2 tablespoons plain flour

- 250ml dry white wine

- 1.2l rich beef stock

- 1 baguette, sliced

- 150g Gruyère cheese, grated

- Optional: a dash of brandy (Cognac)

Method

1. Melt the butter and oil in a large pan over a medium heat. Add the onions and cook with a lid on for 10 minutes to soften. Remove the lid, stir in the sugar and reduce the heat to low. Cook for at least 45 minutes, stirring occasionally, until the onions are deep brown.

2. Add the garlic and cook for 2 minutes. Sprinkle the flour over and stir well for another minute to coat the onions.

3. Pour in the white wine while gradually stirring in the beef stock. Bring to a boil, then lower the heat and simmer gently for 20 minutes. Season generously with salt and pepper.

4. While the soup simmers, toast the baguette slices under a grill until crisp. Ladle the hot soup into oven-proof bowls, top each with two slices of toast and pile the Gruyère thickly over the bread. Optionally, a dash of brandy of your choice!

5. Place the bowls under a hot grill for 2–3 minutes until the cheese is bubbling and melted. Serve immediately and enjoy!